1

I barely said a word until we got to the Yakuza headquarters
in downtown Little Tokyo. Even then, when I was seated
at an oversized oak desk facing Kazuo Yagami—the leader of
the local Yakuza clan and Hannah's father—I still said very
little.

What was there to say, anyway?

Hannah Walker, demon that she was, had killed my wife
and daughter for no apparent reason. In doing so, she had
stuck a knife in my heart that I wanted to pull out and use to
cut her throat from ear to ear.

Hannah was a mad dog, I realized, and like all mad dogs,
she would have to be put down.

But her father, it seemed, had other plans.

He sat across from me in a plush leather chair, framed by
the huge window behind him that afforded a widescreen view
of the city all the way across the river to Bedford.

This was the first time I'd ever met the man in person, and
he came across much how I expected he would. Dressed in a
light gray suit that probably cost more than I make in a
month, he seemed to be every inch the cold and ruthless
Yakuza boss that his reputation made him out to be. Hannah

once described him to me as being disarmingly congenial, which was how he came across now. The shark-smile never left his face as he looked at me with unblinking slate-gray eyes that had probably seen as much death and violence as mine had. He seemed to sense this himself as he gave me a look that bordered on admiration while one of his underlings poured me another whiskey.

"Since you started working with my daughter, I've been watching you from afar, Mr. Drake," he said. "I know you are not a man to be trifled with, and I respect that."

As I lifted my refilled glass, I said, "You do know Hannah isn't your daughter anymore, right?"

"Of course I know." He took a slim cigar from a wooden box on his desk and put it between his lips. A second later, one of his young underlings produced a zippo and held it out so Yagami could light the cigar. When the cigar was lit, Yagami waved the underling away, the boy hitting me with a cold stare that I guess was supposed to intimidate me, which I found laughable since the boy looked barely old enough to shave. Points for trying though. "I've known for a while now. I also know it was she who killed my *Kumi-in* and impaled him on the statue in the square."

"So why haven't you gone after her yet?" I asked him as I took out a cigarette and lit it, glancing at the enormous aquarium to my left, which appeared to be full of piranha. The gravel at the bottom of the tank seemed littered with gleaming white bones, making me wonder if they were human, and who they once belonged to. It didn't surprise me that Yagami enjoyed feeding people to the fishes, or maybe just their hands. I've no doubt it was a great trick to strike fear into people.

"Because if I did, people would die," he said, holding his cigar up, the smoke intermingling with that from my cigarette. "Once I realized what she is and what she is capable of, I decided it would be best to exercise caution."

"And you'd be right. How did you find out she's a demon?"

"I make it my business to know my enemies, Mr. Drake. Hannah has wanted to kill me ever since——"

"You strangled her mother to death?"

Kazuo's face hardened as a tense atmosphere took over the room. Behind me, I sensed his men move slowly toward me. When Yagami gave them a barely perceptible flick of his eyes, his men stopped moving. I got the impression that under other circumstances, my head would be getting submerged into the fish tank so the piranhas could feast on my face. As it was, the Yakuza boss needed me for something, so he let my insolence slide. "In my world, Mr. Drake, loyalty is everything."

"I hope you don't expect it from me," I said. "We might have a problem if you do. In fact——" I shook my head as I sighed, having had enough of this conversation already. "I don't know what I'm even doing here. I owe you nothing, Mr. Yagami. If I hunt down Hannah, it's because she had my fucking wife and daughter killed, not because you want me to find her." Stabbing my cigarette out in the ashtray, I stood up. "Thanks for the drink. I have to be going now."

When I turned around, two of Yagami's men were standing right behind me, eye-fucking me as they flexed their fingers in preparation for a fight. Staring right back at them, I told them to get out of my way, but they stepped in closer.

"I suggest you sit back down, Mr. Drake," Yagami said.

"Or what?" I said over my shoulder, bringing my gaze back to rest on the two Yakuza soldiers in front of me, the youngest of whom looked like he was itching to have a go at me. And the mood I was in, I was itching for him to try.

"I was hoping to keep this encounter conversational," Yagami said.

"Yeah, well," I said, flexing my own fingers now. "We don't always get what we want, do we?"

A pregnant pause settled in the room, during which I noticed the younger Yakuza move his right foot back ever so slightly.

Fucking amateur, I thought.

The guy's shoulders began to turn as he prepared to attack, but I struck first by throwing a lighting-fast right cross, my reinforced knuckles chopping down on the younger guy's chin. The strike was textbook. In shock, the young Yakuza staggered slightly before he collapsed to the carpeted floor in a heap, out cold.

Immediately after, I turned my attention to the other *Kumi-in*, drawing my fist back to hit him. But before I got a chance to throw the punch, he unleashed a snap-kick and drove his boot into my groin, doubling me over for a second, but long enough for him to bring his other leg around in a wide arc, his shin connecting with my thigh, the force of the kick causing me to drop to one knee.

In his arrogance, he stood like he had won, thinking he had gotten the better of me. Until I punched him in the balls, and he cried out in pain. When I hit him again in the same place, his cry was even louder.

As Yagami shouted for me to stop, I ignored him and grabbed the *Kumi-in*, twisting his arm up his back with one hand, grabbing a handful of his hair with the other before pushing him across the floor to the piranha tank. He resisted, of course, but I was too strong for him and too pissed off to give in. Before he could even protest, I dunked his head into the tank and held it there as he started thrashing around, sending water flying everywhere.

"Stop!" Yagami shouted, but again I ignored him, continuing to hold the struggling *Kumi-in's* head underwater. A second later, the water turned crimson with blood as the piranha attacked his face. That's when I let him up, noticing the bite marks in his cheeks as I flung him away across the floor.

As soon as he landed, the *Kumi-in* took out his gun and pointed it at me in a rage. I've no doubt he would've fired if Yagami hadn't shouted something in Japanese, making the guy lower his gun as he continued to glare at me in his rage while blood dripped from his face.

I turned to stare at Yagami, who was glaring at me like he wanted to shoot me himself. "Thanks for the drink," I said.

"I did you a courtesy by bringing you here, Mr. Drake," Yagami said. "And you disrespect me like this?"

"I'm no one's lapdog. You have enough footsoldiers already, anyway." I glanced at the two injured *Kumi-in*. "For all the good they did you."

"If you walk out of here, you'll regret it, Mr. Drake."

"Oh yeah? And why's that? You gonna kill me, Yagami?"

"As easy as that would be—"

"Not that easy."

His face tightened. "As easy as that would be, I'm not going to. I wanted to give you the option of finding Hannah and bringing her to me. But since you seem bent on making things difficult, I will now make you watch as I tear this city apart looking for her. I'll kill anyone who gets in my way, including you, Mr. Drake."

"Why the hell do you even want her?" I asked him. "Do you think you'll be able to tame her, to use her? The very idea is preposterous. She'd kill all of you in a heartbeat, believe me."

"Demon or not, she's still my daughter," he said, sitting back down.

"I don't think she was ever your daughter, was she?"

"On the contrary, Mr. Drake, Hannah has always been dear to me."

I couldn't help but laugh. "Seriously?"

"Just because you don't understand how things are done in my world, doesn't mean I don't care for Hannah. I've always cared for her. I made her strong."

"She became a fucking drug addict thanks to the shit you put her through," I said. "How is that caring for her?"

"*You* clearly still care for her," he said, deflecting my question. "Despite what you think she's done."

My jaw tensed for a second before I turned away from him. "I'm going now. Please stay the fuck away from me."

"I won't allow you to kill her."

Stopping on the way to the door, I turned around. "Then you'll have to kill me now if that's the case."

After staring at me for a moment, Yagami pulled a gun from the drawer in his desk and pointed it at me as he came around and walked toward me. For a second, I thought he would squeeze the trigger. Instead, he lowered the gun as a smile appeared on his lined face. "I don't need to kill you, Mr. Drake," he said. "My daughter will do that for me once you leave her no choice."

Maybe he had a point, but I didn't care. "You're deluded if you think she'll come to you after everything."

Yagami maintained his smile. "I don't think I am. You see, Hannah has only ever wanted one thing, and that's connection. I dare say that hasn't changed now that a demon has taken over her body. From what I understand about demons, they take on the characteristics and personality of the person they possessed. Hannah no doubt found that connection with you, Mr. Drake. But that connection is gone now, and Hannah is out there, alone, emotionally distressed. Lost even. You know her better than anyone. Do you think she'll turn down the chance at connection and belonging that I intend to offer her? And if she does, I have one other option."

"And what's that?"

Yagami smiled. "You aren't the only one to be familiar with the dark arts, Mr. Drake."

"You've no idea of the kind of power you'd be trying to tame."

Yagami's smile widened. "But Mr. Drake," he said. "I have no intention of taming it."

"Then you're even stupider than I thought."

"Watch your mouth, pig," the guy I knocked out said, having just woken up on the floor behind Yagami.

Ignoring the guy on the floor, I said to Yagami, "It's like I said earlier—just stay out of my way."

"You know I can't do that, Mr. Drake," Yagami said. "I'm also not above killing a police officer if it comes to it. I've done it before."

"I'm sure you have."

Yagami turned and went back to his desk. "The next time our paths cross, Mr. Drake, don't count on things being as amiable as they are now. If you chose to have me as an opponent, you will find me to be ruthless…and merciless."

"Right back at you, Yagami," I said, just before I walked out the door.

AFTER I WALKED FROM THE YAKUZA HEADQUARTERS TO Hannah's apartment building to collect my car, I paused outside for a minute and looked up at the broken window as the curtains billowed out of it. Then I looked down at the sidewalk beneath my feet and saw the blood that was already getting washed away by the rain.

Sighing, I went inside the building and made my way up to Hannah's apartment. I knew she wouldn't be there, but I took my gun out nonetheless as I walked inside and checked the living room. When I cleared all the other rooms, I put my gun away and sat down on the couch, resting my head back as I closed my eyes for a few minutes. In my mind, I kept seeing Hannah's face on the video, asking Savage if he had a problem with killing women and children.

I had never felt so betrayed in my life, even though I knew

it wasn't Hannah that caused all this, but Xaglath. It had to be. There was no way the Hannah I knew would do such a heinous act as have my wife and daughter assassinated. The only thing that made sense was that she'd had one of her blackouts, which she used to get quite a lot, during which Xaglath would take over. But even then, why would Xaglath do such a thing?

Because she's a demon, I thought. *And demons don't need a reason to do evil things. Evil is their very nature.*

Still...

Opening my eyes, my gaze fell on the coffee table, and I spotted a white envelope sitting there, realizing it had my name written on it. Frowning, I reached over and lifted the envelope, opening it to find a birthday card inside. I'd forgotten it was my birthday today. Hannah obviously hadn't.

The front of the card depicted a cartoon cop with the words, "Happy birthday to the World's Worst Police Officer," written on it.

Inside, Hannah had written, "Only kidding!" followed by:

Happy birthday, Partner. Hope you don't feel too old :)

She had signed her name underneath, followed by three x's.

Shaking my head, I threw the card back on the table. "Happy fucking birthday," I said bitterly.

2

"Surprise!"

I couldn't believe it when I walked inside my apartment. Party balloons were bobbing around everywhere, and there was a glitzy banner on the wall that said HAPPY BIRTHDAY on it. On the coffee table, there was also a large cake with tiny candles stuck into the icing, which was bright pink.

The five Hellbastards stood in the middle of the living room floor, smiling up at me as I paused in the doorway in shock. I was even more shocked because Daisy Donovan was in the room, standing in the middle of the Hellbastards as if she and they were all great friends now. This, despite the fact that I had never even told her about the demons.

My mouth opened to speak, but I was lost for words.

"Happy birthday, boss!" Scroteface said as if it wasn't ridiculously early in the morning.

"Happy birthday, Ethan," Daisy said smiling, but her smile faltered when she saw the harrowed look on my face. "I hope you don't mind us doing this. We thought it might...help you."

"Yeah, boss," Toast said, wearing what looked to be a

child's superhero costume—Superman, going by the big S on the front. "Miss Hannah told us it was your birthday today."

"When did she tell you that?" I asked, not knowing what else to say.

"The other day," Toast said.

"You want cake, boss?" Cracka said, who was dressed as a tiny Spiderman.

"It's pink," Reggie said, a joint in his mouth as he stood in a Robin outfit. "It's all we could steal. I shoved some magic mushrooms inside, though, so there's that."

Snot Skull, dressed as Wonder Woman, came walking up to me then. The arm that Carlito Martinez had ripped off had now grown back, I saw. Almost in a daze, I accepted the present he handed me. "We got you something," he said. "Hope you like it."

"Open it, boss," Scroteface, dressed as Batman, said.

I stared at the present in my hand for a moment, hardly knowing what to do. The last time I received a birthday present, it was from Callie when she bought me a first press vinyl record of Muddy Waters' debut album, which I still have. With a slight sigh, I proceeded to rip the wrapping paper from the present, unveiling a long black box. Inside the box was a spring-assisted Karambit knife that flicked its curved blade open with the press of a button. The knife was perfectly balanced and beautifully designed, the workmanship like no other.

"Cal made it," Daisy said as if I didn't know. "I hope you like it."

"It's…awesome," I said, mustering a smile for her.

"There this as well," Cracka said, coming up and handing me another wrapped present, although this one looked like it had been wrapped by a drunk child. There was so much tape around it I had to use the knife to cut it open. When I finally got through the tape and wrapping, I uncovered a framed photo of the Hellbastards, all grouped together as they grinned for the camera. Without a doubt, it was the scariest family photo I'd ever seen, and I've seen a few in my time.

After staring at the photo for a moment in part amazement, part horror, I looked up and said, "Who took the photo?"

"Funny story," Toast said, standing with his hands on his hips like a real superhero. "We jumped a kiddie fiddler in the park—"

"Place is full of 'em, boss, as you know," Scroteface interjected.

"Yeah," Toast said as he continued. "Anyway, the guy was terrified. I mean, he shit his pants, like literally." He started laughing, as did the other Hellbastards.

"Shitty Pants," Cracka said, showing all of his teeth.

They laughed harder. "That's what we called him, boss," Snot Skull said. "Shitty Pants."

"Awesome," Toast said, still tittering to himself. "But to finish the story, we persuaded Shitty Pants to take a picture of us on his phone because we said we wouldn't do nothing to him if he did. So he took a picture. His hands shook so much it took him fucking ages, but he got there in the end."

"Turned out well," Reggie said, blowing marijuana smoke out of his large nostrils. "Good lighting, I thought."

The Hellbastards all agreed on that point. Then Toast said, "So we killed the guy and took his phone. We don't have much experience with phones, so we had to jump another guy and ask him how we got a real photo from the one on the phone."

"Don't worry, boss," Scroteface said. "We didn't kill this guy."

"He died of shock after he told us what we wanted to know," Snot Skull said.

"He old guy with beard and everything," Cracka said, his voice muffled behind the Spiderman mask.

"Luckily, he told us what we needed to know," Scroteface said.

"Yeah," Toast said. "So we went into town and found a photo print shop. We waited until closing time before going in. I don't think anyone saw us."

"People never believe they saw us anyway," Snot Skull said. "They just look away like they're going mad."

"It funny," Cracka said.

"Yeah," I said. "I'm sure it's hilarious. Is there much more of this story left? I'd like a drink—"

"Nearly at the end, boss," Toast said. "So anyway, now we asked the guy in the photo shop to make us a photo, and he did."

"Just like that?" I said.

"He took a little persuading," Scroteface said as he adjusted his Batman mask, which didn't fit him properly. The sides had split because of the girth of his substantial skull. "Cracka sorted him out."

"I did, boss," Cracka said. "He soon become Pissy Pants." He laughed at this, and the others tittered. Even Daisy, who was listening on in amusement.

"So now we had our photo," Toast said. "And even though it looked fucking great, Scrotey Face realized we needed a real nice frame to put this fucking work of art into."

Jesus Christ, I thought. *What next?*

"Yeah," Scroteface added. "So we headed to this little shop that was nearby and still open."

"We pile inside," Toast said. "And there's this woman behind the counter, and she obviously screams and all the rest until she realized we weren't going away, not until we got a nice-looking frame for the family photo. But, there's also this other woman in there, and she looks weird and fat until Reggie realizes she's…whatchamacallit—"

"Pregnant," Reggie said.

"I'm not sure I like where this is going," I said.

"Just listen, boss," Scroteface said. "It's beautiful."

"Beautiful?" I asked, perplexed now. How could the Hell-bastards being around a pregnant lady possibly be beautiful in any way?

"So this pregnant lady," Toast said. "She's standing there screaming, and then all this...*stuff* just gushes out of her."

"Her waters broke, boss," Reggie said, then added, "I watch *General Hospital* sometimes."

"Anyway," Toast said as I just stared at him. "The fat lady lies down and starts screaming, and then the other woman who's busy finding us a nice photo frame for the family photo, she says the fat lady must be going into whatyoumacallit..." He looked at Reggie for help.

"Labor," Reggie said.

"Yeah," Toast said, his eyes widening with excitement. "So the photo shop woman, she says she needs to phone a thingy...an ambulance. She goes to phone the ambulance, but Scrotey Face stops her. He just looks up at her and says—"

"We got this," Scroteface said in his best Batman voice.

"Fucking A Right he did!" Toast said, one fist balled in excitement now.

At this point, my jaw was hanging open in horror as I tried to picture the Hellbastards delivering a fucking baby. As imaginings went, it wasn't very pleasant.

"So Reggie, he knows some shit from *General Hospital* or whatever," Toast said. "He asks the shop lady to get some towels and water and some other stuff I can't remember."

"She didn't though," Snot Skull said. "There were none."

"It was a photo frame shop," Scroteface added.

"So what did you do?" I asked in a hoarse whisper, barely able to get the words out.

"Well, Cracka stepped up," Toast said. "He got his little self in there between those fat legs and he pulled that sucker right outta there!"

"Sucker?" I asked.

"The baba, boss," Cracka said softly. "The little baba."

I swallowed. "The little baba?"

"Yeah, boss," Snot Skull said. "That screaming bag of blood and guts that came out of the fat woman."

Daisy's amusement had turned to horror now, unsurprisingly, as she stared at the superhero-costumed demons. "What...did you do...with the baby?" she asked.

"I wanted to eat it," Snot Skull said. "But Cracka wouldn't let me. He just held that thing in his arms, even though it was near as big as him."

"I had to protect the baba, boss," Cracka said, throwing an angry look toward Snot Skull.

"And did you?" Daisy said, almost like she was afraid to ask.

"Yeah," Cracka said. "Cause that's what superheroes do."

"That's good, Cracka," was all I could think to say. "I'm glad to hear that."

"I even bite the thingy of it," Cracka said.

"The thingy, Cracka?" I said.

"The umbilical cord," Reggie said. "There was some blood, but you know..." He shrugged.

"So you gave the nice woman her baby, right?" I asked.

"Oh, yeah, boss," Cracka said. "After I make her promise to call it Kermit."

"Kermit?" I said.

"Like Kermit Frog, boss," he said.

"Anyway," Toast said, pointing at the photo in my hands. "As you can see, we got the nice frame for the family photo."

I looked down at the grinning mugs of the Hellbastards in the photo. "And I'm sure we can all agree that it was totally worth the...*unbelievable* effort you guys went to in order to get it."

"You can put it next to the picture of your old family," Reggie said, holding the joint out for me to take.

"I'm going to pretend you didn't say that, Reggie," I growled, snatching the joint from him.

"I didn't mean——" Reggie started to say.

"Forget it," I said, heading to the bookcase in the corner of the living room and placing the photo on top, next to the other photos there. Toking on the joint, I sat down on the couch as it felt like my body was about to give up the ghost, my mind feeling like it had long since flown the coop.

"You want cake, boss?" Cracka asked.

"No thanks," I said. "You guys knock yourselves out."

"Are you okay, Ethan?" Daisy asked as she joined me on the couch. "You look kind of sad. Is it because you feel old on your birthday?"

I glanced at her as she smiled. "No, it's not because of that. And thank you for the...party."

"You're welcome."

I seemed to remember telling Daisy to stay away, as did her mother, but I decided not to mention this. She clearly had her own agenda anyway, and nothing I or anyone else said was going to stop her. "By the way, how did you end up in here with these cretins?"

"With the little guys? Your front door is broken, so I just walked in and there they were, sitting here watching TV. So I introduced myself."

"They didn't scare you or freak you out any?"

"Of course not, they're adorable. Especially Cracka. He's my favorite." She smiled over at Cracka as he was stuffing his face with cake. "He's too funny."

"Yeah," I said, just wanting to sleep now. "They're all a real hoot."

We sat in silence for a bit as Daisy watched the Hellbastards argue over who was going to get the last piece of cake—the cake that was stuffed with magic mushrooms, according to Reggie. In the end, Cracka stuffed it into his gob until Snot

Skull reached in and took most of it out again, shoving it into his own mouth instead.

"I hope you cretins are going to clean up the mess in here," I said, not caring if they did or not. The only thing I cared about now was getting some sleep, and more important- ly, shutting out the world and my racing thoughts for a blessed time. "Actually, why don't you all go and trip in the park or something? I need sleep."

"Sure, boss," Scroteface said. "Since it's your birthday and all."

"Or since you do what I tell you to do," I said. "Off you go."

When the Hellbastards left, I sat enjoying the silence as Daisy continued to sit beside me on the couch. Just as my eyes were closing, she asked, "Can I tell you something, Ethan?"

"Sure, sweetheart," I mumbled, my eyes half closed. "What is it?"

"I had this really weird dream last night."

"Uh-huh…"

"You were in it, and this other man called The Magician."

My eyes snapped open. "What?"

She stared at me a moment. "You know this person, don't you?"

"Tell me about the dream."

"I'll tell you what I remember," she said. "An angel came to me. I couldn't tell if they were male or female, but they said their name was Malach. They started telling me I would be needed in a war that was coming. That I would soon be a warrior and I would have to help you fight against this man called The Magician. I mean, I thought it was just a silly dream until I saw your face just now."

With my head resting against the back of the couch, I stared into space for a moment as I tried to process what Daisy had just told me. The Magician? There was no way she could know about him, about Wendell Knightsbridge. Unless the dream was about some other person called The Magician, though I doubted it. "Have you had any other dreams?" I asked her.

She shook her head. "None as real as that one. It felt more like a vision or something, like this angel was actually there with me. It's crazy, right?"

"I don't know. A little, I guess."

"Oh, and there's this as well."

"What?"

"Hold on." She got up and retrieved the Karambit knife she and the Hellbastards had given me earlier for my birthday. As she stood holding it, she flicked the blade out and said, "You ready?"

After I nodded, Daisy then began to slash the air with the knife, her movements swift and sure as if she had been practicing for years. She even managed to toss the knife in the air slightly, catching it in a different grip before continuing with the slashing movements. When she finally stopped, she stood staring at me, waiting for my reaction. "I swear I didn't even know I could do that until yesterday when I got the knife from Cal."

I could only stare at her, my mind blown by this point. "You've never handled a blade before?"

"My mom won't even let me near the kitchen knives."

Puffing my cheeks out, I said, "I don't know what to say, Daisy. I mean, clearly something is going on, but I just can't —" I had to stop as I pinched the bridge of my nose between thumb and forefinger. A raging headache had just come out of nowhere, and for a second, I thought I was going to be sick.

"Ethan?" Daisy sat beside me again. "What's wrong? Are you okay?"

Staring hard at the floor, I felt tears sting my eyes, and I hoped she didn't notice. "I need to be alone right now," I said in a near whisper. "I'm just...very tired."

Daisy stared at me, her eyes full of concern. "You're worrying me, Ethan," she said in a small voice.

"I'm fine, sweetheart," I said, squeezing her leg a little. "Why don't you run along and I'll see you later once I've had some sleep. It's been a long few days."

Daisy protested a little, but eventually she left the apartment after she made me promise to get some proper rest.

When she left, I took the Mud bottle out of my pocket and emptied the contents into my mouth before lying down on the couch. When I closed my eyes, I prayed for oblivion to take me.

Thankfully, it soon did.

3

In the dream, I shot Hannah in the chest, just like I'd done before.

I shot her once, and then I shot her four more times in quick succession.

Bang-bang-bang-bang.

With every shot, she staggered back until she finally crashed through the living room window. In slow motion, her face reacted to each shot, her features contorting with pain and...something else.

Sadness.

Deep hurt, as if I'd just ripped the heart from her chest and squeezed until it burst.

Then she fell, her arms waving as she tipped back into mid-air, her eyes never leaving me until she dropped below the window.

As before, I walked toward the window, the wind and rain blowing in and assaulting my face. In the dream, I expected to look out and see that she was gone.

But in the dream, she wasn't.

Before I reached the window, Hannah came floating up and hung in mid-air, hovering in the maelstrom that seemed to have developed outside. As she spread her arms to reveal her blood-stained chest, two massive black wings shot out of her back. Her eyes turned a deep yellow, and her face became a mask of rage and bitter resentment.

"How could you?" she raged. "How could you do this to me? I gave you everything! I gave you my heart! My soul!"

The force of her rage was so great that I staggered back into the room. "You—you killed my family. I had to. I—"

"Had to?" She laughed a bitter laugh before flying toward me at high speed, reaching me in a split second.

With her contorted face before me—filled with pure anger—I looked down as I felt something in my chest, and realized with horror that her clawed hand was right inside me, her fingers clenched around my heart.

I looked up at her again to see a smile form on her face, and then she ripped her hand out, holding it up so I could see my heart clenched in her fist, dark blood dripping off it.

"You're going to pay for what you did to me, Ethan," she said as she crushed my heart into mush.

Below me, I felt the floor begin to move. When I looked down, huge fissures were opening up as the floorboards cracked and split. Muted yellow and red light burst up through the fissures, and I knew I was looking at the light of Hell. I tried to run, but I couldn't move. I was helpless as the floor opened up beneath me.

Then I dropped into the chasm, screaming as I went...

WHEN I WOKE UP ON THE COUCH, I WOKE UP SCREAMING still, only stopping when I realized where I was. Instinctively, my hand went to my chest as if to make sure my heart was still there. With my hand pressed flat against my chest, I felt the pounding of my heart, as if it too had felt the shock of the nightmare for itself; had felt Hannah's fingers wrap around it and crush it to death.

"Jesus Christ…" I breathed as I sat up on the couch, my body bathed in cold sweat, my clothes sticking to me. Looking toward the window, I saw it was still light outside, and the rain was battering the glass. By my watch, it was just after two in the afternoon. The Hellbastards didn't appear to be here either. It was just me and my pounding head and heart in the deathly silence of the apartment.

To kill the silence, I got up off the couch with a loud groan and put on the Muddy Waters record that Callie had bought me for my birthday. It was a record that often helped calm me when I was feeling agitated, not just because of the music itself, but also because Callie had given it to me. When I listened to it, I could almost imagine she was with me in spirit.

As the first bars of "Tell Me Baby" came on, I started to feel better. By the time I'd had a shower and changed my clothes, I was beginning to feel half-way functional again.

After making myself a coffee, I sat on the couch and turned on the TV news. The top story was The Ripper Tripper, the crazed serial killer who seemed to be modeling himself on the infamous Jack the Ripper. In the last twenty-four hours, the killer had claimed two more victims, both prostitutes. The victims were drugged with LSD and then ritually butchered, their bodies found in some seedy hotel room downtown in the Red Light District.

I turned the volume up when I saw Jim Routman come on the screen, standing outside the precinct as he gave a statement to the waiting media who filled the street outside with their news vans. Routman maintained his usual grim expression as he gave the press a cursory rundown of the facts. The only time his expression changed was when some reporter asked him why the FPD were no closer to catching the killer, and if that was because the killer was smarter than they were.

I couldn't help but smile as Routman glared at the insolent reporter. "I can assure you," Routman said. "This killer will be caught. And soon."

"Bold words, Jim," I said as I turned off the TV, glad I wasn't a part of the circus he was ring-mastering. I almost felt sorry for him, for I knew the captain would be up his ass constantly, pushing him to apprehend the killer before he made a fool of the FPD, which, to be honest, the killer was already doing.

As Eric Pike had informed me, the killer was a Mytholite, someone who had taken on the characteristics of a person from legend, thanks to the prevalence of celestial energy in the city.

This was just the start of it.

Pike had said there were a great number of these Mytholites floating around the city now, many of them having powers as real as any MURK. God only knows what effect this was going to have on the city, and on the world for that matter. The characters from myth and legend that these ordinary people were becoming were legends for a reason. They were powerful individuals. Many were even gods.

Was that the next thing? Were we going to see a reincarnation of some god from Greek or Egyptian myth take over the city? Or the whole damn world? And how would the everyday MURKS react to this new breed of Mytholites? What would the vampires, the lycanthropes, the Fallen, and all the rest do when they realized there were people out there more powerful than they were?

Was another war coming? A war that would change things forever?

It didn't bear thinking about.

Speaking of wars, it sounded like Kazuo Yagami was heading for one, even though he didn't know it. Hannah was out there somewhere, no doubt in a deranged state thanks to everything that had happened. She had also probably relinquished full control to Xaglath by now, who wouldn't stand idly by while Yagami hunted her. More than likely, she would hit the Yakuza clan first, and keep on hitting until there was nothing left of it.

Or until I got to her first. Which I planned on doing.

Getting up, I found my trench and fished the flash drive containing the video of Hannah out of the pocket. In the bedroom, I retrieved my ancient laptop and brought it into the living room, placing it on the coffee table after turning the music back on, Muddy Waters once again killing the silence inside the apartment. Sticking the flash drive into the laptop, I waited on it booting up and then hit play on the video.

For the next while, I sat and watched the video of Hannah and Savage's meeting, staring grimly at the screen as I listened to them talk while I watched Hannah's expressions.

After the third run-through, I began to think it didn't seem like Hannah at all. There seemed to be a disconnect between the person on the video and who Hannah actually was. I had assumed before that I was looking at Xaglath on the video, but now I wasn't so sure of that. Xaglath displayed the same cold psychopathy as she always did, but there was something else about her, something not right that I couldn't put my finger on.

When I paused the video and looked in her eyes, I couldn't even be sure it was Xaglath I was looking at. Although it had to be because she was sitting there in the flesh talking to Savage.

But arranging the assassination of my wife and daughter was cold even for Xaglath. No matter how hard I tried, I couldn't figure out her motivation for doing what she did. At the time of the meeting, I had been partners with Hannah for about two weeks. During that time, I had seen her slip back into her demon self more than once, and she told me herself that she often had blackouts that lasted up to several hours before she was able to get a handle on her torment again and wrestle back control of her newer self.

Whatever way you looked at it, it wasn't Hannah on that video, not really. A fact that filled me with guilt. I may have acted too hastily and too harshly when I shot her.

But what was I supposed to do? Just forget about the fact that she was in a video arranging to have my ex-wife and daughter killed?

"Fuck," I breathed as I rubbed at my temples, feeling like my head would explode now.

Lighting a cigarette, I hit play on the video again for the umpteenth time, hoping in vain that another viewing would yield some much-needed enlightenment. As the video started, my phone rang on the coffee table next to the laptop, and I picked it up and answered it without looking at the caller ID. "Yeah?" I said.

"Ethan," said a familiar voice. "It's Jim Routman."

I was surprised to hear from him. The last time I got a call from him was when we were still partners years ago. Which meant he needed something. "What can I do for you, Jim?" I asked as I kept staring at the laptop screen.

"I need a favor, and you owe me for that information I gave you on Jonas Webb," he said, as blunt as ever.

"Fair enough. What is it?"

"A body has turned up in Bricktown. Nelson's Square. It might be murder, it might not be. Either way, I can't get to it."

"Why not?" I asked as I continued to stare at the video in front of me.

"Because I got my fucking hands full with this Ripper Tripper asshole, haven't I? Edwards is all over me to find the guy and bring him in."

"Does the captain know you're asking me to handle a homicide? I doubt he'd want me anywhere near it."

"Fuck the captain," Routman barked, sounding stressed to

the max. "He has everybody else tied up in this fucking task force. What's he want me to do?"

I was about to say that I saw his point when I noticed something on the video that made me take the phone away from my ear and reach out to rewind the footage. As I did, I could hear Routman angrily asking if I was still there, but I ignored him while I concentrated on the video, my finger on the trackpad as I prepared to pause it. When I paused the video, I focused hard on the screen for a moment and then breathed out slowly as I was hit with a sudden realization.

On the phone, Routman was still barking my name, so I held the phone up again while still staring at the screen. "Sorry about that," I said in a distant voice.

"What the fuck, Ethan?" Routman barked. "Are you jerking off or something? I don't have time to fuck around here."

"I'll check out the scene," I said.

"Good. Uniforms are already there. Don't let me down, Ethan."

"Sure. Bye, Jim."

I hung up the phone, my eyes still glued to the screen. To be sure I was right about what I was looking at, I moved the video back-and-forth frame by frame for a moment before shaking my head and flopping back on the couch. "Jesus fucking Christ…"

On the laptop screen was Hannah's face, zoomed-in slightly so I could see better. Her eyes were normally dark brown, but in the frame I had paused, her left eye was clearly green. The color change only lasted for a split second, but it was there, and I didn't think it had anything to do with the video.

The color of her left eye had changed from dark brown to green and then back again.

Upon first noticing this, I thought perhaps it was down to Xaglath. But Xaglath's eyes were always amber or bright yellow when she made herself known. I had never seen Hannah's eyes change to green before. Which meant…

"I was wrong," I breathed.

It all made sense now. It wasn't Hannah in the video because she was never at that meeting with Savage. She had tried to tell me as much, and I didn't listen.

But if it wasn't Hannah, then who was it?

Someone who could make themselves look just like her.

"A fucking shapeshifter," I said.

Shapeshifters were rare, but they were out there.

I clamped both hands to my head as I sighed heavily.

This wasn't over. Someone out there had sent a shapeshifter to impersonate Hannah.

But why? It didn't make any sense.

I fucked up. I shot Hannah for nothing. And now she was probably out there full of hate and resentment, a danger to herself and others.

To me.

More importantly, the person who had arranged this whole thing—who'd had my family killed—was still out there as well.

I was back to square one.

And I didn't even have my partner to help me this time.

4

It was late afternoon when I arrived at Nelson's Square. The rain fell softly on the place, clogged gutters spilling noisily into tight alleys. Countless puddles covered the broken pavement, forcing me to be mindful of my steps when I got out of the car.

The rundown working-class neighborhood is a jigsaw puzzle of tenements and townhouses divided into apartments. At the intersection of its two main streets, there lies the eponymous square, drab and lackluster, surrounded by a handful of stores.

The first thing that caught my eye was the corner-shop convenience store, *One Stop Shop*, which seemed to be closed off by police tape. I guessed that's where the body was. Nearby, the only places that showed any signs of life were *Red Hot Pizza*, *Honeysuckle Florists*, and the *Nelson's Square Liquor Store*. Two more businesses—a laundromat and a hair salon— were closed, despite it being a bit early to be out of hours.

My mind wasn't exactly with it as I trudged across the broken paving stones, my hands shoved deep in my trench pockets as the rain continued to fall. All I could think about was Hannah, and how I'd wronged her. She was the only person I'd had on my side, and I repaid her loyalty by shooting her five times in the fucking chest.

If she came to kill me, she had every right to.

Two uniforms stood outside the convenience store in the rain, looking like they couldn't wait to get away as they each smoked their own cigarettes.

"Look out, Mike," one of them—a big mustachioed guy about my age—said as I approached, "Kolchak: The Night Stalker is here."

The other uniform—a younger guy with a baby face who looked fresh out of the academy—started laughing, though I doubted he even knew who his older partner was referring to. I got the impression Baby Face spent a lot of time laughing at stuff he didn't understand, enthralled by Big Mike and his years of experience as a doughnut-eating wise-cracker.

I stopped beside the two of them as I lit a cigarette. "Big Mike," I said by way of greeting. "I think Dunkin' Donuts is still open. If you hurry, you might catch it."

Big Mike shook his head at me, taking little offense. Guys like him didn't get offended. They didn't give enough of a fuck to get offended by anything unless it affected their bottom line, the only thing most of these guys cared about. They spent more time collecting kickbacks than they did doing any real policing. "Fuck you, Drake," he said casually. "What are you doing here, anyway? Everyone knows you only go after the stuff that goes bump in the night."

"More like the stuff that goes bump in his fuckin' head," Baby Face said in an act of boldness no doubt intended to impress his partner, who did a good job of showing his appreciation by nearly choking on his cigarette as he laughed.

"That's good, Jonny," he spluttered. "I've taught you well."

After taking a few drags of my cigarette, I tossed it away and held my hand up in front of both their faces. "You see this?" I said as the tattoo ink worked its way down my arm and into my palm, swirling enticingly before their eyes. In seconds, they were both enthralled by the ink. "Neither of you can remember where you parked your patrol car."

They both stared and then frowned as if they were trying hard to remember where the car was, despite it being parked right next to my Dodge. When I lowered my hand, they both frowned as they looked at each other. "What the fuck?" Big Mike said. "I can't remember where we parked the car. Weird…"

"Shit, neither can I," Baby Face said. "What the fuck?"

"Who owns that one over there?" Big Mike asked, pointing at his own patrol car.

"Not ours," Baby Face said.

"You sure?"

"Positive."

"Shit."

"Looks like you're walking back to the precinct, boys," I said with a smirk as I moved passed them. "It should stop raining soon."

When I walked inside the convenience store, I came across the head of forensics, Gordon Mackey, leaning over a dead body on the floor at the back of the store. Another female technician was busy taking photographs of the corpse and the scene. "Gordon," I said as I walked up to him. "What do we have here then?"

The forensics tech raised his eyebrows as if he was surprised to see me. "What are you doing here?" he asked.

"Routman asked me to check the scene out," I replied. "His hands are full ring-mastering the Ripper Tripper circus."

"Tell me about it," Mackey said. "There are so many bodies we're running out of room at the morgue. I shouldn't even be here. I still have the latest two victims to autopsy." He ran a hand over his bald head like he was at the edge of his tether.

"Why are you doing autopsies anyway? Why isn't the coroner doing them?"

"You didn't hear? The coroner met with an unfortunate accident last week."

"I never heard. What happened?"

"Car crash. Got himself decapitated."

"Shit."

"Yeah, so now I've been asked to fill in until a replacement is found. Good timing, huh?"

"You look like you need some fun, Gordon. Maybe a little fishing?" I chuckled at the ongoing joke, though he didn't see the funny side.

"Fuck you," he said, glaring at me. "When are you going to stop with that shit."

"Probably never."

"Asshole."

I smiled to myself as I took a pair of black evidence gloves out of my pocket and put them on. The dead guy on the floor was a portly gentleman in his late forties with sandy hair and a short beard. His chubby face was a dark purplish color. His eyes also bulged from their sockets, and his tongue lolled to one side of his gaping mouth. Around his neck was a length of yellow cord like that used for washing lines. Mackey informed me the vic's name was Sam Sidwell, the owner of the convenience store we were now in.

"Are we supposed to believe this was suicide?" I asked Mackey as I looked around the store, noticing how disheveled many of the shelves were as if there was a struggle at some point, and things had got knocked to the floor.

"I guess so," Mackey said as he stood up and removed his gloves. "Seems fishy to me, though. The knot is all wrong for a start. It wouldn't hold a man of his weight."

"Maybe that's how he ended up on the floor." I looked up at the ceiling beam above the body. "Maybe the cord unraveled under his weight."

"Perhaps," Mackey said. "We'll know better when I have time to properly examine the body."

"When will that be?"

He threw me a look. "When I get time, I said."

Looking down at the corpse again, I noticed there was water pooled around it. Crouching down, I dipped a gloved finger into the water and tasted it with the tip of my tongue. "Salt water," I said, raising my eyebrows in surprise. "Why would he be lying in salt water?"

Mackey shook his head. "No clue."

"It's kinda weird," I said. "This whole scene is weird."

"I take it you don't believe this was suicide?"

"Nope, but I'll wait on your report before I jump to any conclusions. For now, I'm treating this as suspicious."

"Well, I'll leave you to it," Mackey said, then looked at the other tech. "Let's go, Janis. We got shit to do."

"When can I expect your report?" I asked him.

"Tomorrow, if you're lucky."

"Tomorrow?"

"Best I can do. Sorry."

"Go on then," I said. "Rejoin the circus. I'll take care of this."

"The meat wagon is on its way. And by the way…"

"What?"

"The victim's niece is upstairs. You might want to talk to her."

"Did she see anything?"

Mackey shrugged. "Do they ever?"

"I'll have a word with her."

When Mackey and the girl left, I had a quick look around the store, concluding after a few minutes that nothing seemed out of the ordinary, except for the dead body on the floor. There was the fact that the vic was supposed to have hung himself, but I didn't think so. The knot around his neck was too shoddy for a start. I doubt it would've held the man's weight long enough for him to get the job done. Then there was the fact that the cord wasn't tied to any of the ceiling

31

beams, as if you were supposed to believe that it slipped off by itself after the vic was dead.

A struggle of some sort also appeared to have taken place going by the disordered shelves. The vic could've kicked the cans and stuff down while he was dying, but once again, I doubted it.

And then there was the strange puddle of salt water under the body. What was that about? My Infernal Itch had reacted when I'd tasted the water. Only slightly, but enough for me to know there was some MURK connection to this whole thing, or at least the salt water on the floor. I still needed Mackey to confirm it, but given everything, it looked a lot like Sam Sidwell was murdered.

I almost smiled when I realized I had a murder on my hands. At least now, I had more to think about than Hannah and the myriad other problems I had, like Kazuo Yagami and the fact that a pack of violence-hungry werewolves would soon be on my trail if they weren't already.

And let's not forget Daisy and her strange dream or vision or whatever it was she had, and that she now appeared to be a dab hand with a blade. That she mentioned The Magician and an upcoming war further unsettled me, but I wasn't prepared to think about all that just yet.

Right now, I had a murder to investigate. Something I was good at. Something I could have at least some control over, unlike everything else in my life at the moment.

At the back of the shop, there was a door that led to a set of stairs. I walked up the stairs until I came to another door, which I then knocked. A few moments later, a nervous sounding voice came from the other side.

"Yeah? Who is it?" a girl's voice said.

"Detective Ethan Drake," I said, holding my badge in front of the peephole. "I'm with the FPD. I'd like to talk to you about what happened downstairs."

A long silence ensued, and I thought she wasn't going to

open the door. But as I was about to knock again, I heard a click, and the door opened a few inches, the security chain still attached. From inside, a young girl's face peered out at me, her hazel eyes full of fear and suspicion.

"It's okay," I said, seeing how rattled she was, showing her my badge again to reassure her. "I just need to talk to you about your uncle."

The girl stared at me a moment longer before releasing the security chain and opening the door wide so I could step inside the apartment.

"Are you with those other two cops?" she asked as I walked down the hallway into the small living room. The place was like a shrine to 1950's rock-and-roll music. All the walls held framed posters of icons like Elvis, Buddy Holly, and Chuck Berry. There was also a genuine Wurlitzer jukebox in the corner stocked with seven-inch vinyls.

"The two uniforms, you mean?" I looked at her before smiling down at the jukebox, approving of the vinyl inside.

"Yes," she said. "Those guys are assholes. They didn't care about my uncle at all."

"Well, I'm not going to disagree with you there." I stepped away from the jukebox and smiled at her. "Those guys *are* assholes. But I'm not like them. Thank god," I added, smiling at her, trying to put her at ease.

The girl seemed to relax a little when I said that, moving her long reddish hair out of her face. "My name's Gemma," she said, seeming no more than eighteen, freckle-faced and sturdily built as if she had grown up on a farm. There was a naivety about her as well that made me think she hadn't long arrived here in the big smoke. "Can I get you get a coffee?"

"Sure. That would be great."

I sat down on the couch as I gazed around the room, taken in by the old posters, not to mention the classic Gretsch guitar hanging above the jukebox. Sam Sidwell took his rock-

and-roll seriously. I almost felt bad for the guy now that he was dead and unable to enjoy his well-curated collection. His ghost might yet turn up back here, not just because he died violently, but also because of his obvious obsession. Sometimes people can't let go of things, even in death. Lots of collectors ended up doomed to haunt the rooms that held the objects of their obsession, at least until said objects were inevitably moved elsewhere. Then the collector ghosts would haunt the storerooms their stuff was moved to. Often, the ghosts would end up in the home of the person who bought the collection in the wake of their death. That's when you'd see the jealousy and resentment coming out because the ghost can't handle seeing their collection being enjoyed by someone else. Bad things would happen after that, usually.

"Here you go," Gemma said as she came in with two mugs of coffee and handed me one.

"Thanks," I said as she took a seat on the other end of the couch, cradling her mug in both hands as if she was trying to extract comfort from it in the wake of a no doubt shocking experience.

"Do you agree with those other two cops that my uncle killed himself?" she asked, staring intently at me.

I shook my head. "From what I've seen, I don't believe your uncle killed himself. We'll have to wait on the autopsy results for full confirmation, but right now, I'm investigating a murder, not a suicide."

She almost smiled with relief. "I'm so glad to hear you say that. The way those two assholes spoke, there wasn't going to be an investigation."

"They said that?"

"Not in so many words, but they sure implied it."

"Tell me, Gemma," I said after taking a sip from my coffee. "What do you think happened?"

"Well, that my uncle was killed, obviously."

"By whom? Did you see it happen?"

She shook her head. "I went out this morning to go to college and when I came back a couple hours ago——" She stopped as emotion overtook her, bringing tears to her already red-rimmed eyes. She pressed her hand against her chest while she took deep breaths to contain herself. "I'm sorry——"

"It's okay. Take as much time as you need. I know how hard this can be."

"I just can't believe this has happened. I've only been here less than two months."

"Where are you from?" I asked, trying to put her at ease.

"Redditch Village," she said as if the name said it all.

"This must be a big culture shock for you then."

"My uncle getting murdered, you mean? Yeah, kind of."

"No, I meant——"

"I'm sorry. I know what you meant."

"It's fine. You don't have to apologize. Were you and your uncle close?"

"Not really, I mean——" She paused for a second as she moved her hair from her face. "I hardly knew him before I moved here. But since I started living in his apartment and working part-time in his store, I was really getting to know him. He was a nice guy. He was nice to me and all the customers who came in, even though half of them are like, total assholes."

"I can imagine."

"Some people are just so entitled. I had no idea until I moved here."

"A place like this breeds some pretty unbalanced people," I said. "Trust me, I know."

"You seem okay."

I smiled. "When was the last time you saw your uncle?"

"This morning before I left for college. Around tennish."

"And you got back at what time?"

"Maybe two?"

"And that's when you found your uncle?"

35

"Kind of. Those two cops were already here."

"Did somebody call them?"

She shrugged. "Maybe. I'm not sure. I guess a customer did or something. Won't you have a record of any calls made?"

"We will," I said, smiling at her acuity. "What are you studying at college, by the way?"

"Mythology and folklore."

"I thought maybe you'd be studying law or something."

"Nope. I want to be a writer. I'm taking a creative writing class as well." She shrugged. "I just love stories."

"Good for you," I said. "There are enough lawyers out there, anyway."

"That's what my uncle used to say."

"You uncle was clearly a wise man."

She smiled and then looked at the floor as more tears ran down her face. "I still can't believe this has happened…"

"I know," I said. "I'll not take up much more of your time. I just need to ask you a few more questions. Is that okay?"

"Sure."

"Great." I placed my coffee mug on the floor and stared intently at her. "Tell me, Gemma, is there anyone you can think of who might have had a grudge or a—"

"Reason to kill my uncle?"

"Yes."

"There's someone I can think of."

"Who might that be?"

"Delphina."

"Delphina? Who's that?"

"She's like…some sort of mob boss, I guess? I dunno exactly."

"You mean she runs a gang?"

Gemma nodded. "There are these three guys and another woman who go around with Delphina all the time. My uncle said they showed up a few months ago out of nowhere and started to terrorize all the business owners in the square. They demand money from everyone, and they call once a week to collect. Sometimes they smash the place up too. As far as I know, all the business owners around here are in debt to Delphina and her gang."

"Like your uncle was?"

"Yes. Sam paid them every week, even though it left him broke most of the time." She paused. "He told me one time he didn't pay up."

"And what happened?"

"He ended up in hospital for a week."

Bunch of fucking shakedown artists, although I'd never heard of any Delphina. She must be new on the scene. "Do you know who Delphina works for?"

"Some guy. I've never met him, but Sam mentioned him a couple times."

"Can you remember his name?"

"I don't think he mentioned his name, or if he did, I can't remember." She thought for a second. "I think Sam referred to the guy as Snake Tongue or something weird like that. Apparently, he showed up before Delphina did."

To pave the way, I thought, *and to talk the unsuspecting business owners into accepting the terms he would soon enforce.*

I knew how it worked. Every gangster organization in the city operated the same way. The talker goes in first to negotiate terms (or at least pretend to), and then the muscle goes in after enforcing said terms. The same thing was going on here, it seemed. "Has the gang ever been violent when you've been around?"

"Not really," she said. "But the violence is always implied, you know what I mean?"

"I do."

"And there's something off about these guys," she said, frowning. "They're strong, for a start. I mean, my daddy has been a farmer his whole life. He can lift a damn cow if he has to. But he's still not as strong as these guys are. I saw one of them lift a refrigerator and throw it across the room like it was nothing. I guess they must be on something to make them that strong."

"I guess so," I said, wondering now if the people she was describing were MURKs, or even the other things…Mytholites. "Tell me about Delphina."

Gemma shook her head as if she didn't want to discuss it, but did so anyway. "She scares the shit out of everyone, including me."

"How come?"

"She's a fucking psycho, that's why. Excuse my French."

"What does she do that makes her so intimidating?"

"It's not so much what she does as what she implies with her manner. You just know she's dangerous as fu—well, you know."

I nodded. "Do you know where Delphina and her crew hang out?"

"No idea. I don't want to know either. Wherever it is, it's a place I don't want to fucking go, I'll tell you that much." She shook her head slightly. "My language has gone terrible since I moved here. My momma would be ashamed if she heard me."

"I don't think you'll go to Hell for using the F word."

"Not according to my momma. According to my momma, you can go to Hell for a lot less than that."

"Your mother is a God-fearing woman, I take it?"

"Damn straight. Goes to church every day. Prays like a dozen times a day."

Jesus, I thought. I'm sure it was fun growing up around that level of zealotry. I'm not surprised this girl fled to the city. "Is everyone in Redditch like your mother?"

She nodded. "Pretty much…and a lot more besides," she added in a whisper.

"What do you mean?"

"Nothing," she said, smiling broadly. "Are we done? I have a lot to do as you can imagine. I've still to tell my folks what happened. They'll probably demand I come home straight away."

"Will you?" I asked as I stood up.

"Will I what?"

"Go home if they ask."

She thought for a moment and then shook her head. "No. I can't go back there. I don't want to."

"Any particular reason?"

"I just don't want to," she said flatly.

"Fair enough." I reached into my trench and took out a card, handing to her. "Call me if you think of anything else. You'll have to give an official statement down at the precinct. Someone will be in touch about that. But in the meantime, if you can think of anything…"

She waved the card a little. "I'll give you a call."

I moved toward the hallway, then stopped by the doorway. "You said the two uniforms were already here when you arrived, is that right?"

"Yes, that's right. Why?"

"Nothing. Just trying to get my facts straight."

"So is this an official murder investigation now?" she asked as I stepped out the front door and stood at the top of the stairs.

"As far as I'm concerned it is."

I SPENT ANOTHER COUPLE HOURS AT THE SQUARE TALKING with the other business owners. Most of them seemed to be decent enough people; hard-working and honest. But they were also tight-lipped when it came to talking about this Delphina person and her gang. They seemed to fear saying anything derogatory in case their words made it back to the wrong ears. Two of them—the woman who owned the florists and the man who ran the pizza place—even sung the gang's praises, telling me how much they appreciated having someone to protect and watch out for them in such a dangerous neighborhood. Having never met any victim of extortion who sang the praises of the person extorting them, I could only conclude that this Delphina character—and the other guy, Snake Tongue—had some strange hold over the people here. The way some of them smiled when they spoke of the gang was just plain weird; even creepy.

"That Mr. Francetti is a lovely man," the florist, Mrs. Honeysuckle, said to me as I interviewed her. "He really does have the best interests of our little square at heart. So does Delphina. Lovely people the pair of them." When I told her that's not what I heard, she scowled and said, "Some people are just so ungrateful."

Evidently, Snake Tongue's real name was Antonio Francetti, according to the florist. I would run a check on him later. As for Delphina, no one knew her surname. The liquor store guy, Jack Talford, did say, however, that Delphina had eyes like a shark. "When that bitch's eyes go dead, you better watch out," Talford informed me. "You know there's gonna be trouble then."

"When's the gang due for the next pick-up?" I asked him.

"Not sure," he said. "They could drop by anytime. They usually show up at least once a week to collect, though."

I would be waiting when they showed up again. Then I'd have a word and see what's what. In the meantime, I'd run Francetti's name through the system. Hopefully, he'd be on there, and I'd get a better idea of who I was dealing with.

Although my gut already knew, without having to check.

I was dealing with the mob.

The fucking Mafia.

5

Darkness had fallen by the time I walked across the square back to my car. I was just a few feet away from the old Dodge when a sudden heat flared up on the back of my neck, followed by the agitation of the tattoo ink on my arms and back.

My Infernal Itch was making itself felt.

But why?

Standing, I began to look around to see if anyone—or anything—was near. The square was quiet, save for a few customers inside the pizza place, and a guy walking out of the liquor store with a bottle wrapped in a brown paper bag. The guy glanced at me briefly but headed off in the opposite direction.

After surveying the whole square and the street beyond, I didn't see anyone who looked suspicious or whose presence further flared up my Infernal Itch.

But just because you can't see someone, doesn't mean they aren't there.

MURKs are masters of stealth and blending in unseen. Such necessary survival skills are in their very genes, making them hard to spot at the best of times.

Someone was out there. Watching me.

I felt it in my bones; felt the unseen eyes boring into me from afar.

For a second, I wondered if it was Hannah. Had she tracked me down? Did she want to kill me now? If she did, I couldn't blame her. If someone had shot me five times, I'd wanna fucking kill them too.

Over time, I'd gotten a good sense of Hannah's presence. My Infernal Itch reacted to her in a certain way, sending not unpleasant sensations down the length of my spine, even from a distance. I wasn't feeling those sensations now, so I concluded it wasn't Hannah watching me.

Someone else then. But who?

As I started to think, my Infernal Itch died down. Whoever had been watching me had moved on now.

Whoever they were, I knew I would feel their presence again soon.

Maybe even up close and personal next time.

~

FROM THE GROWLS OF MY STOMACH, YOU'D THINK I HADN'T eaten in days, which come to think of it, I probably hadn't. On the way home, I pulled into a drive-thru and ordered a couple burgers and some fries, pulling into the parking lot next to the restaurant so I could sit and eat.

While I munched on the burgers, Apex Twin's *Selected Ambient Works* played on the stereo, providing a soothing backing track to my racing thoughts.

I tried to keep my mind on the case, but other thoughts kept breaking my concentration—a series of rapid-fire flash-backs: disturbing images of Scarlet Hood dying in my arms as her blood leaked out onto the floor; Charlotte Webb and her grotesque, spider-like body as she burst through the glass of the tank in which she was created; Derrick Savage's head rolling across the floor after I'd lopped it off; Hannah staggering back and falling out the window after I'd shot her; Callie's butchered body; scores of other bodies combining into a cornucopia of gory violence that represented my life's work. These images and more flashed through my mind as I chewed joylessly on my fast food, prompting me to take a dose of Mud which I washed down with sugary cola.

A bringer of death is what I am. A violent hornet who inevitably stings everyone I come into contact with. I am God's lonely man, beset with violent tendencies and forced to walk a path of blood.

Staring through the windshield, something caught my eye across the parking lot. A movement between two parked cars.

As I chewed slowly, I squinted into the darkness, but couldn't make anything out. Though for a second, I thought I glimpsed a pair of yellow eyes watching me. To be sure, I blinked rapidly three times and activated my infrared vision. But there was nothing there. If someone had been there, they were now gone.

"Quit fucking around," I muttered as I kept staring out the window, "and just fucking show yourself."

After I'd finished my food, I sat smoking a cigarette, almost daring whoever was watching me to make a move.

But nothing happened.

Except that my phone rang in my pocket, startling me slightly. "Yeah?" I said answering it.

"Drake?" said a familiar scathing voice. "It's Captain Edwards."

I rolled my eyes. "Captain. What can I do for you?"

"You can stay away from my cases, for a start."

"Your cases, sir?"

"Routman had no business handing that body in Nelson Square over to you."

"Who else is going to cover it? Everyone is tied up with the Ripper Tripper task force."

"Don't I fucking know it," he muttered.

"You should be grateful I'm helping." I couldn't resist a smile when I said it.

"I'll be grateful when your ass is gone from my precinct," he retorted.

"Seems to me you can't afford to lose me just yet. Besides, this case is now a murder investigation that falls under the remit of Unit X." I smiled again with some satisfaction. "You don't get to toss me off this case…sir."

Edwards sighed audibly down the phone. "Don't tell me. The vic was murdered by vampires? Or a goddamn ghost?"

"Not really, but something's afoot."

"Something's always afoot with you, Drake."

"I'm doing you a favor here," I said. "If you want, I'll hand the case back over, adding to your already full caseload. It's no skin off my nose."

"Fine," he said. "Can I at least get a report?"

"You'd have to ask the commissioner for that."

"The fucking commissioner. See, this is why you get my hump up, Drake. It wouldn't take much for you to keep me in the loop. A simple briefing would do. But no, in your arrogance, you continue to operate as a lone wolf, and then you wonder why I hate you so fucking much." He paused. "What happened with that cult, by the way?"

"Oh, you mean the cult you refused to help me with? That one?"

"I have to be careful where I assign the department's limited resources. You should know that."

And you wonder why I hate you so fucking much.

"I took care of it," I said.

"Took care of it?"

"You really want the gory details?"

He paused before answering. "I think I'll maintain my plausible deniability," he said. "When Unit X inevitably blows up, at least I can say I had nothing do with it."

"That's very political of you to say so. And here was me thinking we were all in this shitstorm together, fighting as one."

For once he had no comeback. "Enjoy working your case," was all he said. "It may be your last one, Drake."

When he hung up, I shook my head at his bullshit and tossed the phone on the passenger seat.

It takes a special breed of asshole to be in charge, I thought, glancing at myself in the rearview mirror.

A special breed indeed.

∾

I HEADED BACK HOME AFTER I'D FILLED MY BELLY BECAUSE NOW I needed to refill the Mud bottle, which I'd forgotten to do earlier. I hadn't taken a dose since this morning and it was beginning to show. My anxiety levels were rising, and I found myself constantly grinding my teeth and clenching my fists, gripping the steering wheel way too tight as I was driving.

Not only that, my thoughts were pinging madly around inside my head, and I felt unable to concentrate on any one thing for longer than a few seconds. This is the downside of relying on a drug to keep yourself in a certain state. When you don't get the drug you end up crashing hard, which only makes you want the drug more because you think to yourself that you can't cope with these horrible feelings of withdrawal.

Yep, I thought as I got out of the car. *I'm a goddamn junkie on top of everything else now.*

But who was I kidding? I've always been a junkie. Hunting monsters? That's not an addiction? Going into battle against something that might kill you? Being a cop? These things are all addictions. And the worst part is, without them, I'm nothing. Just some asshole with a chip on his shoulder.

As I hurried from the car, I stopped when I heard a noise.

Turning around, I thought the noise sounded like it came from the alley.

"Pssst!"

I walked around the corner into the alley to see a massive black shape standing there in the shadows, with two blazing red eyes glaring out at me. "About fucking time," the shape said, coming toward me.

"Haedemus," I said, somewhat surprised to see him. "I assumed you were with Hannah."

"I was," he said as he came closer, his partially decayed head coming to rest near me, his serrated horn stained with blood. "I came to see you. I've been waiting here for hours. Where the fuck have you been? I feel like a fucking creepy stalker waiting in this alley."

"You certainly give off that vibe."

"Fuck you, Ethan. I don't have time to listen to your sorry excuse for humor."

"What's wrong? Where's Hannah?"

"She's gone on the hunt," he said. "I was supposed to wait for her in Little Tokyo behind some fucking neon-lit pagoda, but I galloped here to see you instead."

"Why? Did you miss me?"

"Again, fuck you, Ethan. I don't know how you can joke given what you did. Your little Hannah is back to being Xaglath all the time now. A complete fucking bitch. And, she's on the warpath. Whatever bad shit you stirred up in Hannah by shooting her, Xaglath is now channeling into her war with the Yakuza. I've never seen her so pissed off, not even in Hell when she fell into the Lake of Aborted Fetuses. She was really pissed off that time. Her hair was ruined by that gloopy mess."

With a heavy sigh, I reached into my pocket and took out my cigarettes, stabbing one into my mouth before lighting it up with a zippo. "I—"

"Sure, Ethan, take a smoke why don't you?" he said,

cutting me off before I could say anything. "It's not like you have nothing to worry about. Xaglath has already said that after she's done with the Yakuza, she's coming for you next. Put that in your pipe and smoke it."

"This is a cigarette."

"Whatever." He tossed his mane in a dramatic fashion as he snorted loudly.

"I've never seen you so wound up."

"Well, what do you expect, Ethan, hmm? It's me that has to suffer that demon bitch's foul moods and constant muttering to herself about how she's going to make everyone pay dearly. And by everyone, I mean this whole fucking world. She will not stop at you, Ethan. She plans global revenge, and guess who gets to carry her into it? That's right, me!"

"Alright, calm down, Haedemus," I said. "It won't get that far."

"You haven't seen her. Only this morning, she killed a guy for bumping into her on the street."

"She killed an innocent person?"

"I wasn't around when she did it because she sent me to spy on some Yakuza guy, but yes, she killed an innocent person, and she took great delight in telling me all about how she sent him to Hell."

"Fuck's sake."

"This is all *your* doing, Ethan. Every bit of it."

"Let's not get carried away," I said. "I had good reason to believe she ordered the deaths of my wife and daughter."

"Ex-wife, and you jumped to conclusions." He paused. "Wait, did you just say you *had* good reason? You mean you know she's innocent?"

I looked away. "I do."

"How?"

"Did she tell you about the video?"

"She mentioned something about it, yes. Apparently, it shows her talking to some hitman."

"It does, only it's not her. Not really."

"So who is it?"

"A shapeshifter…I think."

Haedemus turned his head slightly as if he was thinking things over. "I'm not sure how she'll react to this new information. It might make things worse."

"How do you figure?"

"Come on, Ethan. It's not going to make her back down any. She'll just take it as a vindication of her actions. It'll justify her bloody crusade even more."

"Maybe," I said, blowing a stream of smoke into the damp air. "But she has to know the truth."

"Because *you'll* feel better then, right?"

"Fuck you. I made a mistake, alright? Whatta you want me to do?"

"It's not what I want you to do, it's what *she'll* want you to do," he said. "She'll want you on your hands and knees begging for forgiveness, and even that won't save you from going to Hell."

"I need to speak with Hannah, not Xaglath."

"Well, good luck with that. Xaglath is in charge now. And even if you do talk with Hannah, what do you think she'll say?" He adopted a high-pitched voice. "'Oh, thanks so much for shooting me, Ethan. Five gaping bullet holes in my chest is a really great look for me.'"

"Don't be a dick."

Haedemus snorted. "Pot kettle, Ethan, pot kettle."

Tossing the end of my cigarette away, I dug my hands into my trench pockets as the rain started to get heavier. "Is there someplace she's hanging out?"

"Not really. We go from one Yakuza hangout to another, that's all. She plans on making a move on them soon."

"Well," I said. "Kazuo Yagami plans on making a move on her too. He wants Hannah under his thumb, so he can use her as he sees fit."

"That will never happen. Xaglath would never allow it."

"That won't stop Yagami from trying."

"Let him. He'll just be walking into his own death."

"Do you think you can get through to Hannah and deliver a message for me?"

"I don't know, but I guess I'll try. What message?"

"Just tell her to call me. Tell her I know the truth now, and that——"

"You're sorry?"

"Yeah, but not quite as sarcastically."

"I'm sorry, Ethan, but you fucked up. I'm not going to go easy on you."

"I'll remember that the next time you fuck up."

Haedemus opened his mouth to say something else, but as soon as he did he vanished into thin air, leaving me wondering where the hell he had gone to until I realized that Xaglath had probably summoned him back to her.

Sighing, I headed out of the alley and hurried toward the entrance to the apartment building, realizing as I did that things were about to get violent and bloody if I couldn't get through to Hannah. Given everything that Haedemus had told me, getting through to her would prove difficult if not impossible. I was on Xaglath's shitlist now, so I would have to watch my back.

As if I wasn't doing that already every goddamn day.

BEFORE I WENT TO MY APARTMENT, I CALLED UPON THE building super and asked him to come by and fix my front door at some point. The super wasn't happy I was calling so late, but I knew if I didn't say something to him now, I'd just keep forgetting. So I listened to him bitch and moan for a minute before he finally said he would call tomorrow afternoon and get it sorted.

Thanking him, I went to walk away, but as I did, the super called me back. He was a few years younger than me, beefy, his nose bent out of shape as if he'd been a boxer once. "Hey," he said. "You're a cop, ain't you?"

"Yeah," I said. "Why?"

"There's this guy living up on the tenth floor. There's a bad smell coming outta his apartment. People are complaining."

"What kind of smell?"

"Like he's got a fucking dead body in there or somethin'."

I nodded as I thought for a moment. "You want me to check it out?"

"Yeah, I'd appreciate it. The guy comes and goes at odd hours. Sometimes he's carrying black bags."

"Black bags?"

"I think he might be a serial killer."

"Or maybe you watch too many movies."

"The guy's a fuckin' weirdo. He's also a month behind on his rent."

Normally I wouldn't get involved in something like this, but as I needed the super to fix my door, I made an exception. "What number?"

"1013."

"I'll check it out now."

The super nodded. "Thanks. I'll get your door sorted for you tomorrow. Consider it done."

"I appreciate that."

Now on a detour from my apartment, I headed up the stairs to the tenth floor. As soon as I entered the hallway, I almost gagged at the cloying stench that slapped me up the face. "Jesus fuck—"

Covering my mouth and nose with my hand, I reluctantly walked up the dark hallway, the ceiling lights flickering as I went. The smell was undeniably like that of a decomposing body, either animal or human. How the hell the neighbors had been standing this stench was beyond me. Given how suspicious the smell was, I was shocked no one had called the cops before now. Or maybe they did and no one came. Bad smells in a rundown apartment building in a shithole neighborhood were not considered a priority down at the precinct.

Still, this was pretty fucking bad.

As I neared number 1013, I began to think the super's suspicions about the tenant may not have been so farfetched. Maybe there *was* a serial killer living here. Either that, or the guy's wife or dog had died, and he just hadn't told anyone, preferring to keep the body where it was. It happens more than you might think. Someone dies and their spouse can't bear to let them go, so they say nothing and keep the body at home like Norman fucking Bates' mother. The smell gives them away eventually, though. Sooner or later, someone calls it in.

Coming to the green door, I rapped it with my knuckles and stood waiting on someone to answer. My Infernal Itch wasn't flaring up, so I had to figure whatever this situation was, it was mundane. The guy probably had his dead wife in the bedroom. He probably still slept beside her cold corpse every night.

After a few minutes, when no one answered the door, I announced myself as a cop to see if that would bring someone to the door. It didn't. Either no one was home, or they just weren't answering.

I turned to leave, but the smell stopped me in my tracks. It was too damn suspicious to walk away from.

Sighing, I turned around and walked back to the door, banging it harder this time with my fist. "If there's anyone in there, I suggest you open the door or I'll be forced to break it down. You've been warned."

"He's not in," said a voice from behind me.

I turned around to see an old lady sticking her head

around the doorframe of her apartment. "You're sure?" I asked her.

"He left an hour ago. Are you here about the smell?"

"Eh, yeah. That's right. You know anything about it?"

The old lady shook her head. "It started a few months ago. That's when Mr. Dormer started going out at odd hours. I don't really sleep, you see, so I hear everything."

"Do you know Mr. Dormer?" I asked her.

"He keeps himself to himself mostly. He's a shy boy. Never speaks to anyone. I think there's something wrong with him. You know, upstairs like."

"Have you seen him do anything suspicious?"

"I saw him bring a child in there."

I stared at her. "A child?"

"A little boy. He said it was his nephew. That's the only time I heard him speak."

"When was this?"

"A few days ago."

"A few days ago?" I said raising my eyebrows at her. "You never alerted the cops?"

"He said it was his nephew."

"Alright. Why don't you go back inside now and let me handle things?"

When the old lady closed her door, I turned to Mr. Dormer's door again. I liked nothing I heard from the old lady. Not one fucking bit.

After taking my gun from its holster and holding it close to my chest, I booted Mr. Dormer's door, the enhanced strength in my legs allowing me to generate enough force to kick the door in on the first try. The second the door swung open on its now damaged hinges, I recoiled at the stench that hit me like a tidal wave. I did my best not to gag as I pointed my gun in front of me.

"Police!" I announced, just in case anyone was hiding in there. "I'm coming in!"

No one answered, so I moved cautiously inside the apartment, now dreading what I would find.

Aside from the sickening stench, the first thing that drew my attention was the walls. They were painted with a light hue, but you'd never know it from the symbols and writing scrawled all over them. Every single wall in the dark living room was covered in the same gnarly handwriting and painted symbols.

The symbols I recognized as being occult, many of them seeming to relate to demons and dark magic. The living room itself was barely furnished. A battered couch and old TV were pushed to the side of the room, seemingly to make space for the magic circle in the center of the hardwood floor, the carpet having been stripped. Black candles were placed at certain points around the pentagram, and even though it was dark inside the room, I could still make out the bloodstains on the floor in and around the magic circle.

Maybe our Mr. Dormer is a hellot, I thought. *Or just a crazy fuck.*

Whatever the case, he was shit out of luck now, that's for sure.

As I cleared the kitchen and bathroom and then headed toward the bedroom, I glanced at the scrawled handwriting on the wall nearest to me.

The children's souls must be saved, it said. *This world is not for them. Their world is below...*

A few inches over, it said, *I will eat their flesh and vomit their souls...*

I am God's servant, His devourer of innocence...

Christ, I thought as I shook my head at the ominous passages.

Given that every wall was covered in this handwritten nonsense, it must've taken him months, maybe even years, to do it all. These chicken scratchings represented the mind of a severely disturbed individual, there was no doubt about that.

This was Mr. Dormer's psychosis made manifest; the sick outpouring of his twisted mind.

I paused in front of the bedroom door. Fuck knows what I was going to find in there. Given everything I'd seen and read in this nightmare abode, I almost didn't want to find out.

But I knew I had to.

After taking a breath and grasping my gun tighter, I wrapped my fingers around the doorknob and pushed the door open, pointing my gun into the darkness within as the hinges creaked loudly in the heavy silence.

When my eyes finally adjusted to the gloom, I wished they hadn't.

Even in the half-light, I could see the shapes hanging from the ceiling like empty sacks.

It was only when I felt for the light switch and flicked the light on, did I realize exactly what I was looking at.

Human skins.

The skins of children, to be more precise.

Dirty-pink and shapeless like deflated balloons, but not so shapeless that you couldn't make out what they were. There were at least a dozen of the ghoulish things hanging there, all of them stitched at the joints and other places with thick black thread.

But before I could even begin to fully comprehend what I was looking at, my eyes shifted to the corner of the room and I took in the stack of bones there. Small skulls and an assortment of bones—femurs, scapulas, clavicles, ribs, tibias, fibulas, even vertebrae—arranged into something that was clearly meant as a shrine. Black candles adorned some of the skulls, the wax having dripped over the off-white surface of the bones to form a skin of sorts.

"Holy fuck…" I breathed.

Just when you think you've seen it all, some cunt plumbs the depths of depravity and sickness to come up with this gruesome beyond words display.

As I stared at the bones and then the gently swinging skins hanging from the ceiling, it began to feel as if the walls were closing in on me, the twisted scrawls on said walls filling my vision until it was all I could see. With the stench continuing to turn my stomach, I turned and hurried out of the apartment before I threw up the burgers I'd eaten earlier.

Outside in the hallway, I stood taking deep breaths, the air there only marginally better than the cloying air inside the apartment.

It was as I was taking one of these breaths I noticed the figure standing at the end of the hallway. It was a man dressed in a dark raincoat, the hat he wore casting shadows over his face. In his arms, he held a grocery bag. For a long moment, we both stared at each other under the flickering lights, and I knew without a doubt that I was looking at Mr. Dormer.

So did he, for he soon dropped his grocery bag, turned tail, and ran back toward the stairs.

The second he did, I bolted after him, my boots pounding against the floor as I raced down the hallway with my gun still in my hand. I couldn't let this sicko get away. If he escaped, he'd move somewhere else and start killing children again. I didn't give a fuck what compulsion drove him to do what he did. The only thing I knew was that I had to put him down. There'd be no going to jail for this motherfucker.

The only place he was going was Hell.

"Stop! Police!"

The guy wasn't the fastest runner, I have to say. As I chased him down the flights of stairs, I saw he was running with a limp. It wouldn't be long before I caught up with him.

When Dormer got to the third floor—my floor— he opted to cross the landing into the hallway, perhaps to head for the fire escape at the other end.

By the time I crossed the landing and entered the hallway, Dormer was a third of the way down it.

But there was someone else there too, just ahead of him.

Daisy.

She was standing outside my door, either coming out or about to go in. Whatever the case, she stood staring at Dormer as he continued to limp-run in her direction.

"Daisy!" I yelled, hoping she would have the sense to dive into my apartment and avoid Dormer as he continued to lurch toward her. He'd be just the type to grab Daisy and use her as a shield against me.

But Daisy didn't run. Instead, she moved to the center of the hallway and stood her ground as something now glinted in her hand.

What the fuck is she doing?

"Daisy! Get out of the way!"

With horror, I saw that Dormer had a long knife in his hand now, as if he'd had it concealed up his sleeve this whole time.

As he neared Daisy—who continued to boldly stand her ground—I saw him raise his arm and swing the knife in a wide arc as he came upon her.

Coming to a stop, I raised my gun, intending to shoot Dormer in the back before he could harm Daisy.

But before I got my shot off, Daisy rushed forward, ducking under Dormer's arm and the long knife he was holding. As she leaned her body to the side, she drew her arm across Dormer's abdomen, and then came up quickly to face his back just as Dormer froze and the knife dropped from his hand.

A second later, Dormer fell to his knees, and then pitched forward as if dead.

"Daisy!" I shouted as I ran toward her.

Daisy turned around, and I saw the Karambit knife in her hand, the one she got Cal to make for my birthday. Shocked, I saw the blade was dripping with blood.

She stood aside as I kept my gun trained on the downed serial killer. After kicking his knife away, I gripped his shoulder and rolled him over onto his back. He groaned as I did so, his hands clasped across his belly as he struggled to hold his intestines in.

Jesus fuck. She's slit him open like a fucking fish.

Despite his horrific injury, Dormer smiled up at me. "*Hell...awaits...*" he whispered before his eyes closed and he breathed his last breath.

Slowly, I turned to look at Daisy, who merely smiled at me. "He was a bad guy, right?" she said.

I could only stare back at her.

6

Daisy had just left my apartment when Dormer came upon her. She had been hanging with the Hellbastards while I was out and was about to head back to her own apartment when she noticed Dormer coming toward her.

"The knife was already in my hand," she told me after I'd gotten the Hellbastards to drag Dormer's body inside my apartment before anyone saw him. "The knife is never out of my hand. I practice with it all the time."

For someone who'd just killed a guy, Daisy seemed to hold up pretty well. Too well, in fact. She didn't seem at all disturbed or shocked by what she had done. It unsettled me that she had the countenance of someone who had killed before. She was a thirteen-year-old girl, for Christ's sake. How could she do what she did and not be affected by it?

As I sat on the couch with a whiskey in my hand, I watched Daisy as she helped the Hellbastards wrap Dormer's body up in an old sheet. *This isn't right*, I kept thinking to myself. *Thirteen-year-old girls should not be helping demons wrap up dead bodies.*

But there she was, doing exactly that.

And what's more, it didn't even seem to bother her that

much. Dormer's guts were hanging out of his belly, ropes of intestine trailing to the floor. It also didn't help that the Hell-bastards were squishing the intestines underfoot, laughing at the fart noises the gases made. Between Cracka and Toast, they had a damn symphony going they were stomping so much.

"Enough, for Christ's sake!" I snapped at them. "Just wrap the body up so we can get rid of it, will ya?"

"Sure, boss," Cracka tittered as he pressed another thick length of the intestine with his tiny foot, laughing once again at the extended fart noise he summoned.

I would have to report Dormer, or at least his ghoulish apartment, but not the fact that Daisy killed him. Even though there was a good case for self-defense, the last thing I wanted was for Daisy to be drawn into the corrupt, heartless justice system. Once you went into the system—guilty or not guilty—you were marked for life. Daisy didn't deserve that.

In the end, she took out a multiple murderer of children. She did the world a favor.

When I'd finished my drink, I went outside and drove the Dodge around to the back of the building before parking it next to the back exit. With Dormer's body wrapped in a bloodstained blanket, held tight with duct tape, I carried the corpse out to the car and put it in the trunk. I'd already taken the Karambit knife from Daisy, which I'd cleaned up in the kitchen sink, removing the blood from it. I put it now in the glove compartment of the car. By rights, I should get rid of it —it was a murder weapon after all—but it was a birthday present and it meant a lot to me, so I decided to hold on to it.

You never know when you might need a good knife.

Having already told Daisy and the Hellbastards to clean up the blood in the hallway, I drove to an isolated part of the river near the Industrial Zone and dumped the body off the pier into the murky water and watched it sink below the surface in a cloud of bubbles. The currents would carry the body out to sea, assuming it made it that far.

The river that cut through the middle of the city had living things in it that would likely make quick work of devouring Dormer's body.

And I'm not talking about fish.

Dark, alien creatures patrol the murky depths, feasting on anything that enters the water, and sometimes, anything on the bank that gets too close to the water. Dozens of fishermen have gone missing over the years, enough that hardly anyone fishes the river anymore. People know of the rumors about monsters, but very few have ever seen said monsters and lived to tell about it. I have, and I hope to never lay eyes on them again.

Like something from Lovecraft's nightmares, the things in the depths belong in the depths where no one should see them.

A WHILE LATER, WHEN I WAS BACK IN THE APARTMENT, I called Commissioner Lewellyn and told him about Dormer and what was inside his apartment. I told him the super had asked me to check the place out, and while I was there, Dormer happened upon me and I gave chase, but Dormer escaped. Lewellyn said he would send people to the apartment and that I should put a BOLO out on Dormer.

"Only you could stumble upon such horrors, Ethan," Lewellyn said.

"You know me, sir," I said, sitting on the couch with a whiskey in my hand. "This shit has a way of finding me."

"Yes, shit in general has a way of finding you." He paused. "I'll say this much, though—the FPD will have lost a good man when you're gone."

I froze with the whiskey glass near my lips. "When I'm gone, sir?"

"Well, yes, I thought you knew…"

"Knew, sir? Knew what?"

Lewellyn went silent for a second, then sighed. "Captain Edwards has formally requested your removal from the force. I'm sorry, Ethan."

Staring straight ahead as a deep scowl formed on my face, I asked, "How long?"

"I'm not really——"

"How long?" I insisted.

"As long as it takes the paperwork to go through. A few days at most, I would think."

"There's nothing you can do?"

"I'm doing everything I can, Ethan. I'm pulling every string, calling in favors——"

I hung up the phone and dropped it onto the couch as I sat clenching my jaw.

"Ethan?" Daisy stood over by the bathroom, her hair wet because I'd told her to take a shower to remove any blood she may have had on her. I also told her to wash her clothes as soon as she got back to her own place and preferably get rid of them after. "Is everything okay?"

The best I could do was give her a tight smile. The thought of not being a cop anymore was affecting me more than I thought it would. Even though I knew this was coming —that Edwards was out to get me—it was still a shock to hear that he had almost succeeded in his bid to get rid of me. Suddenly I felt adrift like a boat severed from its moorings and was now floating out to the vast, empty ocean.

As I continued to sit in silence, Daisy came over and sat beside me, before somewhat cautiously resting her head against my arm, reminding me so much of Callie it hurt.

"You want to tell me what happened out in that hallway

tonight?" I asked her, as much to force my mind off the current crisis as anything else.

"I don't know," Daisy said quietly after a moment's silence. "I just saw the man running toward me and I knew straight away he was bad…like, really bad."

"How would you have known that?"

"Well, the big knife in his hand was my first clue," she said, causing me to laugh slightly. "But even before that, I just sensed there was something…evil about him, like he did really bad things to people who didn't deserve it."

"He did."

"What did you see in his apartment?"

I shook my head at the memory of the hanging skins and the arranged bones. "You don't want to know."

"Maybe you're right."

"Tell me why you used the knife on him," I said.

"It was in my hand. I didn't even think about it. I just—"

"Reacted?"

"Yeah. It just seemed like the right thing to do."

"But how did you know what way to cut him? I saw you. It was like you'd done the same move dozens of times before." I stared into the memory for a second. "You moved like—"

"Someone else?"

I nodded. "Yeah. Do you feel like someone else?"

She looked worried for a second. "You think I'm possessed?"

"No, I think it's something different."

"Like what?" She slid forward so she could look into my eyes.

I had a strong feeling that Daisy was becoming one of these Mytholites that Pike had mentioned. In the absence of any other reasonable explanation, it was the only thing that seemed to make sense. You didn't just learn to move—to kill— like a warrior overnight, and yet Daisy had done exactly that. I was reluctant to tell her anything just yet in case it freaked her out too much. Plus, I didn't know much about Mytholites myself yet, or how it all worked, or if there were any dire consequences to becoming one.

Until I had a better understanding of what was happening to Daisy, I decided to keep the whole Mytholite thing to myself.

"I'm not sure yet," I said.

"Yes you are," she retorted. "You know something and you're not telling me."

Silly of me to underestimate her acumen. "Just let me make some inquiries first. Then I'll tell you what I know. Have you had any more dreams or visions?"

She pouted for a moment, clearly unhappy I wasn't filling her in. "Yes," she said. "I've had a few."

"What about this time?"

"Battles mostly. Fighting against men in black, and against...others."

"Others?"

"People with superpowers, I guess you'd call them. And monsters."

"Doesn't sound good. Do you think these are premonitions of the future?"

Daisy shrugged. "I don't know. Maybe. It's all a bit overwhelming, to be honest."

"Well, you're not alone in this," I said, smiling down at her. She seemed afraid now, her eyes welling up with tears. I could only imagine how she was feeling, especially after killing a man. "I won't let anything bad happen to you."

"You promise?"

Don't say it. Don't you say it...

"I promise," I said, laying my hand on top of hers. "Nothing bad will happen to you."

❧

When Daisy left, I sat on the couch for another while, drinking whiskey and chain-smoking cigarettes as I tried to deal with the fact that I would soon be out of a job. More than that, I would soon no longer be a cop. As much as I hated the job sometimes, it gave me an identity, a purpose.

Without the job, I didn't know what I was going to do.

Was there even any point in finishing the case I was on?

Yes, there was.

Gemma Sidwell was still relying on me to find her uncle's killer, and I knew if I didn't do it, no one else would. There was also the fact that something fishy was going on at Nelson's Square, and I intended to find out what it was, and maybe even restore order there. If this was to be my last case, I wanted to make sure I solved it before being booted out of the FPD on my ass with not even a pension.

So, first things first. I had to go see Artemis and Pan Demic to get them to run a search on Antonio Francetti for me. I doubted the police database would turn much up on the guy, so I needed the Terrible Twosome to dig deeper. If there was dirt or anything else on Francetti, those two would find it.

As I went to get up, my phone rang on the seat beside me. Picking up the phone, I was shocked to see it was Hannah's number calling. I let the phone ring for several seconds before answering, slowly putting it to my ear.

"Hello?" I said quietly. When there was no answer, I said, "Hannah? Is that you?"

For the longest time, there was just a heavy silence on the line, before a voice—Hannah's voice—said, "Hannah's dead."

There was a beep, and then the line went dead.

7

The following day as I made my way through downtown on the way to Bedford to see Artemis and Pan Demic, I ran into heavy traffic. After inching along for half an hour, I made it into the city center and saw what the holdup was.

A large group of women had gathered in the square around the statue of Joshua Fairview, the city's founder. Dozens of provocatively dressed women were marching around the statue, many of them holding up placards that name-checked The Ripper Tripper.

The city's prostitutes had gathered to protest against the spate of murders by the serial killer, whose name was on everyone's lips thanks to the media who were going fucking hog wild over the guy, using his bloody antics to sell papers and push up ratings.

The usual climate of fear that accompanied these serial killers was absent with The Ripper Tripper, for he only targeted prostitutes. As long as you weren't a streetwalker, you were safe.

Which made it easy for everyone else to revel in sensationalism and point their fingers at the prostitutes as if the women were to blame for being targets in the first place. From what

I'd glimpsed on TV, some were saying the "harlots" deserved what they got for being "whores" in the first place, and that the killer was "doing God's work" in ridding the city of sin.

All of which was ridiculous. The Ripper Tripper was just a crazy motherfucker, and there was nothing biblical in what he was doing aside from persecuting those who didn't deserve it.

Many of the drivers that rolled past the assembled protesters wound down their windows and shouted obscenities at the women, screaming hatred and bile at them. The prostitutes gave back as good as they got, retorting with their own, often witty, responses that I couldn't help but smile at.

Despite standing out in the rain for a protest most of the city was apathetic toward, the women protesters still somehow kept their dignity, or as much dignity as women of their profession could keep.

As I drove slowly by, I spotted a familiar face outside an upmarket clothing store behind the gaggle of protesters, as if standing guard from afar.

It was a woman I hadn't seen nor spoken to in a few years, but she still looked exactly as she did last time I met her. Dressed in a long black coat that almost reached her ankles, her golden brown hair spilled over the shoulders, which were covered in black feathers. With her height, she came across as an elegant black heron waiting by the water to spear its prey.

Her rare beauty and almost dangerous demeanor made her stand out from everybody else around. Hardly a man walked by without shooting her at least a furtive glance, almost like they were too intimidated by her to afford her a proper look.

The men were right to fear her, for she *was* dangerous. Her name was Victoria Belford, but if you got on the wrong side of her, you would know her as The Rook. By then, it would be too late for you, anyway. The Rook was as ruthless as she looked, and if she targeted you, you weren't getting away.

Driving the car around to the other side of the square, I found a parking spot just down from where Victoria was standing. After lighting a cigarette, I got out of the car and walked down the street in the rain, announcing myself before she noticed me coming.

"Excuse me, Miss," I said. "Do you know it's illegal to loiter here?"

Victoria turned her head slowly in my direction as if it was all she could do to give me a second of her attention. When she glanced at my face, she turned her gaze back to the protesters in the center of the square as though she hadn't even recognized me.

"Detective Drake," she said, staring straight ahead again. "Come to join the party, have we?"

"You know me, Vic." I saddled up beside her and stuck one hand in my trench pocket as I held my cigarette with the other. "I can't resist a good party."

She turned her head an inch and gave me a wry smile. "Yes, I remember well."

My mind flashed back for a second to a time when I was still married, but would often meet Vic in hotel rooms and stranger's houses for drug-fueled nights of animalistic sex.

The first time I hooked up with her, it was a revelation. I didn't think it possible for one person to know so much about erotic pleasure. The things she did to me, the heights of orgasmic ecstasy she brought me to, were unmatched before or since.

Vic had a singular talent for driving men crazy with pleasure, to where it became unbearable. Even then, you didn't tell her to stop, for, even though she genuinely had you fearing you would die from pleasure overload, you begged her for more, even if by doing so, you would end up killing yourself.

Thankfully, the only deaths Vic caused were the Little Deaths. At least in the bedroom.

Under other less pleasurable circumstances, she could also cause real deaths if you got on the wrong side of her.

"I warned them against doing this," Vic said as she gestured toward the protesters, who were still getting bawled at by passing motorists, some of whom were throwing things out the window of their cars as they drove past. At one point, I saw one girl get hit up the face with a pink dildo. The few uniformed cops standing around did nothing to stop any of this abuse. They smiled to themselves when it happened.

"I'm sure you did," I said. "Public opinion isn't exactly on their side. Plus, pulling a stunt like this, it's sure to egg the killer on."

"My thoughts exactly. The girls are afraid, though. They feel like they have to do something. The way they see it, they're being targeted by a serial killer and nobody cares very much." She shook her head in disdain, her blood-red lips pressed tight as she watched the spectacle. "The assholes in this city care more for the killer than they do for the victims. Did you know Conan O'Brien offered the Ripper an interview? O'Brien said they could do it over an encrypted satellite link so no one could trace the killer."

"I didn't know that," I said. "Imagine the advertising, though."

"Fuck off, Detective. You're not funny. You never were."

Thanks to my insensitive joke, a tense silence killed the conversation for a long moment, and I stood staring at the protesters before finally asking, "Do you have any leads on the killer yet?"

She shook her head. "Whoever it is, they're like a fucking ghost. One night I saw a man running from what turned out to be the scene of the sixth murder. I chased him, but then he just…vanished. That's the only time I've been close."

"Did you get a description?"

"Tall, dressed in a black cloak, I think…and a top hat."

"Like a Jack the Ripper top hat, you mean?"

"As far as I could make out. It had a red ribbon tied around the base."

"Weird. You tell the cops any of this?"

She threw me a look. "That's a dumb question, Detective. When have you ever known me to tell the cops anything?"

"You told me plenty," I said smiling.

"I told you what you needed to hear," she said, her husky voice cold but enticing at the same time. "I tell all men what they need to hear."

Vic was a former prostitute herself, albeit a high-class one. Now she's a Madam, running her own place out of nearby Astoria.

Besides that, Vic is also The Rook—a ruthless vigilante who targets men that get off on abusing prostitutes. That's how I met her eight years ago, while I was investigating the murder of a high-flying corporate lawyer who'd been found beaten to death in his Bedford apartment. I followed the evidence to Vic, and when I did, she showed me her own evidence that the lawyer was a serial rapist and murderer of prostitutes. I didn't see what good arresting Vic would do, so I let her go. As far as I was concerned, the scumbags she targeted deserved what they got, so I was happy to let her continue with her vigilantism.

As a mark of her gratitude, Vic opened the door for me to a world of pleasure I never even knew existed.

"I'm not on the Ripper Tripper case," I said. "But if I hear anything, I'll let you know. I'd rather you deal with this sick fuck than the justice system, anyway. They'll just make him a folk hero like Manson and all the rest."

"Thank you," she said, a warmth in her hazel eyes for the first time. "And Ethan?"

"Yeah?"

"I'm sorry about your wife and little girl. They didn't deserve what happened to them."

"No, they didn't."

"Have you caught the person who did it?"

"I got the guy, but it turns out he wasn't the only one involved."

"If there's anything I can do to help, let me know."

"Thanks, Vic." I glanced once more at the protesters. "I'll leave you to it."

As I went to walk away, Vic called, "Ethan?"

I turned and looked at her sculpted face, missing looking into those eyes as she did unspeakable things to me. "Yeah?"

"It was good to see you." She paused to smile at me, a smile that could get her anything she wanted and often did, at least as far as I was concerned. "Don't be a stranger. Come and see me sometime. My door is always open."

Grinning like a schoolboy, I said, "Sure thing, Vic. I'll see ya."

❧

Rather than carrying on driving to Bedford, I swung by Cave Hill Cemetery to visit the graves of Angela and Callie because I hadn't been in a while.

As always, I had conflicting emotions as I followed the narrow pathways across the cemetery in the drizzling rain. The guilt would probably never go away, but I wasn't going to let that stop me from visiting the two of them here.

It was the only connection to them I had left.

I had flowers with me, which I split into two bunches, resting one against each grave. I then spent the next fifteen minutes standing in the rain, staring at the headstones as if doing so would bring my family back to me.

Before I left, I placed a kiss on each of the headstones and made my way back across the cemetery again.

On the way back, I made a detour toward Barbara Keane's grave, deciding to pay my respects to the woman. She got a raw deal with what happened to her, and she also seemed like a nice woman when I spoke to her ghost.

When I got to the gravesite, however, I was surprised to see Father John Brown there, bent over as he used a sponge to scrub at the headstone. Someone had vandalized it, covering it in graffiti. The priest had removed most of it, but I could still make out the word "Hell".

"Some people have no respect, eh, Father?" I said.

Father Brown spun around, almost dropping the sponge as I startled him. "Detective," he said once he recognized me. "I didn't hear you come up."

"Just here to pay my respects to Barbara, Father."

The priest nodded. "That's nice to hear, Detective. It seems people would rather deface her grave than show her any respect."

"They think she's a murderer."

"Even though she isn't."

"I know that now."

He looked surprised. "You do?"

"I learned the truth. She didn't kill her husband or her kids. Her husband did that himself."

"How…how do you know this?"

"Would you believe me if I told you I spoke to Barbara herself? Or at least her ghost?"

Father Brown stared at me. "You're not joking, are you?"

I shook my head. "Nope."

"Was she…okay?"

"She's okay. She's with her kids in Heaven," I lied.

The priest smiled at this. "That's…you've no idea what that means to me, knowing Barbara is at peace. Thank you, Detective."

Peace? She didn't seem at peace to me when I spoke to her. There was no peace, according to her. Not for anybody.

Given how much affection he had for Barbara, I was beginning to wonder if maybe Father Brown didn't have a thing for the woman. Was he secretly in love with her? Stranger things have happened. In any case, it was none of my business. "I have to be going now, Father. It was good seeing you again."

"Before you go, Detective Drake," he said, coming over to stand by me. "There's something I'd like to tell you. Last night, a man came into the confessional."

"Should you be telling me this?" I asked him. "Isn't there some vow that stops you from discussing confessions with anyone?"

"There is," he said. "But in this case, I don't know any names. I also think I'm justified in what I'm about to tell you."

"Okay. I'm all ears, Father."

"This man who sat in the confession box with me, I knew there was something strange about him the minute he walked in."

"Strange how?"

"It's hard to explain. There was a power coming off him, almost like electrical energy. It was weird and also…frightening. His energy was…dark, shall we say. Very dark."

By the sounds of it, the priest had been visited by a MURK of some kind. Maybe even a demon, some of whom took pleasure in taunting the agents of God in His own house. "Did something happen?"

"In a way, yes. The man sat down and proceeded to tell me he was a serial killer and that he'd killed over twenty people of late."

Now he had my full attention. "Did he say how he killed them?"

The priest swallowed and took a second to compose himself, the memory of the confession too much for him. "With a knife, and his victims were all women. Prostitutes."

"You don't say."

"I immediately thought what you're thinking now—The

Ripper Tripper was sitting on the other side of the screen. To say my blood ran cold would be an understatement."

"What did he say exactly?"

"He went about describing some of his murders in gruesome detail. I—I threw up in the confessional. When I told him to leave, he wouldn't. He also said he would kill me if I didn't hear the rest of his confession."

"Did he give you any details about himself?"

The priest shook his head. "He was careful in that way. He never told me his name, nor very much about himself."

"Did he tell you anything that might help in catching him?"

"He mentioned he has a family. A wife and son."

"Jesus."

"I believe he said his son was in college and his wife was a lawyer. He bemoaned the lack of intimacy and physical contact between them."

"He's not getting fucking laid, so he takes his frustration out on all those poor girls?" I shook my head in disdain. "Fucking asshole."

"Yes, well. I'm sure there's more to his psychosis than just that, Detective."

Like I care about what makes the cunt tick. "Did he say anything else?"

"That it wasn't his fault, and that something was making him do it, something he couldn't explain. He said he had the power of the Devil in him."

Mytholite power, only this Ripper Tripper asshole didn't understand it. He probably thought he was possessed or something.

"Alright, listen, Father. I'm not on this case, but you need to go down to the precinct and ask for Detective Routman. Tell him what you told me. He's running the task force that's trying to apprehend this guy."

Even though they don't know what kind of killer they're

dealing with. Shit knows what kind of power this asshole has, or what powers he will have.

"I planned on doing that later today," the priest said. "I just wanted to clean Barbara's grave first."

"Okay, Father," I said walking away. "I'll be seeing you then."

"Oh, there's one other thing, Detective."

I stopped and turned around. "What is it?"

"Rather oddly, the man mentioned his hat."

"Let me guess. A top hat with a red ribbon around the base?"

"Yes. How did you know?"

"He was spotted by someone, that's all. What did he say to you exactly?"

"He said when he puts the hat on, that's when the monster in him comes out. The Ripper, as he calls himself. I'm sure there aren't too many places in this city that sell top hats, Detective. Perhaps you could get a lead from that."

"Maybe," I said nodding. "Just tell Detective Routman everything you told me. He'll take it from there."

"Okay. Goodbye, Detective Drake." He paused. "And Detective?"

"Yes, Father?"

"If you ever need someone to hear your confession, I'm here."

I couldn't help but laugh. "Thanks, Father," I said as I walked away. "I'll bear that in mind."

8

"Drakester. How's goes it?"

Artemis was standing before me dressed in what looked like white long johns and some sort of jockstrap thing with straps that crisscrossed his chest before going around his shoulders. He also wore a black bowler hat and held a black cane in one hand. It took me a moment to recognize the outfit.

"Really?" I said as I walked past him into the penthouse. "Why are you dressed as a droog from *A Clockwork Orange*?" I stopped when I noticed the other people in the penthouse, all of whom were women, also dressed as droogs. I spotted four curvaceous females who had to be escorts lying in various states of undress over by the huge corner suite. They all appeared to be sleeping.

"We had a little theme party last night," Artemis said. "You know how we like to keep things spicy, Drakester."

"No, I don't actually. Where's Pan Demic?"

"Right here, Drakester!"

I looked around for the source of the voice and finally located him inside the cinema room. As I walked down the short aisle to the front of the room, I could hardly look at the constantly flashing images up on the screen, most of which were pornographic. Seated in one of the front seats was Pan Demic, his skinny body naked and hairless. On his head was some metal contraption with wires attached to electrodes stuck to his skin. Tiny arms coming from the machine held Pan Demic's eyelids open so he couldn't stop watching the images on the large cinema screen even if he wanted to. Between his legs was a red-headed woman dressed as a droog, but wearing a short white skirt instead of long johns. The woman was busy sucking Pan Demic's surprisingly large cock as he periodically did lines of coke off the back of his hand.

"What the fuck?" I said staring at him.

"Just a little experiment, Drakester," Pan Demic explained. "No need to get freaked out. We thought this might help us reach greater heights of pleasure, jaded motherfuckers that we are."

"And has it?" I asked cautiously, curious despite myself. He gasped as the red-headed escort increased the speed of her head movements, furiously sucking his cock as she tried to bring him to orgasm. "On second thought, don't answer that."

I walked out of the room and back out to Artemis, who was now stationed at his computer. He smiled when he saw the look on my face. "You look freaked out," he said.

"You guys have way too much time on your hands," I said, glancing over at the still sleeping escorts. "Seriously."

Artemis smiled, his eyes encircled with dark makeup. "Help yourself. They're still on the clock."

"No thanks." I sat down next to him in Pan Demic's chair. "I need a favor, though."

"Sure thing," he said. "Just let me get set up here first." Leaning down to his desk, he took a huge blast of coke, making my eyes water just watching him do it. Then he tapped a few keys on his keyboard and death metal came blasting out of the speakers in every corner of the room, and he smiled across at me. "Nothing like a little Napalm Death to get the brain juices flowing again, you know what I mean, Drakester?"

I shook my head as he made devil horns at me. Over on the couch, the four escorts were all up and looking furtively around them as if the fire alarm was going off. When they realized it was just the music, they shook their heads and lay back down again, surrounding themselves with cushions.

When I turned back to Artemis, he was sparking up a fat joint, surrounding us with thick clouds of pungent smoke. When he offered the joint to me, I declined. Shrugging, he placed it in a skull ashtray and out of nowhere started doing air drums in time to the music before adding his own vocals. *"Break down the barriers, That enforce superstition,"* he growled. *"Learn to trust, Overcome suspicion..."*

"Very nice," I said. "You should've been in a band."

"Actually, me and Pan Demic have already recorded some stuff. You wanna hear?"

"No thanks. Some other time."

"You sure? It's like, proper old school early nineties death metal."

"I've no doubt it is, but I'm in a bit of a hurry, so if you don't mind..."

He shook his head at me. "Your loss, Drakester."

"I'll accept said loss with a heavy heart," I said. "Now put this name into your computer—Antonio Francetti."

Artemis shook his head at my lack of interest in his music and begrudgingly started tapping keys. "Who is this guy?"

"A mobster, as far as I know."

"That him?" Artemis pointed to the screen, drawing my attention to the mugshot of a man who looked to be in his fifties. I didn't know what Francetti looked like, but I was pretty sure it wasn't the guy on the screen. Too brutish and not someone who looked to have a silver tongue. Plus, the guy had been arrested for armed robbery.

"Not him," I said, just as a loud cry of orgasmic pleasure

issued from the cinema room, causing me to sigh and shake my head before looking at Artemis again, who sat grinning at Pan Demic's moans of pleasure. "I guess he's done."

"I guess he is," Artemis said with a goofy grin.

"Keep searching."

"So much for the police database…" Artemis tapped the keyboard again, faint blue magical energy arcing across his fingertips as he typed. "Let's try the FBI database instead…"

As we waited on the computer to search the database, Pan Demic walked in wearing a white bathrobe that tented out around his crotch. When he came and stood beside me, he parked his cloaked erection right next to my face. "So what's going on, Drakester?" he asked as if he was just out of the shower.

"Fuck," I said as I drew back. "Get that fucking thing away from me." Pan Demic chuckled as he leaned past me and bent down for a snort of coke, his skinny bare ass in my line of sight now. "Fuck's sake."

I got out of the chair and stood by the other side of Artemis, putting a safe distance between myself and Pan Demic's pork sword.

"Dude," Artemis said to Pan Demic. "How'd it go? Was it mind-blowingly awesome or what? Tell me. Did the shit work?"

A wide smile spread across Pan Demic's face and he started nodding. "Dude," he said. "It was fucking awesome. Better than awesome. It was fucking…*metal!*"

I shook my head as the two of them high-fived. "Hey, Beavis and Butthead," I said. "Talk about your perverted experiments when I'm gone." I glanced at Pan Demic. "I can't help but notice your erection isn't going down there, buddy. Viagra?"

"Nope," Pan Demic said as he looked down at his stiffened manhood with some pride. "Love Pump."

"I'm sorry?"

"Love Pump."

I nodded. "That's what I thought you said. What the hell is Love Pump? Like one of those contraptions you see advertised on porn sites?"

"Just a little concoction we made up ourselves, Drakester," Pan Demic said. "I've been walking around with this bad boy for fourteen straight hours now."

"Sounds painful," I said.

"Only when I try to pee. It's worth it, though."

"I'm sure it is." I turned my attention to the screen again. "Any luck there, Artemis?"

"Almost…done. That your guy?" he asked.

On the screen, I saw a head and shoulders shot of a man in his mid-thirties wearing a dark suit. The photo looked to have been taken on the sly. Probably a surveillance photo. From the guy's impeccably groomed appearance and the calculating look in his dark eyes, I knew I was looking at Snake Tongue even before I read over the dossier the FBI had compiled on him. Not that the dossier held much information. The Feds had arrested Francetti a few years ago along with a number of others in a sting against the Fairview crime family, which was and still is headed by Vito Giordano, a somewhat reclusive mob boss with a fearsome reputation for being ruthless in his methods. But then, aren't they all?

"Seems like the sting was a bust," I said as I looked through the arrest reports. "They all got off."

"The mob has the best lawyers," Artemis said. "Everyone knows that."

"They probably used intimidation too," Pan Demic said. "Just like my impressive manhood is intimidating you, Drakester." He chuckled to himself as he took the joint from the skull ashtray and started puffing on it. "Don't feel bad about it."

"Less intimidated, more grossed out," I said. "Don't flatter yourself."

Pan Demic laughed, not in the least bit offended. "I bet yours is a sight to behold, Drakester."

"I get by."

"Anyway," Artemis said. "Are we done here? I really want to try out our new gadget in the cinema room."

"Almost," I said, reaching into my pocket and taking out the flash drive I got from Derrick Savage, handing it to Artemis. "Take this. It contains a video of someone pretending to be my partner. I need you to pinpoint the exact location on the video and also track the movements of the woman in it. It's from a while ago, so I'm not sure how much luck you'll have tracking her, but try anyway. Any information you glean from it will be helpful."

Artemis placed the flash drive on the desk beside him. "I'll look at it later and call you if I find anything."

"Thanks," I said. "I'll leave you two hellions to it then."

"Before you go," Pan Demic said, sliding into his seat and then yelping in pain as he banged his erection off the edge of the desk, causing me and Artemis to snicker. "Ow, that fucking hurt."

"Serves you right for going against nature," I said. "A stiffy is not meant to last that long."

Pan Demic shook his head at me. "Anyway, there's something I want to show you."

As Pan Demic started tapping keys, Artemis excused himself and headed into the cinema room, and for the first time, I realized he had an erection too. It just wasn't as noticeable as Pan Demic's, who had his friend beat in that respect.

"What's this?" I asked Pan Demic as he brought a video up on the screen.

"Something I thought might interest you," he said. "This is outside The Dripping Fang, that vamp club in Bayside."

"I know it well," I said, remembering my altercation with the Litchghin there, as well as the demon Astaroth. The footage Pan Demic had up on the screen was the view from a security camera above the front doors of the club. The camera pointed toward the road and a black limo that had just pulled up. As the driver of the limo got out and opened the back door, a tall man in a dark suit exited the stretched car, pausing to straighten his jacket for a moment as he looked around.

"I'm not sure if you know this dude or not," Pan Demic said. "But he's one of the top dogs in the Menesis Clan. Or at least, he was…"

"Was?"

"Watch."

Staring at the grainy footage, I saw a black shape suddenly land on the roof of the limo, seemingly from out of nowhere. At that moment, Pan Demic paused the video and zoomed in so I could look at the figure on top of the limo. "Jesus…" I breathed, recognizing straight away who it was. "Charlotte."

"Charlotte?" Pan Demic said. "As in Scarlet's little sister?"

"Yep, that's her alright."

She looked as she did when she burst forth from the tank that time in the mountain lair. Her body was completely black, with four spindly legs coming out of her back. As Pan Demic zoomed in further, I almost drew back in horror at the sight of her face, which appeared to sport multiple eyes—her normal eyes, plus another three across her forehead and one each side of her cheeks.

"Not exactly pretty, is she?"

I shook my head. "Nope."

Pan Demic hit play on the video again, zooming out as he did so. With one swipe of her arm, Charlotte—or the monster she had become—decapitated the limo driver, his head rolling off into the gutter.

Startled, the Menesis vampire turned to face the monster behind him. But before he could even do anything, Charlotte launched herself at him, wrapping all of her legs around the vampire in a tight embrace. Even with all his strength, the vampire couldn't pry Charlotte off him and wasn't able to stop her from sinking her fangs into his neck.

There was no sound on the video, but I've no doubt the vampire cried out in shock when Charlotte bit into him. When she let him go, he staggered back holding his neck, just as his face and body began to distend like a balloon. A second later, he exploded in a burst of blood and gore, leaving nothing behind but a large wet patch on the sidewalk.

With that, Charlotte jumped high into the air and disappeared.

"Crazy, huh?" Pan Demic said. "She made that Menesis look like a fledgling vamp."

"That's what she was made to do," I said. "I guess her war has started."

"Her war?"

"Against the vampires. She'll not stop until she's wiped them all out."

Pan Demic stared at the screen for a second. "Well, I guess that's a good thing, right? I mean, who likes vampires anyway? Arrogant assholes the lot of them."

I couldn't argue with him there, but I doubted it was as simple as that. These situations had a way of escalating out of control, claiming innocent lives in the process. Still, I had no beef with what she was doing. I fucking hated vampires anyway, and couldn't care less if they were all wiped out. I'd keep an eye on the situation, anyway.

As would Blackstar, no doubt. Not only did Blackstar have a relationship with most of the vampire clans, but The Magician's organization would also want Charlotte for themselves if only to use as a weapon. If Scarlet were still here, I don't think she'd want her sister running around slaughtering vampires, or captured by Blackstar.

Damn it, I thought. *Something else I'll have to sort out. For Scarlet if nothing else.*

"Thanks for keeping me in the loop," I said to Pan Demic.

"No problem, Drakester. Anything we can do to help, you know that."

From the cinema room, Artemis cried, "Oh Jesus!"

I shook my head. "Looks like someone's found religion."

"Yeah," Pan Demic said grinning. "Ain't it beautiful?"

9

B ack in the car, I lit a cigarette just as a voice blared from the radio. It was dispatch announcing that shots had reportedly been fired in East First Street in Little Tokyo.

As soon as I heard the report, I knew it had something to do with the Yakuza, and possibly Hannah/Xaglath, so I picked up the radio and announced that I would respond to the incident and that I was on my way.

Given that every cop in the city was out looking for The Ripper Tripper, I doubted anyone else would respond anyway.

And even if units were available, most of them would probably ignore the call. Racism was rife in the police department, so when it came to places like Little Tokyo—places full of ethnic minorities—they were usually left to fend for themselves unless the crime was serious and couldn't be ignored. Such as the time Xaglath impaled the Yakuza soldier on the statue. Hard to turn a blind eye to something as public as that.

Traffic was light on the roads at this time of night so I made it to Little Tokyo in good time, bringing the Dodge to a screeching halt in East First Street. The street was mostly commercial, and all of the businesses were closed, steel shutters down over the doors. In the middle of the street, there were two cars, brightly colored Japanese imports, behind which stood about half a dozen men firing pistols at whoever was ahead of them.

Getting out of the car, I immediately took out my gun and started moving cautiously up the street, sticking to the sidewalk in case I had to duck for cover at any point.

Before announcing myself as a cop to the men who I knew to be Yakuza—I even recognized one of them—I peered up the street to find the target of the Yakuza's bullets. The street didn't have much in the way of lighting, so it was difficult to see at first.

But eventually, I made out a familiar black shape and realized it was Haedemus.

Seated atop him was Xaglath.

The demon had black, feathered wings stretching out behind her back. She also appeared to have curved horns coming out of her forehead now, bright amber eyes glowing fiercely beneath them.

As the Yakuza continued to fire continuously at Xaglath and the Hellicorn, the bullets appeared to stop within an inch of them both before dropping harmlessly to the ground.

She must have some sort of forcefield around her.

I stood with my back against one of the store shutters for a moment, wondering how I should proceed. If I announced myself as a cop to the Yakuza, they'd probably turn their guns on me. And after my meeting with Yagami, the fuckers would probably be itching to take me down. Especially the guy I knocked out in Yagami's office, who I recognized as he leaned across the hood of one of the cars, firing bullet after bullet at Xaglath, even though none of them were hitting her.

Ignorant fucks. They're gonna get themselves killed.

I was tempted to leave them all to it. What did I care if Xaglath killed a bunch of Yakuza? Good riddance, I say.

But I was still a cop, and if I could prevent a massacre, then I had to try.

So stupid ass that I am, I walked out to the edge of the road and shouted, "Police! Stand down!"

The Yakuza soldiers stopped firing for a second as they all turned around to look at me, the one I'd knocked out in Yagami's office eye-fucking me for a few long seconds before raising his gun and firing it at me.

Luckily, he was a terrible shot, and the bullets went wide, hitting the road a few feet away from me.

Once he fired, the rest followed suit.

To avoid the hail of bullets, I dived behind a parked car and let it take the damage as the windows blew out around me, showering glass everywhere.

While I waited for the bullet storm to subside, I suddenly heard a voice come from somewhere, as clear as day as it said, *"I wasn't expecting you, Ethan. Come to see the show, have we?"*

I looked around for a moment until I realized the voice was inside my head.

And it belonged to Xaglath.

Still, I said Hannah's name in the hope that she would answer. "Hannah?"

"Fuck that weak bitch!" Xaglath bit back, her voice different from Hannah's, deep and dripping with hatred. *"Hannah's gone, buried in my darkness and torment where she belongs."*

"I don't believe that."

"Believe what you want…Detective. I'm in charge now, as you will find out to your detriment soon enough. For when I'm done with these fools and their pathetic little clan, I'm coming for you next. Believe that, Ethan."

Despite how adamant she was that Hannah was gone, I still tried to get through to her. "Hannah? Can you hear me? Hannah—"

"Stop wasting your breath, you pathetic human!" Xaglath

snapped as she cut me off. *"Go and wallow in your misery. As I understand it, you have a lot to be miserable about. Missing your little girl, are we? Missing the wife who hated you?"*

As cold laughter began to echo in my head, I gritted my teeth at her words, thinking, *Don't let her get to you.*

"The truth hurts, Ethan, doesn't it?" she went on. *"I have plenty more truth where that came from. Soon enough, I'll drown you in it. In the meantime, watch what I do to those who try to stand against me..."*

With the Yakuza soldiers' attention taken by Xaglath once more, I stood up and looked over the roof of the car toward them. Stupid asses that they were, they were continuing to shoot at the demon, even though a fool could see their actions were doing no good whatsoever. In any case, they were about to pay dearly for their foolishness.

Turning my gaze toward Xaglath as she sat on top of Haedemus, I waited on her to make her move. They made a fearsome pair, Haedemus and Xaglath. I could only imagine how feared they were in Hell, and how damned souls would run from them in terror, having nowhere to go, eventually succumbing to Xaglath's wrath as she inflicted unspeakable torment on them.

Staring in almost rapt fascination, I watched as Xaglath held both hands out by her side, conjuring a huge fireball in each palm. As the light from the fireballs lit up her face, her lips formed into a smile. Then she unleashed both fireballs at the same time, sending them hurtling toward the parked cars.

Almost in slow motion, I watched the Yakuza guys try to run, but I knew before they even made their move that they were too late. They were only feet from the cars when they both exploded.

As I ducked down behind the car I was using for cover, debris from the explosion fell all around me—bits of asphalt and hot, mangled metal—even an arm that was ripped from one of the gangsters by the force of the explosion.

With black smoke now billowing all around me and filling up the street, I stood up again to survey the damage, moving out into the road where I spotted most of the Yakuza soldiers lying mangled, their bodies blackened by fire. Only two of them appeared to be still alive, though they were barely moving.

The sound of hooves made me turn my head to see Xaglath riding through the black smoke, her wings still outstretched behind her, her eyes still glowering beneath her twisted horns. She had turned the street into a mini Hell that she now ruled.

There was nothing I could do as she rode up past the burning cars to survey the damage she'd wrought.

When she spotted me, she stopped and smiled down at me. "They didn't stand a chance," she said. "None of them will. Neither will you, Ethan."

It was disconcerting even to look at her, for despite her newly emerged demonic features, she still looked like Hannah. All I wanted to do was apologize to her and tell her to come back to me, but I knew my words would fall on deaf ears.

At least for now.

I didn't believe Xaglath when she said Hannah was gone. My Infernal Itch and the sensations rippling down my spine were both telling me Hannah was still in there somewhere. Sooner or later, I would find a way to get through to her.

"Hello, Ethan," Haedemus said like he was embarrassed to be a part of this beatdown.

"Hello, Haedemus," I said, nodding my head at him. "Nice night for it."

Haedemus went to laugh but stopped when Xaglath pulled on his mane. "The human is not your friend," she chided him. "Stop pretending like he is."

"Yes, Mistress," Haedemus said, dropping his head.

"Styled any poodles lately, Haedemus?" I said to him, eliciting an involuntary laugh from him I knew would annoy Xaglath.

In response, she trotted to one of the Yakuza soldiers who was still alive. My buddy who I knocked out. He was crawling across the blackened road, still in shock from the explosion, half his clothes burned off him. He stopped crawling when Xaglath reached him, turning over onto his back as he stared up in terror at the Hellicorn and the demon on its back.

"Please…" he whispered, hardly able to form the word.

"Please yourself," Xaglath said. "Haedemus."

Haedemus lifted one heavy hoof and brought it down on the Yakuza soldier's head, crushing it like a melon, splattering his brains all over the road.

On seeing this, the other surviving Yakuza soldier screamed from nearby and got to his feet. But before he could run, Xaglath thrust out a hand and stopped him dead in his tracks with her telekinetic power, raising him into the air before twisting her hand sharply to the left.

In response to this small movement, I heard bones snap in the gangster's body, his arms and legs twisting like pipe-cleaners. When Xaglath turned her hand to the right, more bones snapped, along with the guy's neck.

Suspended in the air, he looked like a mangled string puppet. When he finally hit the ground a few seconds later, it was just as if his strings had been cut.

Xaglath turned her head toward me. "And that as they say, is that," she said. "I hope you enjoyed the show, Ethan. Though just know that the suffering you have seen here is but a fraction of what you will suffer when your time comes. And believe me, Ethan, it *will* come."

Almost languidly, she pointed a finger toward me and it immediately felt as if someone had shot a bullet up my ass that powered up through the length of my spine before exploding out the top of my skull. Crying out, I gripped my head as I sank to my knees, having never felt pain like it in my life, which was saying something. Thankfully, it didn't last long.

Smiling cruelly, Xaglath turned Haedemus around and began to move back up the street without saying another word, and without giving me so much as another glance.

"Goodbye, Ethan," Haedemus said as he moved past me.

"Yeah, bye, Haedemus," I said.

Soon, the smoke from the burning cars swallowed them up, and they were gone, leaving me with six dead bodies that I didn't know how I would explain.

WHEN I CALLED IN THE INCIDENT, I PLEADED IGNORANCE AND said the Yakuza were all dead by the time I got there. As everyone else was busy, I dealt directly with Captain Edwards, which I wasn't happy about. Neither was he. I got a distinct impression as he spoke that he already considered me gone. My continued presence in the force was a mere formality to him now. He didn't seem to give a shit about the dead Yakuza either. "Whoever killed them," he said, "did this city a favor. I hate those slant-eyed fucks, anyway."

And I thought I was the jaded one.

When the uniforms and a couple detectives I didn't know arrived along with the meat wagon, I vacated the scene. They could attach whatever story they wanted to the whole thing. I had other things to be getting on with, anyway.

Like the Sam Sidwell murder, even though it wasn't officially classed as a murder. I called Mackey to see if he'd done the autopsy yet. He said he had, but he was still writing up the report, which would be done in a while if I wanted to call at the precinct later.

Frustrated by the lack of progress on the case and still a little unsettled by my encounter with Xaglath, I went to pay Cal a visit. Earlier today he sent me a text saying he needed to speak to me about something but didn't say what. Which was strange, because Cal hardly ever texts me about anything. Normally he just phones or comes to see me. It was odd, but I was sure there wasn't much to it.

I'll find out soon enough, I thought as I jumped into the Dodge and left behind Xaglath's scene of destruction.

∽

CAL WAS SITTING IN HIS USUAL CHAIR OUTSIDE HIS TRAILER when I got to the scrap yard. The rain had stopped and the dark sky was clear and blanketed with stars. There wasn't much wind either, making for an almost serene atmosphere as I sat beside Cal in the other chair, accepting a beer as he wordlessly handed me one.

"I got your text earlier," I said. "What's up?"

Even before he answered, I could tell from his face that something wasn't right. He was staring off into the distance like he was lost in his own mind. Even the dogs, who sat huddled together nearby, looked subdued. Forlorn even.

"I'm dying," he said, keeping his gaze directly ahead as if he was afraid to look at me.

I paused with my beer halfway to my mouth and stared at him. "What?"

"You heard me."

A frown creased my brow as I shook my head in confusion. "I don't…I don't understand."

"Yes, you do."

He was right. I understood full well, but I just didn't want to believe it. How the fuck could he be dying? This was Cal, the toughest motherfucker I knew. There was no way…

"What—" I stopped, hardly able to form the words. "What's wrong with you?"

"Brain tumor." He still hadn't looked at me, which was disconcerting me even more.

I took a deep breath and let it out. "Are you shitting me? Like that time you told me—"

"I'm not shitting you." He finally looked at me, his slate-gray eyes deadly serious. "I'm dying, Ethan."

"Fuck, Cal…"

"Yeah."

"Surely there's something—"

"There's nothing," he said shaking his head. "I have an inoperable brain tumor and that's that."

"How long have you known this?"

"About six months."

"Six months? And you're only telling me now?"

"I thought I could fix it. Turns out, I can't."

As I let out a shuddering breath, I thought, *This can't be happening. Not Cal of all people, not him…*

"How long?"

"How long what?"

"How long…do you have?"

He shrugged. "Docs say not long. Few weeks maybe, if I'm lucky."

Tears stung my eyes. "Cal, I—"

"Don't. It is what it is." He sighed and sipped on his beer. "Fuck it. I always thought I'd go down in a blaze of glory, not from a fucking brain tumor."

I lapsed into a long silence as I stared straight ahead, not knowing what to say nor how to feel beyond shocked and gutted. Cal was family—the only family I had—and I always knew I'd miss him when he was gone.

But now that that possibility had become a reality, it was even more heart wrenching than I thought it would be. On top of everything else, it was fucking devastating.

"I'm sorry, kiddo," he said. "I hate to leave you in the lurch and all, but…"

Putting my beer down, I stood up and started walking to the car.

"Ethan. Where you going? Ethan…there's stuff we have to talk about, things to discuss—Ethan!"

He was still calling my name as I drove away with tears streaming down my face, tears that were quickly becoming tainted with anger as I gripped the steering wheel and spun the wheels of the Dodge in the dirt while I rounded a corner, almost sliding into a mound of scrap.

But before I got to the gates, I slammed on the brakes and stumbled out of the car and started walking around in circles with my hands on top of my head, cursing the very air that I breathed.

Which is when I got slammed from behind and went flying face-first into the dirt.

~

THERE WAS SOMEONE ON TOP OF ME, SOMEONE WHO SMELLED of musk and wood smoke and…blood.

A little too late, my Infernal Itch went wild, sending my tattoos into a spin.

Then I felt something hard and sharp pressing against my throat.

A claw. Pressing so hard it drew blood.

"Don't fight me," my attacker said in a growly voice, a voice that was unmistakably female despite the low pitch. "I only wanna talk."

Despite what my attacker said, I struggled to get up, but couldn't because she had one knee pressed into the center of my spine. So I slid my hand toward my gun instead but soon found my arm trapped.

"I said not to struggle," my attacker said. "Don't you listen?"

"What the fuck do you want? Who are you?"

"I'll explain if you promise not to try anything when I let

you up." I felt the claw press deeper into the flesh of my throat. "Believe me, mister, you don't want to fuck with me."

"Fine," I said. "Just get the fuck off me, will ya?"

When my attacker removed herself from my back, I turned around on the ground and lay there staring up at her for a moment. I was looking at a woman in her early thirties, with long dirty blonde hair and eyes that glowed a faint yellow. She was average height and slimly built, wearing blue jeans and a short brown leather jacket with a black T-shirt underneath.

As she stood a few feet back, she held her hands out by her sides slightly, her claws long and sharp. When I made eye contact with her, she bared her teeth, flashing me her fangs. "Get up slowly," she said in the same growl as earlier.

Getting to my feet, I brushed the dirt off myself before looking at the woman again. "You're one of *them*, aren't you?" I said, reaching into my trench for my cigarettes.

"One of who?" she asked as she eyed me warily.

"One of Savage's pack."

"You must have known we'd come. I've been following you for days."

"I know. Where's the rest of your pack?" I asked, popping a cigarette into my mouth as I looked around for a second, expecting to see glowing eyes watching me from among the mounds of scrap metal.

"They aren't here," she said. "Least not yet. They will be, though."

I leaned against the car as I puffed on my cigarette, my head still spinning from Cal's devastating news. "That right? Why aren't they here now?"

"Because first I had to find you." She seemed to relax slightly as she came closer, her teeth and claws retracting. She was pretty in a rural sort of way. No doubt a total hellcat in bed. Not that I intended to ever find that out.

"So your pack leader sent you to sniff me out. Doesn't make much sense that you would warn me like this."

She stared at me a second before saying, "Toss me one of those."

Taking out a cigarette, I tossed it over to her, followed by my zippo lighter. When she lit the cigarette, she threw the lighter back to me, which I caught and pocketed again. "You probably could've killed me just then. Why didn't you?"

"I thought about it."

"So what stopped you? My cuddly demeanor?"

"Yeah," she said, looking me up and down with a half-smile on her face. "You're a real panda bear, Mr. Policeman."

"A panda bear who killed one of yours, though Savage was more of a psychopathic grizzly."

"You aren't far wrong on that score."

"I'm sensing you didn't have much love for him either."

"What'd he do to you to make you kill him?" she asked.

"The cunt killed my wife and daughter, that's what."

"Oh. I'm sorry."

"Are you? Or maybe you're just as bad as he was. Maybe your whole pack is."

"You're wrong about me." She took a drag of her cigarette. "But you're right about the others."

"Oh? What makes you so different?"

"I run with the pack because my brother is the pack leader," she said. "But that don't make me like them. They're all dog soldiers, mercenaries, and they don't have a conscience between 'em."

"And you do?"

"I'm here, aren't I?"

"So," I said as I wiped away the blood trickling down my neck, "you're just here to warn me, is that it?"

She came closer. "I'm here because my brother ordered me to track you down, the person who killed his best friend. Derrick and my brother were real close."

"So you're gonna run on back to your pack and tell them where to find me?"

"I don't have a choice. If they even knew I was talking to you like this, they'd kill me."

"Your own brother would kill you?"

"Like I said, no conscience."

"Maybe I should just kill *you* now, save us all a lot of trouble."

A growl left her mouth. "You can try."

I thought about rushing her, using my bulk to take her down and then choking the life out of her. She was going to sic the rest of her pack on me, after all. But, at the same time, she was here warning me ahead of time. She could've just said nothing. In my book, that counted for something. "So maybe you tell me where your pack hangs out, and I get to them first."

She snorted derisively at the idea. "What'd you take me for? They're still my pack. You're just some stranger who killed one of us. I don't owe you shit."

"And yet, here you are. I'm guessing Savage did something to you. What he do? Rape you or something?"

Her eyes glowed yellow as she snarled. "Mind your own fucking business."

"Alright, look," I said, tossing the butt of my cigarette away. "I appreciate the warning. You can run on back to your pack now, whatever your name is."

"You think you can take them on, don't you?" She shook her head at me like I was some stupid fool, which maybe I was. "You'll have no chance against them. Best thing you can do is run as far from here as possible. That's the only way you'll live."

"I don't run from anything, lady."

Oh yeah? Didn't you just run from Cal?

"Then you're stupider than I thought, mister."

"We'll see about that."

"Yeah," she said as she walked past me. "You can count on it. Next time we meet, things won't be so friendly like. I suggest you get your affairs in order, for you won't be around much longer."

Like someone else I know, I thought to myself as I looked ruefully toward Cal's trailer.

10

After the werewolf tracker left me to it—heading off to tell her pack where to find me—I got back in the Dodge and sat chain-smoking after dosing myself with Mud. A voice in my head was telling me I should never have let the woman go, that I should've killed her. But I could tell she was in a bind and had to do what her pack leader told her. Besides, even if I'd killed her, the pack would send someone else to track me. It was inevitable they would catch up with me at some point. I knew that the second I chopped Savage's head off.

But if the pack thought I'd be easy meat, they'd be mistaken.

Let them come.

I'd be ready for them when they did.

In the meantime, the person I was closest to in the world was at death's door, and I was too chicken shit to talk to him about it. You'd think being around death so much, I'd be used to it by now. But you never get used to it, especially when the reaper is in your own backyard.

Death doesn't just take those closest to you; it also takes a part of you with it.

A part of your soul.

Jesus, I thought. *The closest thing I have to a father is about to die, and all I can think about is myself. Way to go as usual, Ethan.*

Disgusted in myself, I pushed a CD into the stereo and a second later the brooding electronic tones of Gary Numan's "A Question of Faith" filled the car as I sped off in the direction of the precinct.

~

THE PRECINCT WAS AS EMPTY AS I'D EVER SEEN IT WHEN I GOT there. The duty Sergeant informed me that everyone was downtown in the Red Light District. Apparently, the mayor wanted everyone there as a show of force, hoping it would deter The Ripper Tripper from murdering any more prostitutes.

Given what Vic had told me about the killer's ability to vanish into thin air, I doubted this vain show of force would do much good. If anything, the sick fuck would see it as a challenge probably, like some video game—kill the hooker without getting caught by the cops. Bonus level: send a taunting note to the cops telling them how useless they are and how they will never catch you.

I'd be very surprised if another vic didn't turn up tonight.

The precinct may have been empty, but thankfully the morgue wasn't. Mackey was down there with a room full of bodies, many of which were the mutilated corpses left behind by The Ripper Tripper. I pulled the plastic sheet off a few of them to have a look and was horrified by what I saw. The motherfucker didn't half go to town on these poor girls, slicing every inch of flesh that could be sliced, leaving them looking like they'd been on full spin in a washing machine filled with razor blades.

"Pretty, aren't they?" Mackey said in a weary voice with

about as much compassion as a slaughterhouse worker talking about a side of beef he'd just carved up.

"Not anymore," I said, pulling the sheet back over one of the vics. "You get any evidence from any of them?"

"Not much. A few fibers that are all but useless when we have nothing to match them to."

I thought about telling Mackey that they weren't dealing with a run of the mill serial killer, that they were dealing with a supernaturally empowered freak, but I doubted he would've listened. Mackey was firmly in the category of those who turned a blind eye—for the sake of sanity—to anything that didn't match their model of reality. Vampires? Lycans? Demons? There's no such thing to the people in this category, which encompassed the whole damn precinct and most of the city.

Ignorance, as they say, is bliss. A luxury I could never afford.

I was never given the chance to.

"So what about my vic?" I asked him. "What'd you find out?"

Mackey sighed with some frustration as he pulled the sheet back from Sam Sidwell's body, which by now had the familiar Y-shaped incision in his chest and abdomen, fully stitched up by Mackey's well-practiced hands. "Okay, so it was no surprise to discover that the cause of death was asphyxiation."

"From hanging?" I asked as I came over and joined him by the gurney, lighting a cigarette as I did.

"You can't smoke in here."

"I hear that all the time. It's cute. Carry on."

Mackey shook his head at me, seeming pent up, and not just by my smoking. Something else seemed to be bothering him. Years of interrogating suspects who thought they could hide things from me told me told me he was doing the same.

"That's all," he said. "Your vic died from asphyxiation caused by hanging. I'm ruling it as a suicide."

"Like fuck you are. What are you not telling me, Gordon?"

He looked shifty as he shook his head. "Nothing. There's nothing more to tell."

"Gordon," I said in a quiet voice with more than a hint of menace. "The biggest mistake you can make is to take me for a fool. I've been around this shit for a lot longer than you have. I know when someone's hiding something from me. Don't make me beat it outta ya."

Mackey stared down at the floor for a long moment before giving a heavy sigh. "I swear, I hate this fucking job sometimes. I just want to move to Fiji and spend my days fishing in a nice boat with a hunky local to keep me company."

"I'm sure you do." I reached out and put a firm hand on his shoulder. "Tell me what's bothering you, Gordon. Did someone say something to you? Is that why you're being so reticent? It's okay, you can tell me. I promise no harm will come to you if you do."

He fixed his gaze on me for the first time. "You can't guarantee that."

"I can if you tell me who muscled you into keeping your mouth shut." I smiled. "You know me, Gordon. No one intimidates me, and by extension, you."

"Alright," he said, finally relenting. "I'll spill, but you have to promise not to tell them I told you."

"Tell who?" I already had a good idea who, but I needed him to say their names.

"Officers Mike Williams and Jonny Eastwood."

"Big Mike and Baby Face," I sneered. "No surprise. I knew they were covering this shit up when I met them at the crime scene."

"You knew?"

"Yeah. They were at the scene even before the incident was called in."

"Which means they were called in by someone else."

"By the gang who killed Mr. Sidwell here."

Mackey frowned like things still didn't add up. "Williams told me to make sure my report ruled suicide, which is fair enough if that's how they want things to appear officially. But the thing is, if this man was murdered, I'm not quite sure *how* he was murdered."

"What do you mean?" I asked.

"Well," Mackey said. "Mr. Sidwell died from asphyxiation, that much is true, but the way in which he was asphyxiated is…well, it doesn't add up."

"Explain."

"The guy has water in his lungs. He died from drowning."

"Drowning?"

"That's what I said."

I frowned down at Sam Sidwell's waxy corpse. "That makes no sense."

"As there were no signs of struggle—not much anyway—I'm assuming the body was moved from somewhere else. The water in his lungs—and around the body at the scene—is sea water. The closest source of seawater is the old aquarium, and then the docks after that. There are also no ligature marks on the neck. The cord around his neck was tied posthumously."

"Which we knew anyway," I said.

"Given the cause of death, I doubt Williams and his partner killed Mr. Sidwell," Mackey said. "But they covered the tracks of the real killer."

"Do you think Sidwell was taken away and drowned before being brought back to his shop?"

Mackey shrugged. "It's possible, I suppose. But why not just dump the body? Why bring it back to the store and pretend that he killed himself?"

"I don't know," I said. "There's obviously more going on here."

"Like what?"

"I intend to find that out. I'm going to need the room for a while."

"What for?"

"I'm bringing in a consultant."

"A consultant?" Mackey seemed a little offended that I would bring an outsider in, as though his work wasn't good enough.

"Someone with a particular set of skills."

"What kind of skills?"

"Believe me, Gordon," I said, stabbing my cigarette out in a kidney dish. "You don't want to know."

A SHORT TIME LATER, MACKEY LEFT FOR HOME, COMING OFF the back of a triple shift. He was happy enough to leave me alone in the morgue, too tired and stressed to argue with me. I locked the door from the inside when he left and then called my "consultant" who said he would come down to the precinct as soon as he could.

Having made the call, there was nothing left to do but wait, so I climbed atop an empty gurney and lay down on it, using my trench as a pillow as I lay back and closed my eyes. It used to be I could go for days without sleep, but these days, tiredness seemed to get the better of me more often than not. For long stints awake, I needed Snake Bite to keep me going, which I didn't have with me. So while I waited on my consultant to arrive, I closed my eyes and tried to grab some Z's.

Within minutes of shutting my eyes, my mind got busy with putting on a raucous stage show comprising major characters like Hannah, Daisy, Cal and a whole host of walk-on characters, some of whom barely spoke, others who hung around long enough to deliver a few cutting lines that made me wish I had never closed my eyes in the first place.

When an outside voice made me open my eyes again, I was already wondering if my mind was now just a desolate, nightmarish land haunted by the ghosts of my past and present.

"Bad dreams, Ethan?" the voice asked quietly.

I sat up to see Richard Solomon standing by the side of the gurney, looking down on me like a tall, thin specter, his pale face a mass of shadow under the brim of his hat, though his eyes still seemed to shine out, his gaze as penetrative as always.

"You took your time," I said as I swung my legs off the gurney, sitting long enough to light a cigarette before standing to face Solomon. The lights in the room appeared to have dimmed in his presence as though the darkness in his soul was too overwhelming even for the light.

I almost recoiled when he outstretched his skeletal arm and placed a bony hand on my shoulder, sending a chill through me.

"You have been through much suffering since we last met," he said, his eyes half closed, a tangible pleasure in his voice. "You even crossed over into death. Tell me, how was it? What did Death teach you?"

I swatted his hand from my shoulder as you would a bothersome fly. "It taught me not to fucking die again, that's what."

"You gave yourself willingly to Death, but yet you pulled away at the last moment." He made a tutting sound. "What a wasted opportunity."

"Yeah," I said as I searched in my pockets for my cigarettes, "a real wasted opportunity. I'm sure I would've learned much floating in the Void with the rest of the miserable souls."

"Once again you presume to know Death's workings, Ethan," he said. "Death does not have the same plans for everyone."

"Death is death." I stabbed a cigarette into my mouth and lit it. "There's only ever one outcome."

"On the contrary, I've crossed over into Death's realm

many times, and each time I learn something new. I am Death's student; its loyal subject."

"Oh really? And what have you learned exactly?"

"I have learned that Death's powers can be harnessed," he said, beginning to walk slowly around the gurneys containing the victims of The Ripper Tripper, running his hand over the plastic sheets that covered the cadavers. "I've learned that Death is not something to be feared but to be embraced."

"You embrace floating in the Void for eternity?"

Solomon smiled slightly with his gash of a mouth. "Only the uninitiated end up in the Void, or as lost, lonely ghosts haunting the Earth. The initiated, on the other hand, get to explore the dark corners of the universe, travel between dimensions, even back and forth across time as the secrets of the universe are imparted to them." He paused in his traversing of the gurneys to look at me. "I could teach you, Ethan. I could make you an initiate of Death. The wonders of the universe would be open to you, and your soul would be free."

"Studying under you, Solomon?" I shook my head. "No thanks. My life is dark enough without that."

Solomon shook his own head. "Still so much ignorance. You have such potential, Ethan, and yet you smother it beneath a facade of misplaced respectability and a dogged sense of duty to so-called justice. Tell me, where has that duty gotten you? Everyone you love is dead, including your friend Scarlet. Her death has created much pain in you. I can feel it. I can tell that you had deep feelings for her."

"Stop it," I growled.

"And what about Hannah the delectable demon?" he went on. "You really messed up there, didn't you? You turned her against you. Your guilt is destroying you from the inside. Don't you want to transcend all that useless emotion, Ethan? This connection that you seek—that you've always sought—is not to be found in others as you wrongly think. True connection can only be found by giving yourself to Death, by sacrificing the humanity that only serves to keep you down and hold you back. Hannah has fully embraced her true self once more, and she is all the better for it. If you want a true connection with her, you need to do the same. You need to embrace that part of yourself that you have run from since the night your mother died—"

"I said stop it," I growled again. "I'm warning you, Solomon. Just stop it."

Solomon tutted and shook his head. "Why can't you see I'm just trying to help you, Ethan? That I'm trying to free you from—"

"Being a human being?" I snapped. "You want to turn me into a monster like you?"

"A monster? That's how you think of me? Perhaps you should take a look in the mirror, Ethan. I'm not the one who shot his partner, the woman he loves despite never admitting such to himself."

"Get the fuck out of my head, Solomon, or I swear to fuck, I'll—"

"What, Ethan? You'll what? You could never hurt me. I'm beyond hurt at this point. Wouldn't you like to be the same? Wouldn't you like to transcend your own suffering and misery?" He pulled back the sheet on one of the corpses and stared down at the mutilated meat with derision. "Humanity is overrated. You want to end up like this pathetic soul? Laid out on a slab, humiliated in death instead of lauded by Death itself?"

"I'll take my chances."

Solomon replaced the sheet over the corpse again. "Of course you will, but I won't stop trying to save you, Ethan."

"And why's that? Because you love me so fucking much?"

His piercing stare fell upon me, and it felt like he was looking right into my soul...or what was left of it. "Our destinies are intertwined," he said. "Someday you will realize that, and then you will accept my teachings."

"You're deluded."

He smiled, not offended in the slightest by my rejection of him and his so-called teachings. "We will see, won't we? Someday you will come to me, Ethan, with hand outstretched, asking for what I can give you."

"Don't hold your breath."

Turning away from me as he fell into silence, he continued to move through the maze of cadaver gurneys, pulling back plastic sheets to examine the bodies underneath, closing his eyes as he ran his long fingers over the cold, waxy flesh, his fingertips tracing the contours of the sliced muscle and exposed bone. "The man who killed all these women walks in Death's shadow." He closed his eyes as his fingers sank into the exposed flesh of the corpse. "A part of him embraces Death as a friend, and yet…he also fears Death. He fears dying and ending up like the women on these slabs."

"What can you tell me about him?" I asked, glad the conversation wasn't about me any longer.

"His compulsion to kill is strong," he said, touching the pubis of the corpse as one finger slid inside. "In some strange way, his compulsion is not his own. It's like…he has a separate being in him." His finger went deeper. "No, not separate…conjoined and…old. He carries with him a dark passenger that threatens to take him over completely. You are looking for a man who hides behind a mask of respectability, perhaps with a family, a high-flying job. He struggles to maintain his mask, however. He longs to discard it completely, to walk permanently in Death's shadow."

"Sounds like your ideal student," I said sarcastically.

"There's a new power at work here," he said, looking around at all the bodies. "I've sensed it for a while now. It grows stronger by the day."

"It's down to the Fallen, according to Pike."

"You spoke with Eric Pike?"

"Yeah, we met up a couple times. He said the combined celestial energy of the Fallen has formed into something called a Creation Rift. Least that's what Knightsbridge calls it. This new energy is having a profound effect on some people, turning them into what our dear Wendell calls Mytholites."

"Mytholites?" Solomon smiled. "Wendell always did have a knack for naming things."

"The Ripper Tripper is a Mytholite. He's a version of—"

"Let me guess. Jack the Ripper?"

"Yep. Some version of him anyway. A worse version going by how many lives he's claimed."

"And I suppose Wendell is trying to control these people, is he? To use them for his own ends?"

"I don't know. You tell me. Pike said he's still in contact with you sometimes. That true?"

"You make it sound like I've betrayed you somehow."

"I couldn't care less. I'm just asking."

"Well, as you are just asking, yes, I still have some ties to Blackstar. Not many, though, and they are mostly for my own benefit."

"How so?"

"I don't have to tell you everything, Ethan, especially when you insist on holding back with me."

"Because I refuse to let you lead me down a dark path, you mean?"

"My dear Ethan, you are already on a dark path. I only wish to steer you in the right direction."

"I'm sure you do." I turned away from him as I walked toward the body of Sam Sidwell. "Come and do what I brought you here to do before someone comes."

"Who is this person?" Solomon asked as he came to stand opposite me, Sam Sidwell's body between us on the slab.

"Just a guy who was murdered. He was drowned. I need to know what happened."

"Very well," he said, then smiled at me. "I'm sure you know what I want in return."

I knew before he even got here what he would want, but it pissed me off nonetheless. "What do you want to know?"

"Let's see…" His dark eyes reflected his enjoyment of seeing me squirm. "Why don't you tell me about how you avenged your father's death."

My jaw set as I stared hard at him for long seconds. "Fuck you, Solomon. I'm not talking about that. How do you even know about that?"

"Please, Ethan. You forget I was an interviewer at Black-star. I had access to everyone's tapes, including yours."

"And of course you watched them all."

"How do you think I know so much about you, Ethan? About everyone at Blackstar for that matter?"

"You know what happened and you're still asking me to talk about it? You're a sick fuck, Solomon."

"The past shouldn't hurt you, Ethan. It's the past, after all."

"Something tells me if I got a hold of your tapes, you wouldn't be saying that. Maybe I'll ask Pike to get them for me sometime."

Solomon's smile faltered for a second. "Pike would know better than to hand over my interview tapes to you."

I smiled at his rare discomfort. "For someone who believes the past can't hurt them, you sure seem jittery."

He stared at me a moment before his thin smile returned. "This isn't about me. It's about you, Ethan. If you didn't need my help, you wouldn't have to leave yourself open to me like this, but since you clearly *do* need my help, why don't you start talking while I seek out this man's soul."

Asshole. Some day I'll turn the tables on him…

"Fine. Just get on with it then."

"Ditto."

A sigh left me as Solomon closed his eyes and laid his

hands on Sam Sidwell's corpse while I cast my mind back to an incident I hadn't thought about in a long, long time. An incident I had buried deep after it happened for the sake of my sanity, and because Cal told me if I didn't, I would end up eating my gun. *Shit happens*, Cal had said at the time, *and you can either get over it or let it drag you down…or kill you.*

After it happened, I buried the incident as deep as I could in the recesses of my mind, so it only ever emerged in my nightmares. In my waking hours, it was a scab in my mind, and now here was Solomon asking me to pick at it, releasing its septic fluid to poison my conscious mind once more. The things I do for the sake of justice.

So as Solomon did his necromancy thing, I lit a cigarette and began to dredge up what should never be dredged up.

"Shortly after I met Cal, he helped me track down the man who killed my father."

"Yes, the man who killed the father you hardly knew… right in front of you," Solomon said with some glee. "And speaking of Cal, I'm sensing some pain in you—"

"We're not going there. Don't even ask."

"Very well. Carry on then."

I took a long drag of my cigarette before speaking again. "Cal hooked me up with a mentalist who could take me back, in my mind, to the time my father was killed. And yeah, I didn't know my father because I was only four when he died, and he wasn't around much before that, but still…"

"He was your father." Solomon's eyes were open and rolled back into their sockets, so only the whites showed. I'd seen him do this ritual countless times now, and it still creeped me out.

"Yeah, that's right. I still felt the need to avenge his death. Anyone who kills a man in front of his kid like that deserves to die, anyway."

"Hmm," Solomon said as he began to whisper to himself the words that would allow him to find the soul of Sam

Sidwell. It was possible he could summon Sam's ghost here, but that could only happen if his ghost was already on the Earthly Plane. If it wasn't, Solomon would connect with Sam's soul in the Void.

"So thanks to the mentalist, I relived the whole experience."

"How...did you feel?"

"How do you think? I was traumatized all over again, but I was angry as hell."

"Filled with wrath."

"Yes. I got a good look at the bastard as he garroted my father. I saw how much the killer enjoyed it, and how he smiled at my four-year-old self as he bloodied my face with my father's blood."

"And you think of me as twisted." Solomon smiled as he continued to press his hands on Sam Sidwell's body.

"Yeah, well, this guy was a real psychopath. I eventually identified him as Tommy 'The Animal' Testa."

The anger and need for revenge I'd felt at the time burned through me once more as I gritted my teeth against it. My rage back then was powerful and often made me unhinged and dangerous to be around. Cal eventually taught me how to control it, but until he did, I was happy to lash out at anything or anyone in my path, including and especially Testa, who as it turned out, was one of the most feared Mafia hitmen in the whole city. By the time I got to him, he was reported to have had over two hundred kills under his belt.

"Once we found out it was Testa," I went on, "I was all for confronting the guy head-on, but Cal thought that would be a bad idea. First, the guy wasn't a feared killer for nothing, and wouldn't be easy to put down, and second, Cal reasoned that even if I killed the guy, I'd have the rest of the Mafia after me and my life wouldn't be worth living. So we opted for stealthy assassination instead."

"Hold that thought," Solomon said. "I've found him. Take my hand."

Reluctantly, I took Solomon's hand, gasping at how ice-cold it was. Within seconds, I was hit with rapid-fire images that strobed across my mind, snapshots of Sam Sidwell's life: helping his father on the farm, learning to drive a tractor, his pain and sadness when he had to leave to work in the city, the awkwardness of his first sexual experience, the anger and stress of being mugged numerous times, his loneliness in the big city, his joy at having his niece come to stay with him, and finally, the agony of his death, which Solomon somehow slowed down so I could witness the whole thing like a third party who was actually there.

As the images filled my vision, I felt like a ghost watching the living as they went about their business oblivious to my presence. The visions were fuzzy like on an old TV with dodgy reception and bad sound, but I could get the gist of what was going on.

I was looking at Sam Sidwell, alive and surrounded by three men and a woman, with another much younger woman directly in front of him. Sam Sidwell's face was full of fear as he pleaded with the younger woman. "Please, Delphina," he was saying. "Just give me one more week and I'll get your money. Call Antonio, he'll understand—"

"Sorry, Sammy," Delphina said as she swayed from side to side like a cobra with a bad attitude, looking like she was barely into her twenties. "But I ain't calling no one, and I especially ain't calling Snake Tongue to tell him you're late on your payments again, not when we've given you how many extensions now?"

"Three," one of the men surrounding them said, and for the first time, I noticed they were all wearing dark slacks, held up with braces over a white shirt. Bizarrely, they also wore black bowler hats, even the woman, looking like upmarket versions of droogs.

"Three," Delphina repeated in a Southern twang, leaning into Sam as she said it. Unlike the others, who were all Caucasian, Delphina had light brown skin. She was also dressed differently, in black jeans and a black leather jacket, her dark hair cut short, giving her a somewhat boyish appearance. Her large brown eyes were wide as she leaned in toward Sam, who drew back from her in fear. "Three goddamn extensions and you still haven't paid up. I'm sorry, Sammy, but we just can't let that go, I'm afraid."

"I'll go to the cops!" Sam shouted. "I'll tell the newspapers what y'all are up to! I mean it!"

Delphina stared hard at Sam, who seemed to instantly regret what he said. "You'll what?" she said.

"Delphina, I—"

"Take him down!"

As one of the bowler-hatted men moved to grab Sam, Sam pushed him in defense and knocked the guy back into the shelves. As produce fell from the shelves to the floor, another of the men grabbed Sam by the throat and lifted him clean off his feet with one hand, holding him up for a second before slamming him down to the floor.

As Sam lay there in a daze, Delphina then sat on top of him, straddling his chest.

"We can't have people missing payments," she said as she placed her hands either side of Sam's head. "If people in the square hear about it, they'll think we're soft and that they can get away with missing payments too, and we can't have that, can we boys?"

"No, boss," the rest of the gang replied in unison.

"Course not," Delphina said. "Which is why, Sammy boy, we gotta make an example of you. Now, just lie there, and I'll make this as painless as possible. Let yourself drown, Sammy, just let it happen."

As Delphina kept her hands on Sam's head, water suddenly bubbled forth from his mouth, and he started to choke and gag, bucking under Delphina as he struggled to breathe air that wasn't there anymore. With water gushing from his mouth, Sam's eyes widened as he realized he was actually drowning.

"That's it, Sammy," Delphina said gently. "Just let it happen. It'll all be over soon. There's a good boy."

A minute later, Sam Sidwell stopped his struggling and went completely still, having just drowned at Delphina's hands somehow.

What the hell is she? I wondered. *Some kind of MURK? A Mytholite?*

"Now what?" the red-headed woman in the bowler hat said. "What do we do with him?"

Delphina stood up, seemingly unaffected by what she'd just done, even going as far as to grab a lollipop from one of the shelves, tearing off the plastic wrapping before beginning to suck on it. "Call the two goons, Williams and the other one, whatever his name is. Tell them to get down here and fix this, so it looks like a suicide."

"Will do, boss," the woman said, taking out a phone and walking away.

Delphina looked satisfied with a job well done. "Damn," she said as she pulled the lollipop out of her mouth. "These taste *good*…"

At that point, the vision ended abruptly, and I was back in the morgue staring at Solomon. "I assume you got what you needed?" he asked.

"Yeah," I said. "I did."

"A crude lot, whoever they are."

"Crude, but dangerous."

"I could help you kill them all if you like. Their energy would be useful to me."

"I'm sure it would, but I can handle them myself."

Solomon smiled. "Of course you can, just like you

handled Testa. Perhaps you can finish telling me about that now."

"If I must."

"You must."

"Fine," I said as I lit a cigarette and leaned back against the autopsy table, forcing myself to cast my mind back to that time I've since tried to forget, telling myself this will be the last time I'll have to think about it. After this, Jack goes back in the box and gets locked up for good. "Cal and I tracked Testa down, found out where he lived, which was an apartment in Little Italy, one of the more expensive ones because being a Mafia hitman pays well. I waited until the small hours hit, and then I went in."

"What happened when you went inside?" Solomon asked as if he didn't know already.

I threw him a look. "You know what fucking happened. Why're you making me say it?"

He merely smiled. "You know why, Ethan. Carry on."

'Cause you're a sick fuck, that's why.

Let's just get this over with…

"I picked the lock on the front door," I said, feeling that I was there all over again, to where I could even smell the disinfectant in the hallway, and the lingering smell of spaghetti sauce inside the apartment as I went in. "Once I'm inside, I take out my gun—a suppressed Beretta. It's after three a.m., and the place is silent. I figure Testa is sleeping, so I make my way down the hallway toward the bedroom. But halfway down the hallway, I stop when I hear the bedroom door open, and I backtrack and hide around the corner. This'll make things easier, I thought to myself. He's coming to me." I stop for a second to take a drag of my cigarette and then found myself staring at the tiled floor, wishing I didn't have to continue with this story, the old associated feelings turning me sick.

Solomon was staring at me with rapt attention as if he was

afraid of missing a single second of my pain and discomfort. "What happened next?" he asked in a near whisper.

Fucker. I wanted to punch the guy, for all the good it would do. He'd make me suffer for even trying.

"The hallway was dark," I said, continuing with the story in a subdued voice, cigarette smoke rising around me, stinging my eyes. "I couldn't see much, but as soon as I heard the bedroom door open, I dropped to a crouch, and then I raised my gun and—"

I stopped to swallow back the bile that threatened to come up. My belly was suddenly cramped, painful. To make matters worse, I kept getting flashbacks to the night I held Callie in my arms, her lifeless body unresponsive to my cries of pain. "I fired two shots. I double-tapped Testa as he came out of the bedroom."

I wanted to leave it at that, to pretend that's what happened and walk away from Solomon, but the bastard wouldn't let me if I tried.

"Only that's not what happened, is it, Ethan?" he said. "Who did you really shoot?"

"Fuck you, Solomon…"

"Tell me."

Staring hard at him, I said, "A kid. I shot a fucking kid."

"You shot a little boy, didn't you? Age ten, I believe. Mr. Testa's son."

"I didn't know he had a kid, I—"

"You didn't do your homework properly, did you? You were so bent on revenge—on fueling your own out-of-control bloodlust—that you rushed in and shot the wrong person. Tell me, when Mr. Testa inevitably came out to see what was happening, what was his face like? Was he shocked, considering how many people he himself had killed? Do you think it was different because it was his son?"

This was like The Interview all over again. Dredging up painful memories. Stuff that should stay buried, not dragged into the light again for someone else's amusement, in this case, Solomon's. He could go fuck himself. I was done.

"I'm done," I told him, about to walk away.

"What about Testa? What did he do?"

"What the fuck do you think he did?" I snapped. "I turned the lights on, and he screamed once at the sight of his son lying with two bullets in him. Then he went for his gun in the bedroom. I got to him before he grabbed it. Shot him in the back, turned him over and told him who he was looking at. He registered no emotion. Nothing. I shot him in the head and left."

"And the child you shot?" Solomon asked. "What about him? Did you just leave him there?"

"Goodbye, Solomon," I said as I walked out the door.

11

Thanks to Solomon stirring the pot of my mind with his wicked hand, I was now all over the fucking place as I stumbled out of the precinct with decades of long-buried memories pinging around inside my mind like angry wasps—images of MURKs I'd killed, people that I'd killed, my dead wife and daughter, Scarlet with her slit throat, Hannah with her bullet-ridden chest crashing out of that window...

It was too much.

I needed to forget for a while, to give my mind a chance to capture all those painful memories again and lock them up in the darkness where they belonged.

Fucking Solomon.

He does this to me every time, harvesting my pain before discarding me like so much chaff.

Every bar in town had people in it. There was only one that didn't—The Brokedown Palace.

It was still lying empty and untouched. Sooner or later, someone would come along and claim it, but for now, it was a place where I could go to be alone and get quietly drunk.

After getting into the Dodge, however, I just sat there

staring out the window at nothing, my eyes unfocused as my burdensome emotions weighed down on me.

At times like this, I wish I had kept the Spock Chip in while I was at Blackstar. Sure, the chip turned you into an emotionless automaton, but that was also its chief strength. With it in, you didn't suffer at the hands of your conscience or get dragged down by guilt and depression. You were free from all that, and like an insect or a shark, you could do what you had to do, cleanly, efficiently, and without remorse. It made going through life fucking people over—either by accident or by design—so much easier.

Fuck it.

I'd have to make do with what I had.

Alcohol and Mud did nearly the same thing as the Spock Chip. Only the effects were more temporary.

Reaching into my pocket, I took out the Mud bottle. It was about half full. Not bothering with the dropper, I emptied the contents of the bottle into my mouth and swallowed, wincing at the acrid taste.

After putting the empty bottle back in my pocket, I found my hip flask and drained what was left in that, which was about three measures of Jack Daniels.

After a few minutes, a welcome numbness settled over me, and the thoughts in my head began to get fuzzed-out, becoming too indistinguishable to focus on and worry about.

Sliding down in my seat, I lit a cigarette and sat for a while as I watched the occasional patrol car come and go in the street. The world around me was becoming more fluent, the street lamps and lights on the passing cars becoming brighter, the after-burn remaining on my retinas for a long time afterward, the glare stretching to infinity it seemed like. People walking down the street seemed to be doing so in slow motion, their heads turning to look at me as I sat staring at them from inside the car.

Then I spotted a familiar face walking out of the precinct

—a tall figure dressed in a dark suit that looked too expensive for a cop.

Detective John Striker, IAB's finest.

He stopped at the bottom of the steps leading out of the precinct to stare at me. It was the first time I'd seen him since I let myself into his apartment that night to warn him off and essentially blackmail him into staying away from me. No longer a hellot now that his demon master was dead, he didn't seem to carry himself with quite the same arrogance as before, though I could tell he was still up on himself from the look in his eyes. I didn't need to be near him to feel his resentment.

Smiling, I lifted my hand and slowly waved at him.

Striker didn't respond but continued to stare at me, his eyes saying it all.

You think you've won, they said, *but you've only won the battle, not the war.*

At least, that's how I interrupted his gaze as he returned my smile with a smug one of his own before walking off in the opposite direction.

"Asshole," I muttered as I watched him go. "I should've just killed you."

The world seemed to be spinning now, my vision soft around the edges thanks to the Mud. I wasn't quite tripping, but it felt like I was. At least my mind had calmed, and my emotions had dulled down.

Fuck Solomon if he thought he could unsettle me. Fuck Xaglath too, and Captain Edwards, and Lewellyn and the cunt who had my family killed. Fuck them all if they thought they could control me, deflate me, fuck me. I've put up with assholes trying to do all those things my whole life, and none have succeeded yet.

And none would.

"Not when I'm doing such a stellar fucking job myself," I

said, laughing and then shaking my head as I glimpsed my red-rimmed eyes in the mirror.

I averted my gaze to the window again, realizing there was now a massive black spider crawling across the glass, which immediately made me think of Charlotte, and then Scarlet, and how Charlotte had carried her sister's body away…

"Where are you going?"

"I'm taking my sister home…"

Home.

To the woods.

I needed to go there.

I needed to see her.

I needed to see Scarlet.

Or her grave at least.

~

WITH AT TIMES IMPAIRED VISION THANKS TO THE MUD, I MADE the journey to the Great Woods. When I hit the highway, the hypnotic noise of the Dodge's engine lulled me into a state of semi-consciousness that drew me across lanes until I almost collided with a huge semi, managing to turn the wheel just in time before the truck's massive wheels pulled the Dodge under itself.

After that, I put a CD in the stereo and turned it up loud. Gary Numan's *Sacrifice* album blared inside the car on repeat for the rest of the journey, ensuring I didn't nod off again.

It was close to dawn when I finally arrived at the Great Woods. Unlike my last trip here with Haedemus, I knew exactly where I was going this time. Rather than having to make a ridiculously long trek through the woods like last time, I located the private road at the edge of the woods where Jonas Webb had taken Charlotte to before he made off with her.

After parking up, it didn't take me long to make my way

through the woods to the cottage. Sounds around me were heightened through the Mud. Every hoot from an owl sounded amplified. Coyotes howled, sounding like they were right next to me.

At times, I fancied I could even hear the chattering of the Wyldefae as they went about their nocturnal business. Not that I paid much attention. My focus was singular, subservient to the overwhelming urge I had to be near Scarlet again.

You want the truth. I missed the hell out of her. Which is strange for me, becoming so close to someone I hardly even knew at the end of the day. But I couldn't deny I enjoyed being around her. Her presence had a calming effect on me, and she was one of the few people who made me feel good about myself. I'm not saying I was in love with her. I don't know what I'm saying. The only thing I know is that there's a hole in my life now that she's gone.

Scarlet was a kindred spirit, and I hadn't come across many of those in my lifetime.

As I neared the cottage, I soon came across what looked to be massive spiderwebs stretching between the trees, forming a barrier around the cottage and its gardens. The webs were everywhere, and I noticed that many unfortunate animals had been caught up in the sticky substance. A rabbit bucked its legs as it tried to free itself, but all it succeeded in doing was entangling itself further. Above me, a pigeon flapped its wings in similar fashion, but it was going nowhere.

The webbing was impenetrable until I took out the machete-like blade I had under my trench and started cutting my way through it like I was trekking through thick jungle.

As I made inroads toward the cottage, I soon came across something slightly more disturbing than a trapped animal.

There appeared to be a person wrapped up tight in the spiderweb, with only their head visible, their body covered in the sticky white webbing.

"Help me…" the person whispered.

When I hacked my way toward them, I realized it wasn't a human wrapped up in the web, but a vampire.

And she wasn't the only one.

Looking around, I spotted three more of them ensnared in the spiderweb, suspended between the trees as they stared down at me with pleading red eyes.

"What the fuck?" I said.

Charlotte had obviously been busy, though why she felt the need to trap the vampires like that, I didn't know. Did she plan on torturing them? Eating them? Not that I cared about the well-being of a bunch of vampires. I had no love for them, and frankly, couldn't care less if they were all wiped out of existence. What use were they anyway? They were just parasites, feeding off humans and gathering as much power for themselves as they could.

Yeah, like humans are any different.

"She'll kill you."

I looked up to see a female vampire hanging upside down from a tree, her body wrapped in webbing. "Why hasn't she killed *you* yet?" I asked the vampire.

"I don't know," she said. "She's an abomination."

"And you aren't?"

The vampire hissed angrily. "I hope she bites your fucking head off, human!"

"Keep hanging in there, bloodsucker."

"Stinking human!"

Ignoring the angry vampire, I continued to hack my way through the spiderweb, occasionally getting caught up in it myself, having to cut myself free with the blade.

How did she even make this web? I wondered.

Had she further mutated since she escaped the mountain facility? Was she a complete monster now?

Something told me I would soon find out.

Through the webbing, I could make out the dark shape of the cottage.

"Charlotte?" I called, half-hoping she wasn't here, genuinely afraid that I would end up cocooned in her spiderweb along with the vampires. "It's Ethan Drake. You remember me?"

Of course she remembered me. She probably still blamed me for her sister's death, even though it was she who killed her. But people have a way of shifting blame, don't they? Not that I blamed Charlotte for killing Scarlet anyway. She didn't know what she was doing. I blamed Jonas Webb for turning her into a monster in the first place.

As I paused to see if I would get a response to my announcement, I felt the spiderweb around me begin to vibrate slightly and to pulse as if something was moving across it.

"She's com-ing," one of the trapped vampires hissed softly in a sing-song voice. "You're going to get eaten, human."

I hoped not as I looked around for signs of Charlotte, half expecting to see a giant spider coming toward me, but through the maze of webbing, I couldn't see very much in the thick darkness.

My Infernal Itch, however, was reacting to something.

It could've been responding to the presence of the vampires, or it could've been responding to something else, I wasn't sure. At any rate, I continued to hack my way through the webbing as I tried to make it to the cottage. A few more feet and I would—

Something grabbed me from behind.

Hard, black limbs.

By the time I was gripped and spun around, I knew it was too late to do anything, especially since the arm holding my blade was now glued to the webbing along with one of my legs.

When I was spun around with those powerful black limbs, I found myself face to face with Charlotte, only some monstrous version of her.

The top half of her body was still vaguely human in shape, her skin black and shiny like liquid obsidian. Smooth dark hair fell either side of her face, and two glowing red eyes stared right at me as her mouth opened to reveal a pair of long, needle-sharp fangs. She held me with two of her thick spider legs, the barbs of which pierced my coat and pricked my skin. Her body was attached to an enormous, bulbous abdomen, which explained how she could spin so many webs.

As she held me, she put both her hands under my chin, pressing her extremely long fingernails into my flesh. It would only take one push, and those hard, black nails would stab into my skull, killing me instantly.

"What…are you doing here?" she hissed.

"You remember me?" I asked her, doing my best to stay calm in the face of such monstrosity. "I'm Scarlet's friend."

She hissed loudly and pushed her fingernails further into my flesh, causing me to yelp slightly. "It's your fault she's dead!"

"No…we were trying to help you, Charlotte. Your sister wanted to save you, to—"

"Kill him!" one of the cocooned vampires shouted. "Suck him dry!"

"Silence fiend!" Charlotte snapped, turning her head to glare at the vampire behind her, before fixing her attention on me again.

"I came to pay my respects to Scarlet," I said, hoping to get through to her. "You buried her here, right?"

She stared at me for a long time as venom dripped from her fangs—stared at me so long that I felt sure she was going to eat me there and then.

Which is why I was surprised when she released me from her grip, using her legs to slice the webbing I was stuck in. Now able to move, I started backing away from her out of the spiderweb until I was standing in the clearing surrounding the cottage.

"Why did you let him go?" the vampire behind her raged. "And yet, you keep us trapped here!"

Charlotte turned on the web suddenly and scuttled toward the vampire at high speed. In a split second, she was above the vampire, and I winced as she sank her fangs into his skull, crushing half his head. Within his cocoon, the vampire screamed and then turned to dust, the webbing that once held him so securely now deflated.

Charlotte's red eyes glared at me for a second before she scurried back across the web and down onto the ground. For a second, I thought she was going to kill me the same way she did the vampire, but instead, she stood as her monstrous arachnid body began to transform itself, her limbs retracting, her bulbous abdomen turning into human legs.

Soon she stood before me as a person, albeit a naked one as her black arachnid skin gave way to the pale skin underneath.

"You have some nerve coming here," she said, just a girl now, young and innocent-looking, harmless even, though I wasn't about to underestimate her ability to kill me if she chose to do so.

Slowly, cautiously, I lit a cigarette and blew the smoke into the cold night air before speaking. "Thanks for not killing me."

"I owe you nothing."

"I didn't say you did."

"You should go. You have no business being here."

Perhaps she was right. What did I hope to get out of coming here, anyway? It wasn't like I could speak to Scarlet again, was it? Nor did I have any obligation toward Charlotte.

And yet, it felt like I did, for I knew if Scarlet were still alive, she wouldn't be happy that her little sister had become a monstrous vampire hunter-killer. I didn't think even Charlotte was happy with what she had become, but she seemed accepting of it nonetheless, perhaps because there was no one around to tell her any different.

Seemingly done with me, Charlotte went to walk toward the cottage until I stopped her by asking her where she buried Scarlet. She stood with her back to me for a moment before turning around. "I buried her body around back. Why?"

"I'd like to see," I said. "That's the main reason I came here. Whatever you might think of me, I had a lot of respect for your sister. She was good people."

Charlotte stared at me with dark eyes that were once blue. "My sister didn't have friends. All she had was me. What made you so special?"

"We helped each other out, that's all." I took a drag of my cigarette. "Though, to be honest, she helped me more than I helped her. She almost died for me."

"Almost?" Charlotte said, her eyes blazing. "She did die for you!"

There were tears in her eyes. Clearly, she felt the same guilt that I did, though probably far more considering she delivered the death stroke.

"It wasn't your fault what happened, you know," I said. "You didn't know what you were doing."

"I knew." She turned her head away. "I just couldn't stop myself."

"What your father did to you—"

"That man was not my father, no matter what he said."

"But you went with him when he came here for you."

"I didn't know any better, and he was convincing. He made me think he cared, but—" She sighed heavily, the victim of an insane conman. "I should never have left here. Everything that happened after is my fault."

"Charlotte," I began, walking toward her, but she held a hand out to stop me.

"I don't want to hear your platitudes," she said bitterly. "Whatever you have to say, it doesn't matter. It won't change anything, and it won't bring my sister back." As tears ran down her cheeks, she said, "Just do what you have to do and then leave, whatever your name is."

"It's Ethan. Ethan Drake."

"Whatever."

Turning, she walked inside the cottage, leaving me standing there as I smoked the rest of my cigarette, feeling about as useless as it was possible to feel.

So much for getting through to her. What did I expect anyway? I was nothing but a stranger to her, a man who, in her mind, facilitated her sister's death. I was lucky she didn't bite my damn head off like she did to that vampire.

Grinding my cigarette underfoot, I headed around back until I spotted a patch of recently dug earth that had a crudely carved wooden plaque sitting on top of it. Scrawled into the plaque was Scarlet's name. It was something of shock seeing it, like bumping into Scarlet herself, the first real contact I'd had with her since she died.

Sighing as I was overcome with sadness, I crouched down by the gravesite and placed my hand on the damp earth for a moment.

"Hey," I said quietly as if she could hear me. "It's me, Ethan. You probably think I have some nerve coming here. Or maybe you don't. I never—I never got a chance to thank you for saving me. Although, if you were here right now, I'd kick your damn ass for doing what you did. That's twice you stuck your neck out for me when you knew I didn't deserve it. Anyway, I just wanted to say I'm sorry, and that I—I miss you, Scarlet. I know we hardly knew each other, but it felt like we'd known each other for years. You were a cool motherfucker, girl—"

I had to stop as I choked up. This was harder than I thought it would be. If she were here now, she'd probably tut and tell me to go get a grip, a thought which made me laugh to myself. "You were one of the good ones, and I'm going to miss the hell outta you. Goodbye, Scarlet."

As I stood up, I saw Charlotte inside the cottage, staring at me through the window. When she saw me looking, she stepped back into the shadows, disappearing.

Around the front of the cottage, I paused by the front door, expecting Charlotte to come back out. When she didn't, I said, "Just to let you know, Charlotte, you don't have to do what you're doing. You don't have to be the monster that Webb wanted you to be. You can still be the person who Scarlet wanted you to be. It's not too late to make her proud."

There was no response from inside. Just silence.

Turning around, I walked away from the cottage so I could make my way back to the car again.

So much for closure.

12

I was exhausted by the time I got home. It was early morning, but I had no intention of sleeping. My priority now was bringing Sam Sidwell's killers to justice, and that included not just Delphina, but her whole gang and the two fuckwit cops who helped her cover up the murder. I had maybe a couple days left of being a cop if I was lucky, and I wanted to get it all done before Edwards came demanding my badge and gun. If possible, I would go to him first and hand in my badge myself before he could take it off me. At least then I could deprive him of the satisfaction.

It's the little victories, right?

Upon entering my apartment building, I bumped into the super who informed me that he'd fixed my door and that the new keys were under the mat. He'd installed a heavy-duty security door in thanks for sorting out Dormer, though he obviously didn't know Dormer was dead. All the super cared about was that the apartment was now empty and ready to be rented out again. It made me queasy to think some unsuspecting person or family would end up in that place, sleeping in a bedroom that once had the skins of dead children hanging in it.

As per usual, the Hellbastards were huddled on the couch watching TV when I walked in, though I knew something was up as soon as they all went quiet, and also because every one of them had raging erections.

To make matters even more bizarre, all five of them wore balaclavas over their heads. As I paused by the bedroom door to stare at them, they kept their attention on the TV, suspiciously quiet like naughty children.

"I have many questions I'm not sure I want to know the answers to," I said. "Let's start with the balaclavas. Why are you wearing them?"

"We did a job, boss," Scroteface said.

"Excuse me?" I said. "A job? What kind of 'job'?"

"We did a daylight raid on the stash house up the street," Reggie elaborated.

"It was awesome, boss," Cracka said with his hand wrapped around his erection as he tugged at it gently.

"Please stop doing that, Cracka," I told him. "It creeps me out. The fact that *all* of you have hard-ons is creeping me out. Why—"

The sound of a chainsaw coming from the TV interrupted me, followed by a loud, blood-curdling scream that was too convincing to be anything other than real. Frowning, I looked at the Hellbastards and then walked around so I could see the TV. On the screen, a masked man was busy cutting up a woman with a chainsaw while several other men watched on.

"What the fuck?" I said. "You're watching *snuff?*"

Scroteface looked at me again. "I told you we did a raid on the stash house up—"

"Yeah, up the street," I said. "You already said. You did a raid just for snuff? In fact, you did a raid at all? What the fuck, guys? What did we say about keeping a low profile? I mean, how did you even do a hold-up?"

"With these," Toast said, lifting one blackened hand to show me the silver pistol he held.

"We're packing now, boss," Reggie said, raising what seemed to be a Mach 10 so I could see it.

"All of you?" I said in disbelief.

"Oh yeah, boss," Cracka said as they all raised their weapons at once. Scroteface had a .357 Magnum, Snot Skull a Scorpion machine pistol and Cracka, well, he seemed to have acquired a Colt Peacemaker that he could barely hold up it was so big.

I shook my head. "Where the hell did you get all those? Wait, on second thoughts, I don't want to know."

"It's a funny story," Reggie said.

"Yeah, I'm sure it is," I said as my stomach growled with hunger, despite the fact that there was a woman on TV getting her head chainsawed off while a bunch of guys jerked off around her. "Some other time, maybe. I hope you don't plan on doing any more stickups. That shit attracts attention we don't need, you understand me? Pretty soon, I'm not gonna be able to protect us the way I've been doing because I won't have the law on my side anymore."

Scroteface turned to look at me, his eyes bulging through the eyeholes of his balaclava. "Why not, boss?"

"'Cause I'm being pushed outta the force, that's why," I said, the words like a punch to my gut. Fucking politicking, bureaucratic assholes. Their ignorance would fuck them up the ass someday. I fucking hoped so anyway.

"You not going to be cop anymore?" Cracka asked sadly.

"No, Cracka, it doesn't look like it."

"So what's the plan, boss?" Snot Skull asked. "You need to sit down and maybe bounce some ideas off us or something? We could help you figure out a new career plan."

"Maybe draw you up a CV," Reggie said, sounding proud of himself that he'd thought of that.

"I know!" Cracka said. "We all do stickups. Rob banks."

"No, Cracka," I said.

"How about solve mysteries like Scooby and the gang?" Toast suggested.

"Yeah!" Cracka said, enthused by the idea. "I be Scrappy Doo! Ta dadada ta daaa! Puppy power!"

"Get a grip, little guy," Snot Skull said, chuckling.

"No," Cracka said as he put the barrel of the Colt to Snot Skull's head. "You get a grip, asshole!"

"Go on," Snot Skull growled, pointing his Scorpion pistol at Cracka's massive boner. "I'll make a fucking flute out of your todger!"

"Hey!" I shouted. "Put the fucking guns away! Now!"

Cracka lowered his gun immediately, followed by Snot Skull. "Sorry, boss," Snot Skull said. "We were just screwing around."

"Exactly," I said. "I'm not happy with you guys having guns. You're all dangerous enough as it is. Get rid of them."

"But boss—" Scroteface began.

"Boss nothing," I said. "Lose the guns, and no more stick-ups, you hear me?"

"Yeah, boss," Scroteface said.

"And turn off the fucking snuff, will ya?" I said. "Besides being in bad taste, fucking Daisy could walk in here and see it. Get rid of it."

Toast sighed audibly. "There goes my masturbation session later. I got lube and everything."

"You got lube?" Snot Skull asked.

"Yeah," Toast said. "You want some?"

"Sure," Snot Skull said. "I'll take some off you. You have any good skin mags?"

"No, but Cracka does."

They both looked at Cracka as he shook his head. "Na. They mine. Get your own."

"Where'd you stash them, you little shit?" Snot Skull asked. "I'll find them. They can't be far."

"Boss," Cracka whined. "Tell them."

Sighing, I shook my head. "I'm gonna make myself something to eat. You guys fight over porn mags. And lose the fucking masks. I feel like I'm being held hostage by a bunch of over-sized Gremlins."

Reggie laughed. "Yeah, don't feed us after midnight."

"That's Mogwai, you tool," Scroteface said.

"Same shit," Reggie said.

"No, it isn't," Scroteface argued. "Maybe if you weren't so fuckin' stoned out of your tree all the time, you would—"

Shaking my head, I closed the kitchen door on them, wondering as I did what kind of monsters I had created.

AFTER A NOT VERY SATISFYING MEAL OF BAKED BEANS ON toasted stale bread washed down with beer, I came out of the kitchen to find that the Hellbastards had discarded their balaclavas, all except Cracka, who insisted on wearing his for the duration of the slasher flick they were now watching, which apparently helped him "walk in shoes of killer". Whatever. At least they weren't watching snuff anymore. I might have to pay this infamous stash house a visit myself some time. Girls getting cut up with chainsaws for the amusement of twisted pervs didn't sit well with me. Who knows, maybe it'll be my first case as a private dick should I go down that road in the near future.

With my belly full and growling with indigestion now instead of hunger, I went into the bedroom and blasted two lines of Snake Bite up my nose, my nostrils feeling like they were on fire afterward.

As I stood taking deep breaths to quell the rush, a text came through on my phone from Artemis, telling me he had something for me regarding the footage I'd asked him to examine. Texting him back, I told him I'd swing by later.

"I'm heading out again," I told the Hellbastards when I went back into the living room. "Stay outta trouble while I'm gone."

"We'll do our best, boss," Scroteface said, hardly looking at me.

"Gee, thanks for inspiring me with confidence that I won't come home to total fucking chaos later, Scroteface," I said. "I look forward to hearing how you were unable to obey a simple command when I get back."

Scroteface kept his eyes on the slasher flick, which I realized was *Nightmare On Elm Street*. "What?"

I shook my head. "Nothing. I'll see ya later."

Walking down the hallway, I paused for a second by Daisy's door as I considered knocking on it, but I decided against it when I realized she was probably at school. I also didn't want to incur the wrath of her mother when she saw it was me at her door.

I'd be lying if I said I wasn't worried about Daisy. Given her newfound skills and strange visions, it was a safe bet that she was becoming one of these Mytholite characters, which to be honest, I wasn't happy about. I mean, look at this Ripper Tripper guy and what a murderous son of a bitch he is. Would Daisy end up the same way? What character from legend was she becoming, anyway? And how much more of an effect was this new power going to have on her?

I liked sweet little Daisy as she was. I didn't want to see her transformed into someone else with murderous tendencies. Not only that, if she was becoming one of these Mytholites, it also meant she would have a target on her back. Blackstar would no doubt be interested in her for nefarious reasons, and God knows who else.

Whatever the outcome of her unsettling transformation, I vowed to protect her no matter what. As best I could anyway. I'd lost too many people now to ever think I could protect anyone completely. In fact, I'd be a fool to think otherwise.

It wouldn't stop me from trying, though, that's for damn sure.

On the way out to the car, I got a phone call from a number I didn't recognize. "Hello?" I said as I braced myself against the gusts of cold wind blowing through the empty street. "Who's this?"

"Detective Drake," a girl's voice said. "It's Gemma Sidwell. You're investigating my uncle's death?"

"Yeah, hi, Gemma. What can I do for you?"

"I just thought I'd let you know that Delphina and her gang have arrived at the square again. I saw them go into the florists."

"That's good," I said as I stood by the car. "I was just about to head over there, anyway."

"Have you made any progress in the investigation?"

"Yeah, a little," I said, wondering how much I should tell her, and if she'd even believe me when I told her. "I'll call in and see you after I talk to Delphina."

"Okay," she said. "Be careful, Detective."

Hanging up the phone, I got into the Dodge and turned the ignition, but the engine didn't start. "Fuck's sake, come on, baby…"

I tried again, but the car refused to start. I'd been meaning to get the ancient Dodge serviced because it had been doing this for a while now, taking its time about starting. It was probably on its last legs, but I was reluctant to get rid of it. I'd been driving it for years now, and I'd become fond of it. Besides, I couldn't afford a new car anyway, especially as I was soon to be out of a job.

Thankfully, the Dodge started up after a few more turns of the ignition and away I went, turning on the radio as I took the corner at the top of the street. The news was on, and as usual, The Ripper Tripper was the top story. He'd taken another victim last night, despite the heavy police presence in the Red Light District. It made me wonder if the guy would ever get caught, given how adept he seemed to be at avoiding detection. Routman was probably fuming, not to mention red-faced at his task force's seeming inability to catch this guy. I doubted Routman would be making any grand statements to the media anytime soon, at least not until he had something to give them other than failure.

Hyped up and wide awake thanks to the Snake Bite igniting my nervous system, I switched out the news for an old Godflesh CD, and soon the car reverberated with the heavy, pounding industrial rhythms of "Like Rats". If ever there was a song that summed up this city—this *world*—it was this one.

"*You breed...like rats,*" I sang in my gruffest voice as I banged the steering wheel with my hands in time to the music. "*You breed...like rats.*"

The city this morning was heaving with traffic, which annoyed me no end, having to sit in line as I inched along. Not good when you haven't long taken two lines of Snake Bite.

All I could do was turn the music up and wait as I continued to sing along. "Don't *look back...You were dead from the beginning...*"

When I made it downtown after an age crawling along at a snail's pace, I saw the cause of the gridlock—a motor vehicle accident involving two cars, a bus and several downed pedestrians.

As usual with these situations, motorists were slowing down as they passed so they could get a good look at the carnage. Getting my own stare on as I passed, I spotted a MURK looking on from the sidewalk.

A demon; his dark Visage hovering menacingly over him.

The smile on the asshole's face said it all—he had caused the accident somehow, and he was now feeding off of the hurt and misery to satisfy his own sick desires. I had a good mind to park up somewhere and confront him, drag him into an alley and kill the cunt. But I knew by the time I even found somewhere to park that the demon would be gone. These Fallen assholes did shit like this all the time, causing accidents, turning people against each other and sitting back to watch the resulting carnage. They got a kick out of it, sick fucks that they are.

And speaking of sick, evil fucks, I wondered what Xaglath was up to as I carried on toward Nelson's Square, the traffic moving better now that the accident had been left behind. The demon bitch was probably planning her next move against Yagami.

Meanwhile, Yagami was most likely raging over the fact that Xaglath had killed six of his men with little effort on her part. I also wondered if he knew I was present at that incident, and if he did, did he think I was in league with Xaglath?

Not that I cared if he did. Something told me I would end up going head to head with him at some point, anyway. Yagami was the type that if he couldn't control you, he'd kill you instead.

Who knows, he may be my ticket out of here. I can only hope.

Kidding.

Or am I?

Even I don't know these days.

With traffic moving steadily now, I drove the rest of the way to Nelson's Square, parking the Dodge next to a large SUV with blacked-out windows. I hadn't seen the car here before, but I knew immediately who it belonged to—Delphina and her gang of wannabe droogs.

The florist's shop was near the edge of the square a few doors down, which is where Gemma said she saw the gang go into.

Before I headed in that direction, however, I went around the back of the SUV and stuck a small magnetized tracking device underneath the car. I'd taken the device from my apartment earlier. I figured it would make things easier if I knew where these assholes hang out. Maybe they would lead me to Snake Tongue.

We'll see.

In the meantime, I headed to the florists to see what was what.

When I walked inside the small shop, my nostrils immediately filling with an abundance of not unpleasant floral scents, I saw the four members of Delphina's gang, though there didn't seem to be any sign of Delphina herself. Maybe she was in another shop, causing havoc. Or perhaps she was in the convenience store intimidating Gemma Sidwell. Delphina seemed the type to gloat over someone's death. If she was, I'd soon put a stop to it. But first, I decided to fuck with her gang a little, rattle their cages to see what fell out.

When I walked in, every member of the gang stopped what they were doing to stare at me. Just like in the vision, they were all dressed in black slacks, white shirts and bowler hats. What I didn't notice in the vision—but noticed now—was the fact that they all appeared to have small Egyptian ankhs hanging from gold chains around their necks.

I thought it slightly strange that they were all wearing the same jewelry. I also wondered at the significance of it. Why an ankh? What did that have to with anything? They were all part of the Italian mob, so why would they be wearing a friggin' ankh of all things?

They all appeared to be in their twenties, fresh-faced, arrogant as hell and seemingly always up for trouble, as demonstrated when one of them looked at me and said, "You're no customer."

"No," said one of the others as he took a few steps toward me, looking me up and down as he did so. "You're that cop that's been sniffing around here, aren't you?"

I held my hands up and smiled. "You got me. There's no foolin' you guys, is there?"

"What are you doing here, copper? This square is none of your business."

"Yeah," said the only female of the gang, good-looking with bobbed red hair under her hat. "We own this square, and we say what goes on in it. Isn't that right, Mrs. Honeysuckle?"

"Oh yes," Mrs. Honeysuckle—a gray-haired woman in her sixties—smiled from behind the counter. "That's right, dear. Everyone knows Mr. Francetti is the boss here."

"And we work for Mr. Francetti," another of the male gang members said. "Which means we run things here on the ground. So any ideas you have of arresting us or anything else, you can forget it."

"Wow," I said, walking further into the shop. "You're a confident lot, aren't you? I'm sure old Snake Tongue is real proud of his drones."

"Drones?" one of them said. "We are not drones. We are essential parts of the business."

"And what business might that be?" I asked them as I picked up a red rose and sniffed it. "Extortion? Intimidation? Murder?"

"We have every right to be here," the redhead said, and then hit me with a load of legal speak that I guess was supposed to justify all of their actions, past and present, and also to intimidate me. I barely listened as she droned on while the others nodded smugly in agreement. Francetti had them well-schooled, I'll give him that much. But if they thought quoting the law to me was going to somehow intimidate me into leaving them alone, they thought wrong.

"Are you finished now?" I asked. "Because if you are, I'd like to question you all on the murder of Sam Sidwell. Where's your other boss, by the way? Delphina."

"We know nothing about any murder," one of them said. "And Delphina will be along shortly, unfortunately for you."

"Sam Sidwell killed himself," another said. "You need to speak with Officer Mike Williams. He'll set you straight."

"Oh, I'll be speaking with Big Mike, alright," I said. "Only, I'll be the one setting him straight. In the meantime, I'm gonna need y'all to come down the station with me for questioning about the murder of Sam Sidwell and the extortion racket you're all a part of here."

They all stared at me a moment and then burst out laughing, which is kinda what I expected from them. I knew they'd defy me, and I also knew that even if they came to the precinct with me, some fancy lawyer would have them out in no time at all. It would be a waste of time arresting these arrogant bunch of drones.

That didn't mean I couldn't rattle their cages a little, however.

I soon got my chance when the redhead came charging at me, her fist primed to smack me in the face.

As soon as I saw her move, I took a few steps back before timing my next move to perfection, grabbing the arm she was gonna use to punch me and redirecting her forward momentum, Aikido style, toward the glass front door. Unable to stop herself, she went crashing through the glass and landed on the broken paving stones outside.

"What the fuck?" one of the other gang members said as the three of them now advanced toward me. "You're gonna pay for that, copper."

Rather than try to fight these assholes in the confines of the shop—and wrecking the place in the process—I backed out through the smashed front door.

But I never counted on the redhead getting back to her feet so quickly, and the next thing I knew, she'd jumped on my back and had locked her arms into a chokehold around my neck.

"I don't go down that easy," she hissed as she started to apply a shocking amount of pressure to the chokehold.

As my vision began to blur around the edges, I noticed the other three goons exit the shop, but they hung back, probably thinking their redheaded companion would take care of me on her own.

To buy myself some time before I got put to sleep, I slipped one finger into the crook of the woman's arm and pulled down on it, taking at least some pressure off my neck. I then reached around with my right arm and felt for my assailant's head, closing my fingers around a clump of her hair and then pulling as hard as I could until the bitch squealed with pain.

At that point, one of the other goons came forward and punched me hard in the stomach, forcing the wind out of me as my knees gave way a little.

But I didn't let go of the redhead's hair as I kept my balance, pulling harder until she finally relinquished her hold on my neck, and I could pull her right around, dumping her down on the ground in front of me.

The gang gave me no time to recover, however, and within seconds, the three guys were on me, taking it in turns to come at me with fancy kicks and punches. I did my best to block and evade the blows, but inevitably, a few got through. A punch to the face bloodied my nose and made my eyes water like crazy, and a low kick to my thigh almost broke my balance.

Fuck this. I'm nobodies fucking punching bag.

The next guy to come at me got a rude awakening when I rushed forward at him, using my weight and momentum to drive him back as I repeated the same punch several times to his face. Considering how hard I was hitting him, the guy didn't seem too bothered and even smiled as my fist smashed into his cheekbone.

What the fuck are these guys on? They shouldn't be this strong.

The guy ducked under my next punch and slammed into my waist, wrapping his arms around the tops of my legs before hoisting me clean off the ground and slamming me onto my back, seemingly with little effort. Bear in mind, I'm over 250lbs, and this guy lifted me like I was barely half that.

Despite the pain in my back from the crash landing, I scrambled back to my feet again and immediately drew my gun.

"Back off!" I shouted as the four of them advanced toward me, stopping when they saw the gun, although they didn't seem too worried about getting shot.

"You gonna shoot us, copper?" one of them sneeringly asked.

"If I have to," I said as I wiped blood from my nose. "Don't think I won't."

"I don't think that'll be necessary," said another voice with a Southern twang to it.

I looked to my left to see a smallish female coming toward me, dressed in jeans and leather jacket, her black hair boyishly short, all attitude as she took her time getting to me.

"Delphina, I take it?" I said as I flanked further to the right so I could keep my gun trained on all of them, Delphina included.

"That's right," Delphina said, smiling, seeming happy that I knew who she was. "And you are?"

"He's the cop who's been sniffing around," one of Delphina's crew said. "You want us to kill him, Delphina?"

Delphina stood looking at me like she wasn't impressed by what she saw.

"Nah," she said, putting her hands on her hips. "He ain't no threat to us, are you, Detective? 'Cause that would be damn near impossible. You know why?"

Before I could answer, Delphina suddenly raised herself off the ground until she was floating above it somehow, gently moving her arms and legs as if she was floating underwater. "'Cause no one is a threat to us," she finished.

I kept my gun trained on her as she positioned herself nearly horizontal in the air and then began to swim toward me like a shark with her arms held back by her sides. Almost languidly, she began to circle me, swimming through the air as her lithe body swayed from side to side.

"What the fuck are you?" I asked her, still glancing from her to the other four goons in case one of them made a move, though they seemed happy enough to stand back while Delphina put on her little show.

"That's a real good question there, Detective," Delphina said as she swam from side to side in front of me, just as the heavens opened and the rain began to pour, making it look like Delphina was swimming in the rain itself. "You see, I'm still figuring that one out myself."

"Yeah?" I said. "And what have you come up with so far?"

"I'm glad you asked," she said, smiling. "You see, there was once a great shark Goddess called Ka'ahu Pahau, and for whatever reason, she—or at least her power—has been reborn in me. So I guess that makes me her, but also, you know, me. To be honest with you, Detective, I don't give a shit how or why I ended up with these awesome powers. I'm just happy to have 'em, 'cause then I can do shit like this."

She shot toward me then, her mouth opened impossibly wide as she hovered menacingly in front of me, her mouth which was now full of shark's teeth.

Taking a step back, I pointed my gun at the freak's head. "Stay the fuck back."

Delphina's mouth returned to normal as quickly as it had widened in the first place. "Relax, Detective," she said, smiling now. "I ain't gonna hurt you. Least not if you get the hell outta here and leave us to our business. This is my square, and I say what happens here."

"What about your boss, Francetti?" I asked. "Doesn't he get a say?"

"Snake Tongue handles the business side of things," Delphina said as she came to stand on the ground again. "Security is my job, and I don't take lightly to anyone threatening that security, you hear me? If you know what's good for you, Detective, you best take your gun and get on outta here. I see you back here again—cop or no cop—I'll take a chunk outta ya so big, it'll look like you were attacked by a Great White."

Jesus, the balls on this bitch.

"Not too many Great White sharks around here last time I checked," I said.

Taking a step forward, Delphina slowly tilted her head to the side. "You just haven't been looking properly. Heed my warning, Detective. After today, don't come back here, or things will most definitely turn nasty. You feel me?"

Staring back at her, I said nothing, letting my eyes do the talking, and they said, *This isn't over. We'll see each other again.*

A slight smile appeared on Delphina's face, her whiskey brown eyes saying, *I know, and I'm counting on it.*

Without another word, she moved past me and ushered her crew to follow her.

"Be seeing you, copper," the redhead said with a sneering smile as she and her three companions headed toward the black SUV.

"Damn right you will," I said to myself as I watched them get into the vehicle. Delphina sat up front as one of her crew drove, and she opened the window half-way so she could peer out at me, her cold, shark eyes staying on me until the SUV sped away.

Taking out my phone, I brought up the app for the tracker. A street map appeared on the screen, showing the square I was standing in. Moving away from the square, heading east, was a red dot, representing the SUV.

Smiling, I put the phone back in my trench pocket.

I'll be seeing you all again very soon.

Before I left the square, I went to check on Gemma Sidwell, just in case Delphina had paid her a visit.

As it turned out, she had.

Gemma was behind the counter in the convenience store, her reddish hair tied back in a ponytail over a black T-shirt that showed a hissing female vampire with the words VAMPIRE: THE MASQUERADE emblazoned underneath.

Gemma was staring into space as I walked in. When she saw me, she smiled as she awkwardly wiped tears from her eyes.

"Detective," she said as if she hadn't been crying at all. "You're hurt."

"I'm fine," I said, touching my nose. "It's not broken."

"At least let me get you something to wipe it."

"I take it you had a visit from Delphina?" I asked her as she handed me a wet wipe that I used to wipe the blood from my nose and face.

Gemma nodded as she went back behind the counter. "She was in here asking what I'd said to the cops. She was blaming me for you being around here."

"Don't worry about Delphina." I tossed the bloodstained wet wipe into a nearby garbage can. "I'll sort her out soon enough."

"How?" she asked.

"Whatever way I have to."

She stared at me for a moment, perhaps sensing the darkness underneath my cop facade for the first time, which didn't seem to unsettle her much. "I'm glad to hear you say that. I'm not sure how much more I can take of those people. Have you found out anything about my uncle's death?"

"Well," I said, "he didn't kill himself, that's for sure."

"How do you know?"

"Because there was sea water found in his lungs, which means he was drowned."

"Drowned? How? Where?"

How much do I tell her? How much does she know already about the hidden world?

"Delphina and her little gang are not what they seem," I said. "Especially Delphina. She's...different."

Gemma frowned. "Different how?"

I nodded at her T-shirt. "You a gamer?"

Looking down at her T-shirt for a second, Gemma said, "Yes. Why?"

"Do you believe that stuff is real? Vampires and such."

"Well," she said, "myths and legends are kinda my forte, and these stories have to come from somewhere, I suppose. I'd say it's not beyond the realm of possibility that monsters exist. I mean, I've never met a vampire or anything, so..."

"You've met Delphina."

"Are you saying she's a vampire, Detective?" She was giving me a weird look now as if the conversation was getting a little far out.

"Not a vampire, but something else."

"Like what?"

"Would you believe me if I said the reincarnation of an ancient shark Goddess?"

Gemma stared deep into my eyes to see if I was serious. When she realized I was, she asked, "Ka'ahu Pahau, by any chance?"

"You really do know your stuff."

"Well, there aren't many shark goddesses in myth and legend." She shook her head. "What you're saying is crazy, Detective."

"Think about it," I told her. "How else could your uncle have been drowned when he never left this store? And why was his murder covered up? Believe me, Gemma, a lot more exists in this world—in this city—than you know."

"Like what? Monsters?"

"Among other things."

Gemma shook her head as she laughed slightly. "If I was having this conversation with anyone else, I'd think they were crazy," she said. "But for some reason, I believe you, Detective. I mean, you don't look crazy—"

"Wait until you get to me know better," I joked.

"Well, I guess we're all a little crazy, right?"

"Yeah, some more than others."

"Like Delphina?"

I nodded. "She's definitely crazy."

"Crazy as a shark, it turns out. What about the others? Her gang? Why are they so strong?"

"I've no idea," I said. "Could be that they're just on something. They don't strike me as being unusual, apart from their shitty dress sense."

Just then, an old man walked into the shop, nodding at me as he went to the counter. "Gemma, sweetheart," he said by way of greeting. "How are you today?"

"I'm good, Mr. Hawthorne," Gemma said, smiling at the old man. "And you?"

"How long have you got?" Mr. Hawthorne said, then cackled. "I'm just kidding. My arthritis isn't playing up, so I'd call today a good day."

"Glad to hear it. Are you here for your hunting magazines? They came in this morning."

"Yes, please," he said before turning to look at me with rheumy eyes. "I'm too old to hunt now. Reading about it is all I can do these days…when my eyes don't play me up that is."

I smiled over at him. "We take our pleasures where we can get them, right?"

"Indeed we do, sonny, indeed we do," he said with a slight cackle.

Gemma put three magazines into a brown paper bag and placed the bag on the counter after telling Mr. Hawthorne how much he owed. Mr. Hawthorne then spent a full minute searching his pockets before saying, "Goddamn it. I've come out without my wallet again. I'm sorry, I'll have to go back and get it."

As the old man went to hobble away, Gemma said, "It's okay, Mr. Hawthorne, you can just pay me the next time you come in."

The old man smiled a gummy smile. "You're sure?"

"Of course." Gemma handed him the bag with the magazines in. "There you go."

"You're a real angel, young Gemma," he said. "Your uncle would be proud."

Gemma smiled as tears threatened to spill out of her eyes.

When the old man left, I approached the counter and took out my wallet, handing Gemma a twenty. "Here," I said. "For the old guy's magazines."

"You don't have to," she said. "He's always good for it."

"I've no doubt he is, but I'd like to pay, anyway."

"That's very gentlemanly of you, Detective."

"Call me Ethan."

"Okay…Ethan. Thank you for coming in to check on me. I know you didn't have to."

"Don't mention it. You have my card, right? Call me if Delphina comes back. I'll come right away."

"You've no idea how much that means to me."

Before I left, I paused by the door and looked over at her. "What we talked about? Don't mention it to anyone. They'll think you're crazy."

"Okay," she said. "But I'd like to talk more about it. I have so many questions, you've no idea."

"I know, and I'll be happy to answer them. Once I sort Delphina out, we'll have a sit-down, and you can ask me whatever you like."

"Great," she said, smiling. "I look forward to it. And Ethan?"

I paused with the door held open. "Yeah?"

"Thank you for all that you're doing. My uncle would really appreciate it."

A rare sense of warmth filled my chest that almost brought tears to my eyes. "My pleasure, Gemma."

A while later, I was inside Artemis and Pan Demic's penthouse as I stood staring down into the living room in mild disbelief at the makeshift stage erected there.

A stage that was occupied by three young Japanese girls dressed in black and red outfits. Each of the girls had a microphone in their hands and were pretending to sing as they danced energetically along to the music blaring out of the speakers in every corner of the room.

To the side of the stage stood a burly security guy in a dark suit, who watched on impassively as the girls did their thing.

The music coming out of the speakers sounded like metal —all heavy guitar riffs and frantic drumming, underpinned by breakneck synths—but the singing over the top of the music wasn't exactly metal in style. The vocals were female and sung in a cutesy Japanese voice. It was a strange combination, but somehow it worked.

"Babymetal!" Artemis shouted over the music as he and Pan Demic stood down near the stage, off their heads on coke as usual as they head-banged and pogoed around to the frantic beats.

"What?" I shouted back to Artemis as I stood behind the bank of computer screens on the level above. "Come up here, will ya!"

Artemis practically ran up the steps to where I was standing and then began to pogo around me as a particularly heavy guitar riff blasted from the speakers. "Babymetal!" he shouted again. "They're a Japanese band."

"Yeah, I can see that," I said as I looked down at the frantically dancing girls on stage, who looked like they were barely over eighteen.

"Not them," Artemis said as he finally came to a stop and grabbed a half-full bottle of beer off his desk. "Those cute little things are just a tribute act. They aren't even singing; they're just miming. But still, they look awesome, don't they?"

"They look like jailbait."

"That's why the security guy is here."

"Thank god."

Drawing back in mock offense, Artemis said, "Drakester... whatta you take us for?"

"A couple o' pervs."

Artemis smiled, his dark eyes like saucers. "You're totally right, we are. What do you think of the music then? Babymetal are our latest obsession. Pan Demic and me go to every show they play here. We've seen them dozens of times. Their guitarist died last year, though. Fell off an observation deck while stargazing with his wife. You believe that? And then Yuimetal left the band, which was so sad, and a massive shock to us all."

"I'm sure it was."

"She's sorely missed by everyone," he went on as his lower jaw rotated, seemingly of its own accord thanks to the drugs he was on. "Poor Moametal had to take up the slack for a while there. It was sad seeing her on stage behind Su-metal. She looked like a spare part. Luckily, the band found a replacement for Yuimetal, but me personally, I don't think anyone will ever replace Yuimetal."

"I have no idea what the fuck you are rambling on about," I said. "You said you had information for me. Hit me up so I can leave you to your...*Babymetal*."

"Admit it, Drakester, you love it," he said as he dropped into his seat in front of his computer. "How could you not?"

Surprisingly, I had to agree as I sat down next to him in Pan Demic's chair while Pan Demic himself continued to dance like a crazy person in front of the three Japanese girls, the security guy still looking on like he was used to coked-up guys going mad around the girls. "I shouldn't like this shit, but...I can't help liking it. They put fucking heroin in these songs or something?"

Artemis laughed while he tapped away on his computer. "I know, right? I'll give you a day until you have the CDs bought for your car." As another song came on, he started singing in Japanese in a high-pitched voice, "*Seiya sessesse seiya...*"

I just shook my head at him, a smile on my face nonetheless. "I'm overwhelmed with cuteness."

Artemis laughed. "Welcome to the club, Drakester."

"Anyway, what've you got for me?"

"Really weird shit is what I got. Hang on a sec..." He tapped furiously at his keys and the footage of the shifter posing as Hannah came up on the screen. "Okay, this is like, a diner on the edge of downtown called A Taste of Heaven. I've never heard of it, but apparently they do nice pancakes there."

"I know the place," I said, unsettled once more by the image of Hannah on the screen. "It's opposite the Belfry Theater."

"Yeah, that's right. So—" He pointed at the screen, still half-shouting to be heard over the music. "Here's your partner, or the person pretending to be her, anyway. She leaves the diner about two minutes after the other guy she was sitting with." He taps a few keys. "This is street-cam footage of her leaving the diner. As you can see, she walks down the street and then turns the corner into…" More key-tapping and the image on the screen changes. "This street right here. Now watch."

I deliberately didn't tell Artemis that the person in the footage was a shifter because I wanted to make sure I wasn't mistaken. I was glad now that I wasn't as I stared intently at the large screen, watching the person pretending to be Hannah walk down the empty side-street. In the time it took me to blink, the impostor had transformed into a teenage boy decked out in full goth gear, including a long black leather jacket and chunky boots.

Amazed at the speed of the transformation, I asked Artemis to slow the video down, which he did, advancing it frame by frame. Even then, it was near impossible to see the transition it happened so fast.

"How did they do that?" I asked. "It's not like shifting, it's more like—"

"Glamouring?"

"Yeah."

"That's what I thought too. It's all done with magic, hence the ability to change the clothes."

"So maybe this person isn't an actual shifter, but more of a—"

"Wizard? Witch? Warlock?"

"Maybe one of those, yeah. Where do they go next?"

Artemis changed the footage to show a different street. "I tracked them to here, a couple streets over. They get in a taxi and head across town, emerging from the taxi as a woman, as you can see. The woman then gets another taxi, which I tracked across the bridge to here in Bedford. They get dropped off outside this brownstone, only now they seem to be a tall guy in a suit."

"I can see that," I said as I stared at the screen, not recognizing the light-haired man at all as he went inside the brown-stone. "You get a name to go with the address?"

"I did, but I don't think it's who you're looking for."

"Why not?"

"The building seems to be owned by a real estate company, which, after a little more digging, turned out to be a shell company."

"I see." I leaned down and rewound the footage myself, pausing on the tall stranger's face. "This might not even be him. This might be just another glamour. Who the fuck knows who this person really is."

"Only one way to find out, eh, Drakester?"

"Yep," I said. "Thanks Artemis, I appreciate you doing this. I'll let you get back to your Babymetal now."

"Awesome," Artemis said, already on his feet and about to join Pan Demic down at the stage again. As I was walking toward the front door, he asked me what the person in the video did, anyway.

I stopped and turned to look at him before I said, "The worst thing anyone could ever do to me."

"Yikes," Artemis said, making a cringe face. "Wouldn't wanna be him...or her."

"No," I said as all sorts of violent thoughts went through my head. "You most definitely wouldn't."

THE SUN WAS ALMOST SET AS I SAT OUTSIDE IN THE CAR, though you could barely see it behind the darkening clouds. As I lit a cigarette, night began to engulf the surrounding buildings, their gleaming facades fading as the buildings became blocks of shadow interspersed with yellow lights. Night was almost upon the city once more, turning the place into a hunting ground for MURKs and Mytholites like The

Ripper Tripper, who would no doubt be on his way to stalk some poor prostitute in the Red Light District soon.

Cracking the window to let the smoke out, I took out my phone and gave Routman a call, surprised when he answered after the second ring. "Jim," I said. "How goes the investigation?"

"It's a fucking nightmare is what it is," he barked, sounding like he was on the move. "Although we may have a lead finally."

"The priest came to see you?"

"Yeah. He said he spoke to you first. Hold on." Down the phone, I heard him bark orders at someone. "We're gearing up now to hit an address we got."

"You tracked down the top hat, I'm guessing?"

"Yeah. Lucky for us, top hats aren't exactly a popular item in this city, especially ones with red ribbons around the base."

"You get a name?"

"We did."

"Who?"

"I can't say. You know the drill."

I sighed. "Sure, whatever. Just don't let the asshole escape. He seems to have a special ability for vanishing."

"Yeah, don't we know it? I gotta go, Ethan. I'm trying to organize a strike team here."

"Good luck. Let me know if you need any help."

"Yeah, sure."

When Routman hung up, I sat and smoked the rest of my cigarette. So they'd finally tracked the infamous Ripper Tripper down. About fucking time. I hoped they caught him, but something told me the guy wouldn't be that easy to catch, even if they did have his address. Routman thought he was chasing a normal guy. He wasn't factoring in The Ripper Tripper's special ability for disappearing at will. Hopefully, the asshole wouldn't get a chance to use it before the strike team nabbed him.

We'd soon see.

In the meantime, I had my own psychopath to catch whoever he was. Or she was. Not that I cared about this asshole's gender. They could be a fucking hermaphrodite elephant with ten titties and three cocks. It didn't matter.

I was still gonna kill them.

But I wasn't stupid either. Whoever this person was, they were powerful.

Powerful enough to change their appearance at will, which meant they were also powerful enough to do other things as well that were potentially far more deadly, and all in the blink of an eye.

In Blackstar, my team had dealt with a few individuals that you might call witches or warlocks—humans with the ability to wield dark magic to devastating effect. And although we were able to apprehend these individuals, their apprehension didn't come without loss of life, and in one case, massive destruction resulting in a lot of collateral damage in the form of innocent lives being lost.

Dark Spreaks (as in Spell Freaks) were invariably clever, sneaky, and willing to kill anybody who got in their way. They often had big plans, plans that involved grabs for power that would upset the delicate balance that existed in the city.

Which is why Wendell Knightsbridge wanted them brought in, so he could contain them. God forbid anyone else should threaten his plans or grab for power.

The last Spreak my team and I brought in almost killed me in the resultant battle. In fact, if it weren't for Richard Solomon of all people (a proud Spreak himself), I'd probably be dead now, torn apart by the black magic that was thrown at me. When they brought me back to the Blackstar Facility, Solomon was able to cleanse me of the insidious, destructive magic.

And speaking of Solomon, I realized I would probably have to consult him before making any kind of move on this particular Spreak. Spreaks invariably had so many wards and traps surrounding their abodes that walking straight into one without sufficient protection would be akin to a fly walking straight into a spider's web. As much as I wanted to drive straight over to the Spreak's address right now, I had to force myself to hold off.

I could still wonder, though, why this Spreak had targeted my family and me. Was this whole thing about getting revenge against me? If so, for what exactly? Because of something I'd done as a Blackstar operative? If that was the case, why wait ten years to do anything about it?

Or perhaps this fucking Spell Freak was, in fact, hired by someone else to fuck with me. And if that was the case, who would've hired them? And why?

"Jesus Christ…" I breathed as I felt a headache coming on. This shit can't get any murkier or confounding.

This is what happens when you spend your life tangling with the darkness. It drags you down, taking away everything you love along the way—every*one* you love—until there's nothing left.

And then, when there's nothing left, the darkness swallows you whole and forces you to live in its belly—the Void—forever, just as a final act of degradation.

No matter where light goes, darkness is already waiting. That's how it's always been. And that's how it will always be.

There is no escaping darkness.

Not for anyone.

A WHILE LATER, I CROSSED TOWN INTO LITTLE ITALY, THE tracker I'd placed on Delphina and her gang's SUV having brought me here.

When they'd left Nelson's Square earlier, the gang drove here to Little Italy first, making a quick stop before heading back across town to the docks area, where they made a stop at the aquarium before heading back here.

The black SUV they were driving was parked outside an Italian restaurant that I was pretty sure was owned by the mob, and a favorite hangout for mob boss Vito Giordano, who I now knew the gang worked for.

I was parked across the road in the Dodge with the window half down as I smoked on a cigarette, staring over at the restaurant, watching who was coming and going, which seemed to be regular customers for the most part. I'd seen a few guys in dark suits who looked like mobsters, though none I recognized, at least not until the redhead belonging to Delphina's gang came walking out along with one of her male cohorts.

Tossing my cigarette away, I slouched down in my seat a little as I peered out the window. The redhead bitch was waiting by the front door while the other guy climbed inside the SUV and started the engine.

A moment later, a tall man with dark hair came walking out of the restaurant. As he did, the redhead walked ahead and opened the back passenger door of the SUV so the tall man could get inside. But before he did, he paused for a second to look both ways up and down the street. Just by his gait and general demeanor, I could see he was an arrogant son of a bitch, flushed with power and the belief he was smarter than everyone else.

"Francetti," I said, recognizing him from the FBI surveillance photo.

When the SUV pulled out into traffic, I started the Dodge and pulled out as well, staying a few car lengths behind. I wasn't worried about keeping eyes on the vehicle as I had my phone clipped to the dash with the tracking app open, so I knew exactly where the SUV was at all times.

For the next couple hours, I followed the black SUV as it made its way across town, stopping only twice. The first stop was a pawn shop around the corner from Nelson's Square. Francetti and the redhead both went inside the shop, staying there for ten minutes before coming out again and driving away. Then they stopped again at a shoe repair shop. Francetti went in alone and came back out fifteen minutes later, carrying what looked like a shoebox.

"What's going on there?" I wondered aloud. "Francetti doesn't look the type to repair his shoes."

No, he looked more the type just to buy a brand new pair. Whatever was in that box, I doubted it was shoes.

As the black SUV pulled away again, I pondered for a second whether to follow it or go inside the cobbler's to see if anything was amiss in there. In the end, I decided to keep following the SUV. If I went inside the cobbler's and flashed my badge, started asking awkward questions, I doubted I would get much information. At least not the kind of information I was looking for. If I had to guess, the cobblers was probably part of a money-laundering operation. The mob had businesses all over that they used to launder the money they made from their various criminal enterprises, including gun-running, racketeering, and these days, even drug and people trafficking.

Jesus, I thought as I pulled off again. It was only recently that I was admonishing Hannah for wanting to take on the Yakuza, and now here I was about to take on the goddamn mob. Or part of it at least. At present, I was only interested in taking down Delphina and her gang.

But who was I kidding? Did I think Don Vito Giordano was just gonna turn a blind eye?

If he didn't, there was nothing I could do about it. Gemma Sidwell and the other good people of Nelson's Square were being victimized and extorted out of their hard-earned money, and I wasn't about to sit by and let that continue. Gemma especially deserved better, and the last thing I wanted was for her to end up murdered like her uncle.

I followed the SUV discreetly for another twenty minutes until it rolled up outside a bar called Rusties. Parked down the street, I watched as the redhead got out and opened the back door so Francetti could exit the vehicle. He seemed to exchange a few words with her before going alone inside the bar. When he was gone, the redhead got back inside the SUV and drove off.

"Doesn't seem his type of hangout," I said as I stared at the bar. "Seems a bit lowbrow."

Who knows? Maybe old Snake Tongue liked to slum it. Or maybe there was more to the bar than meets the eye. He may have been meeting someone inside.

Only one way to find out.

I got out of the Dodge and started walking toward the bar, intending to get a drink or three while I was in there. I wasn't sure if Francetti knew me or not. Delphina had probably told him about me by now, but that didn't mean he knew what I looked like.

Even if he did recognize me, so what? I wanted the bastard to know I was onto him. In fact, I was interested to see what he'd do. Would he try to browbeat me into staying away, threatening me with the mob fist? Or would he try to persuade me by subtler means? Maybe even try to buy me off like he'd obviously done with Big Mike.

About to head inside the bar, I stopped when my phone rang. Taking it out, I answered it as I stepped away from the front door of the bar. "Yeah?" I said.

"Ethan, it's Daisy."

"Daisy." I was surprised to hear from her. "What's up? Is something wrong? Are you okay?"

"I'm fine," she said, her tone implying she would always be fine, her burgeoning Mytholite status having increased her confidence as well as her fighting skills. "I just wanted to let you know that you had visitors earlier."

"Visitors? Who?"

"Couple big, mean-looking guys. I saw them at your door as I was coming out of my apartment. Don't worry, they didn't break down your new door or anything."

"Well, that's something at least," I said. "Are they still hanging around?"

"I'm not sure," she said. "I'm looking out the window to the street right now. I get the feeling they're out there some-where along with——"

"Along with what?"

"A big dog, maybe? I'm not sure. I can sorta see its shape in the alleyway across."

Shit. The werewolves have come for me.

"Alright, I'm on my way," I said to Daisy as I hurried back to the car. "Do me a favor and stay in your apartment no matter what happens, you hear me? Don't go outside."

"Who are these people, Ethan?" she asked.

"Bad men," I said as I got into the car. "Just make sure you stay indoors."

"Okay, I will. Be careful, Ethan. I get the sense these men want to…"

"Kill me?"

"Yeah."

"You're not wrong."

Starting the engine, I turned the car around and sped toward Bricktown.

14

I'm not usually in the habit of rushing toward a fight with a bunch of murderous werewolves. For a start, werewolves are nothing if not perfect fighting machines. They're freakishly strong and powerful, to where one could pick up a man and throw him half a city block. They also have razor-sharp teeth and claws that can make a mess of a man in seconds, tearing through armor and then flesh and bone like it was wet clay.

When fully transformed, a werewolf can be hard as fuck to kill because they can regenerate whole limbs if they have to. The only way to kill a werewolf is to fill it so full of silver that it dies of poisoning, or to do so much damage that it can't come back from it. Decapitation is good. Burning is good. Chopping it into little pieces is good. Chocolate is also good. Works on dogs, right? I'm kidding. If only it were that easy.

Werewolves are also susceptible to asphyxiation and drowning. But to do any of this damage, you first you have to get near enough to them and then survive when they inevitably try to kill you. Hard enough against one, never mind a whole pack.

As I sped through downtown, I reflected that I was

heading into a trap. Ordinarily, I would've avoided the waiting werewolves until I could figure out the best plan of attack against them.

But Daisy was there, and I didn't trust her not to do something foolish, like try to confront the dog soldiers herself. She already knew she could fight—and kill—if she had to, which gave her confidence, sure, but that didn't mean she was equipped to go up against a werewolf, or several werewolves at once.

Werewolves who would probably rip her apart in an instant, and without a second thought, caring not that she was just a little girl.

The last thing I needed was another death on my conscience, especially Daisy's.

And as much as I could use his help, I didn't want to involve Cal either. Not that Cal couldn't handle himself, but he was old and not the warrior he once was. He was also dying—a fact that I could barely bring myself to think about.

It tore at my guts that I would soon be living in a world without Cal in it, a world that was seeming emptier already.

Parking the car a block away from my street, I got out and went to the trunk, popping the lid to reveal the weapons I had stashed in there for just this occasion—for when Derrick Savage's pack caught up with me.

With a lit cigarette hanging from my mouth, I took out a solid silver blade—the same one I'd used against the undead werewolves at Scarlet's place in the woods—and slid it inside my trench.

Taking the magazine out of my Sig Sauer pistol, I replaced it with a magazine filled with silver-tipped bullets, putting the pistol back in the holster on my hip when I was done.

Also in the trunk was a Mossberg 500 Tactical shotgun that I'd procured from Cal a while ago. Cal also supplied me with a box of special buckshot shells. About half of the buckshot was made from silver, enough to significantly slow down a werewolf at close proximity. I slid five shells into the Mossberg and loaded my trench pockets with another ten.

Finally, I took out a fragmentation grenade and slipped it into my pocket. You never know, right?

Taking a final drag on my cigarette, I tossed the butt away and closed the trunk of the Dodge just as the sound of a wolf howling filled the cold night air. I froze when I heard the sound, which was quickly followed up by three more howls, each of them slightly different in tone.

The werewolves knew I was here. They'd probably caught my scent already.

And they'd be waiting.

Not exactly nervous, but on edge, I started heading down the street toward the next block. On the way over, I passed a group of young guys—wannabe gangsters—hanging around outside a boarded-up row house.

"Jesus," one of them said as they all clocked me coming with the shotgun by my side. "Look at this fucking guy."

"Hey man," another of them said. "Where you heading? You gonna ghost somebody with that thing?"

"Fuck off," I said as I passed them.

"Hey!" One of them had jumped in front of me, blocking my way. "I think you should hand that thing over. Thing of beauty like that belongs with us, right?" The guy cockily looked over at his pals, who all cheered in agreement. "Hand it over, man. *Now.*"

Jesus, how fucking stupid are these assholes? You see a man walking down the street with a shotgun, you don't try to steal it from him.

So when the guy in front of me went to slip his hand inside his jacket—probably to pull his own piece—I brought the Mossberg around in a wide arc until the butt caught the guy across the face, flooring him instantly.

In the same movement, I spun around and pointed the

shotgun at the other guys, some of whom had their guns out as they pointed them at me. "Don't be fucking stupid," I growled as the guy on the ground moaned beside me. "Unless you wanna see what this thing can really do."

The guys holding the guns stared at me with defiance, but I could see in their eyes they had no intention of shooting me. I doubted they even had it in them. Plus, neither of them wanted to take the chance of getting blasted by the Mossberg, so after a second, they all lowered their guns.

"Fuck off outta here, man," one of them said. "Before we change our minds."

That's right, I thought. *Save face by making it seem they controlled the situation. Assholes.*

Without saying another word, I turned and walked away from them, focusing once more on the real killers I was about to go up against, any one of whom would decimate the whole gang behind me before any of them could even draw.

Another howl split the night air as I neared my apartment block, a howl that didn't sound that far away this time. Coming to the corner, I peered around it into the street and saw a lone dealer standing by the curb under a broken street lamp. "Hey, buddy," I hissed.

The dealer turned to look at me, pistol barely concealed in the waistband of his sagging jeans. "You want something, man?" he asked with a scowl on his face.

"Yeah," I said. "I want you to—"

Before I could even finish, a massive dark shape burst from the alley behind the dealer. Before the dealer even knew what was happening, the figure from the alley had punched through his back, one arm going right through him and exploding out his chest, blood spraying everywhere.

The dealer never even had time to scream as the dog soldier held him up and then threw him at me.

As the dealer's body whacked against the wall, I ducked

around the corner for a second before moving back around again, this time with the Mossberg shouldered.

But the street was now empty, the werewolf gone.

"Son of a bitch," I said as I stared down at the dealer's body, a massive hole in his chest where his heart used to be.

Another howl issued from nearby.

They were trying to scare me. Intimidate me into making a mistake.

If they thought that, they didn't know who they were dealing with.

As I stood on the corner, my eyes moved to my apartment building, and the window on the third floor. Through the grimy glass, a figure stood looking down.

Daisy.

"God damn it, Daisy," I hissed.

So much for her staying inside her apartment. As long as she didn't come out here. I'd kick her ass myself if she did.

"You're gonna die, copper," a deep voice said from nearby, though it was hard to tell where it was coming from exactly. There were a number of cars parked in the street. I guessed the person speaking was crouched behind one of them. "Derrick was my brother, he was all our brothers, and you killed him. So now, we're gonna kill you. We're gonna tear you to fucking pieces and eat your flesh because no one fucks with us and gets away with it, you hear? No one!"

Another howl echoed through the street, quickly followed by another.

Then I heard a loud growling noise, and I turned just in time to see a dog soldier burst from the alley and come charging toward me, yellow eyes blazing in the darkness as he ran.

Immediately, I shouldered the Mossberg and fired, hitting the charging werewolf in the chest as it howled in pain, the blast stopping it in its tracks, but not putting it down.

Pumping the shotgun to eject the shell, I fired again,

pumped, and then fired once more as I moved toward the half-transformed beast, who was now howling in pain from the silver buckshot in its body.

As I moved in to finish the downed werewolf, however, another one came at me from the left, leaping over a car and landing right in front of me.

I fired the shotgun, catching the massive werewolf in the stomach, but the blast wasn't enough to stop it, and he grabbed the gun and ripped it from my hands, tossing it away where it landed on the road somewhere nearby.

Backing away as the werewolf roared at me, I drew my sidearm and shot the beast three times in the chest, buying me just enough time to pull the blade out from underneath my trench.

As the werewolf lurched forward to grab me, I swung the blade downward and chopped off one of his arms at the elbow.

The beast roared in pain and rage as blood jetted from the stump of his arm, soaking the sidewalk.

I swung the blade once more in a backward movement, aiming for his neck this time, but as the blade neared him, the werewolf ducked and then charged into me, driving me down to the ground as its weight came down on top of me.

I still had my pistol in my hand, so I shoved it into the werewolf's side and fired three times, pumping it full of silver-tipped bullets.

But the motherfucker was tough and didn't budge from me.

As the blood from his stump dripped over my face, he brought his head down to bite my neck, but I was able to shove my hand into his throat to stop him, just about.

His gnashing teeth were only inches from my turned face.

Despite the damage he'd taken, this mutt still had plenty of strength left in him. That strength would dwindle as the silver weakened him, but by then, he would probably over-power me, so there was only one thing left to do.

Fumbling in my trench pocket with my other hand, my fingers found the grenade in there, and I pulled it out and brought it to my mouth so I could use my teeth to pull the pin, and while the werewolf continued to try to bite me, I shoved the grenade into his enormous mouth.

He was so riled up, he ended up sucking that thing back, nearly choking on it. His eyes widened in fear as he realized what I'd done.

But before he could think to eject the grenade from his mouth, I scrambled back a little, just enough to get my knees up so I could kick the asshole off me, sending him tumbling back.

A second later, the grenade exploded inside the werewolf's mouth, and his entire head was obliterated in the blast, show-ering me with blood and bone fragments that sliced into the skin of my hands and face.

Now dripping with blood, I scrambled to my feet and quickly grabbed the blade that was lying on the ground. The werewolf I'd put down earlier was just sitting up, his face a mask of pain from the amount of silver in his body.

"You're dead meat!" he roared.

But before he got fully up, I rushed at him with the blade and swung it as hard as I could at his neck, decapitating him in an instant.

"*You're* fucking dead meat, asshole," I said as I rushed back to retrieve my pistol, which was on the ground near the other headless werewolf.

"NO!" a voice roared nearby, and suddenly there were three more dog soldiers standing in the middle of the road, their yellow eyes blazing with rage as they looked upon their fallen comrades.

"What's the matter?" I said after I'd picked up the pistol. "You thought killing me was gonna be easy? You toothless fucks don't know who you're dealing with. I used to eat mutts like you for breakfast."

The three of them roared at once, pushing their chests out as they did so.

Behind them, up by the window, Daisy still stood looking on, her face clear in the light, her expression neutral as if she watched this sort of thing go down every day, and for a second, this disturbed me more than the werewolves in the street.

At present, the werewolves were only half-transformed. But as I changed the magazine on my Sig, I did a double-take as I saw all three of the dog soldiers drop onto all-fours as their bodies began to change at an incredible rate.

Within seconds it seemed, the increased girth of their limbs and bulging muscles tore the black tactical clothing from their bodies, their naked skin now covered in a thick layer of hair, their faces no longer recognizable as human, now monstrous and wolf-like.

Shit.

If these assholes were hard to stop before, they'd be even harder to stop now.

Especially when all I had was a pistol and a blade.

My eyes flicked up to the window of the apartment building again.

Daisy wasn't there anymore.

As dread filled me, I hoped she had gone inside her apartment where it was safe.

Alright. Time to call in reinforcements.

Scroteface.

A second later, his voice came through.

Yes, boss?

I need all of you here now. Get your game face on.

Before he could even reply, I had the five Hellbastards summoned and standing next to me in the street. I didn't need to explain anything to them. They saw the towering beasts for themselves.

They knew what to do.

As for the werewolves, they continued standing in the middle of the road as their yellow eyes fell upon the diminutive demons standing in front of me.

Didn't expect this, did you, assholes?

Before any of the werewolves could make a move, I raised my pistol and started firing, concentrating most of my shots on the pack leader, who appeared to be a foot taller than the other two.

But despite the fact that I shot him several times, he barely flinched, and in response, he just roared, and the other two wolfs came charging toward us.

As the wolves roared, so too did the Hellbastards. Or at least they screeched and screamed as they ran to meet the massive beasts without fear or trepidation.

I had to give it to the little bastards. They always had my back, no matter what.

The Hellbastards leaped en masse at the werewolves, Scroteface and Cracka hanging off the arms of the pack leader as they used their sharp teeth to bite into the werewolf's flesh, snapping their heads back to rip off chunks of skin and muscle.

Reggie and Snot Skull went for the other two werewolves, while Toast shot a fireball from his mouth that hit one of the wolves on the chest, setting fire to the wolf's thick, matted fur. The wolf screamed as the fire spread up his chest and the flames licked his face. Werewolves hate fire because it can do them real damage that's hard to come back from.

And going by the screams of the other wolf, they don't like acid either, as evidenced when Snot Skull vomited his load down the back of the wolf he was hanging off.

With the three werewolves preoccupied with the ferocious

attacks of the Hellbastards, I thought it time to rush in with my blade.

I went for the one that was on fire first, going in low and chopping the blade down on his leg until it met bone. The werewolf screamed and fell to the ground, but as I went to finish him, I felt razor-sharp claws get raked down my back, slicing right through my trench and deep into my skin.

With a roar that was half pain, half rage, I spun around just as the pack leader—having gotten rid of Scroteface and Cracka—grabbed my lapels, lifting me off the ground before running forward and slamming me down onto the hood of a parked car.

Dazed by the impact, I was now staring up at a monstrous face displaying nothing but pure rage. The werewolf's jaws opened wide as it prepared to bring its head down to bite my face off, but as it did, Cracka appeared on top of the werewolf's massive shoulder.

"Get off my boss, you hairy butthole!" Cracka screamed before sinking his tiny, needle-like teeth into the werewolf's pointed ear.

With a roar, the werewolf let go of me with one hand so he could make a grab for Cracka. But Cracka was too fast for him, and scurried across the werewolf's back to the other side of him, this time raking his claws across the werewolf's face, catching one of his eyes as he did so, which only further infuriated the werewolf as he grabbed for Cracka again, this time catching him in his massive hand.

"Let me go, you fucking big dog!"

The werewolf's mouth opened wide, and I realized what he was going to do as he brought Cracka toward his waiting maw.

Throughout all this, I had kept a hold of my blade, so I stabbed it into the werewolf's side, causing him to roar in pain as he flung Cracka away from him.

But despite everything, I still wasn't able to break loose

from the werewolf's grip, and he still had me pinned to the hood of the car.

With his free hand, he took my blade out of his side and let it drop to the ground with a metallic clang.

Once again, the werewolf opened its jaws, saliva dripping down onto my face as it lowered its head slowly toward mine, the stench of its breath disgusting as all I could do was turn my head away.

So this is it? I thought. *I'm gonna die from having a fucking bastard werewolf bite my face off?*

This wasn't how I expected to go out.

But as the werewolf's jaws came to within inches of my face, he suddenly reared back again and roared as if something had attacked him from behind.

And was still attacking him, for I could see arcs of blood fly up from behind him as if someone was shredding his back non-stop.

As he let go of me to turn and face this new opponent, I finally saw who it was, and whatever color was left in my face suddenly drained.

It was Daisy.

She stood facing the werewolf with two karambit knives in her hands, dwarfed by the beast in front of her.

Just behind her, the other two werewolves were still preoccupied with the Hellbastards. Both beasts were partially on fire thanks to Toast, and Snot Skull's acid vomit was eating into them in various places, with at least one hand almost melted off one of the werewolves.

Turning my attention back to Daisy, I saw she was circling the pack leader. When the werewolf took a swipe at her, she went underneath his arm and slashed his belly with one of her knives, which infuriated the beast to no end.

But I wasn't about to let her take on the werewolf alone, who would surely get the better of her before long.

I rolled off the trunk of the car and grabbed the blade

from off the ground, rushing forward and skewering it into the werewolf's back.

At that precise moment, Daisy came forward and went to slash the werewolf again with her knives, but as she did, the werewolf grabbed her by the throat and lifted her, holding her out in front him so she couldn't reach him with her knives, and even though she slashed at his arm, he still held her.

Pulling the blade from the werewolf's back, I went to bring it down on his shoulder, intending to chop his arm off, but as I did, something grabbed me from behind, and the next thing I knew, I was being flung through the air.

Several feet away, I landed with a hard thump in the middle of the road, looking up to see that two more were-wolves had joined the fray.

Where the fuck did they come from?

It didn't matter. They were here, and now there were five of the bastards instead of three.

We're fucked.

I could only watch in horror as the pack leader, still holding Daisy up by the throat, turned to stare at me.

As I went to get up, a massive foot pressed down on my chest as one of the new arrivals held me down.

If the pack leader could smile, he would have.

Daisy's face turned red and then purple as the pack leader squeezed her throat, the knives falling from her hands.

"No!" I shouted. "Don't!"

The Hellbastards continued to attack, but they couldn't get near the pack leader thanks to the other three werewolves, who fought the demons off.

As the pack leader choked the life out of Daisy, I struggled to free myself off the ground, but the crushing weight of the massive werewolf standing on my chest ensured I couldn't move.

All I could do was watch helplessly as Daisy's bulging, fear-filled eyes stared at me.

Another useless scream of frustration left my mouth.

Daisy's body went limp as her eyes started to close.

With horror, I realized she'd be dead in another second or two.

No, not Daisy, please not her...

As Daisy's eyes closed, so did mine.

But my eyes snapped open again as soon as I heard something.

Or rather felt something.

A rush of wind.

When my eyes opened again, I saw that the pack leader was gone and Daisy was lying on the ground, dead or unconscious, I couldn't tell which.

A second later, the werewolf holding me down lifted his foot and moved behind me as he roared in anger. The other werewolves also moved past me, posturing and growling at something or someone I couldn't see.

But I didn't care who or what had gotten the werewolves' attention.

I only cared about Daisy.

Getting to my feet, I ran to her and then dropped onto my knees beside her, placing two fingers on her neck as I felt for a pulse.

But there was none.

"No," I said as I immediately started to do chest compressions on her, stopping only to open her mouth and breathe air into her unmoving lungs. "Come on, Daisy, come back to me, come back to me, plea—"

Daisy's eyes snapped open suddenly as she took in a huge breath and then started coughing and choking.

"Daisy," I said with tears in my eyes. "Oh Jesus...you're alive." I held her up as she struggled to catch her breath. "I thought I'd lost you."

She seemed dazed and confused for a moment until her eyes finally focused on me. "Ethan?"

"I'm here," I said. "You're okay…you're okay."

"Close call, eh, Ethan?" a voice said.

I looked to see none other than Haedemus standing behind us.

From somewhere, Cracka yelled, "Yea! The big horsey!"

"Haedemus, what are…" I started to say.

He moved his massive head to point my attention down the street. "Look there," he said.

I turned and looked down the street to see a figure clad in some sort of black, leather-type outfit with a long bit at the back that trailed the ground. The person's face didn't look human, the eyes shining cobalt against bone-colored skin. It took me a moment to realize I was looking at Xaglath, who seemed more demonic than ever with her twisting horns and some massive scythe-type weapon held in one hand.

In her other hand, she held the werewolves' pack leader by the throat, holding him aloft as easily as he had held Daisy aloft only moments ago. The werewolf bucked in her grip and kicked his legs frantically, but no matter what he did, he couldn't break Xaglath's iron grip.

As the other werewolves stood looking on in fear and help-lessness, Xaglath turned her head and smiled at them, her face seeming different from the last time I saw her, the cheekbones higher and sharper, the eyes larger, the chin more pointed.

Then she turned to look at the werewolf in her grip again, and with one single swipe of her scythe, she sliced the pack leader clean in half, holding his upper body as his lower half fell to the ground, his cleanly cut innards spilling down over his severed legs.

In response to seeing their pack leader cut in half, the other werewolves roared, but none of them made any move to attack Xaglath.

They knew, instinctively, that they didn't stand a chance.

As if to add insult to injury, Xaglath then mumbled a few familiar-sounding words, and a second later, a hole opened up in the ground beside her, and the reddish-yellow light of Hell spilled forth, illuminating the darkness around her.

Casually, she kicked the two halves of the pack leader's body into the Hell Hole before looking up at the other werewolves.

"There's plenty more room in Hell if any of you would like to join him," she said.

Needless to say, none of the werewolves took her up on her offer.

With a final roar, they all dropped to all-fours and ran off into the night.

"Stupid dogs," Haedemus said dismissively. "You do get yourself into these scrapes, don't you, Ethan?"

"Shut up, Haedemus," I said as I stood up with Daisy.

"I miss you, too, Ethan," Haedemus said, then mumbled, "More than you know."

Xaglath came toward us, seeming to glide across the ground without effort, coming to a stop a few feet away from Daisy and me.

"Hello again, Ethan," she said, and I saw just how much she had changed since I last saw her. It was like she was becoming as she was in Hell. She even seemed taller, her voice carrying a new authority as if she now ruled this city.

It made me wonder if the Hannah I knew was even in there anymore, which was a despairing thought.

"Xaglath," I said, unsure of how to be around her. "What are you—"

"Doing here? Why, I came to save you, Ethan." Her new cobalt eyes shifted to Daisy as she held her scythe out, using the point of the bloodstained blade to raise Daisy's chin. "And who is this little mouse? Ah yes, I remember now. Daisy, isn't it? You seem...different. You're one of these new breeds of creatures, aren't you? They appear to be springing up all over like vermin. Not to worry, though. I'll have you all under my control soon enough."

I have to give it to Daisy, she showed no fear in front of Xaglath, even though she should have.

"Why?" I said, still not understanding what she was doing here. "Why would you come here just to help us?"

"I've been keeping an eye on you," she said, lowering her scythe. "You see, my dear Ethan, no one but me will get to kill you. You and I have much torture and suffering to go through, or at least, you have anyway. I'll be the one inflicting it."

"So you saved me just so you could kill me down the line?" I said.

"Yes," she said. "That's about the height of it. Take care of yourself, won't you, Ethan? I'd hate to see anyone but me damage that body of yours."

She walked past me to Haedemus and floated up onto his back. "I must go now. There's another soul I want to send to Hell before I turn my full attention to you, Ethan."

"Yagami?" I asked.

"Yes, father dearest." She chuckled as if she found this funny. "I'm tired of toying with him, and I'm anxious to get started on you, Ethan. So it's time to finish this little spat with the Yakuza. It will all be over soon, and then I'm coming back for you. Keep your blood warm for me, won't you?"

Laughing, Xaglath grabbed Haedemus' mane and turned him around. Then she galloped up the street, soon disappearing into the darkness as the sound of hooves hitting the road faded away.

"I miss big horsey," Cracka said as he came to stand by my feet. "When he coming back?"

As I stared off into the darkness, I said, "Not too soon, I hope."

15

Inside my apartment, I checked Daisy over for injuries. Apart from bruising around her neck, she seemed fine, if a little shaken up. This didn't stop me from admonishing her, though.

"What the hell, Daisy?" I said as we stood in the living room, the Hellbastards outside disposing of the two were-wolves I'd killed, and the dead dealer. "What did I say to you on the phone?"

Daisy dropped her gaze to the floor. "To stay inside," she muttered.

"Yes, to stay inside, and what do you do? The exact fucking opposite. You almost died, for Christ's sake. Hell, you did die!"

"What?"

"You had no pulse," I said, dialing back my anger when I saw how upset she was getting. "You were damn lucky I was able to bring you back."

Tears were now streaming down her face. "I—I'm sorry."

Sighing, I went to her and put my arms around her, hugging her into me.

"It's okay," I said, unable to keep thoughts of Callie out of my mind, of all the times I'd comforted her as she cried over something or other. "But you have to realize, this is no game, Daisy. Dealing with MURKs is dangerous, even for someone as experienced as me."

She pulled away and stared up at me with wet eyes. "I thought they would kill you. I just wanted to help."

I nodded. "I know you did, and I appreciate you trying. I just don't want to see you get hurt, Daisy. You're too special for some MURK just to kill."

"You think I'm special?" she asked, a slight smile on her face now.

"A special pain in my ass," I said.

"You love me really." Still smiling, she walked toward the kitchen. "I'm thirsty. You want anything?"

I looked toward the bottle of whiskey sitting on the coffee table. "No, thanks."

As Daisy went into the kitchen, I sat down on the couch and opened the whiskey, taking a slug straight from the bottle as I thought about what just happened outside. With the pack leader dead—and his soul in Hell—I hoped that was the last I'd see of the werewolves. If I didn't exactly scare them off, Xaglath certainly did. Hopefully, the rest of the pack would think twice about coming after me again if they thought Xaglath would arrive on the scene once more.

Which was messed up, by the way, her showing up like that. Saving my ass just so she could torture it in the near future? Fucking crazy bitch.

Though as crazy as she was, I knew that she would follow through on her promise to come for me once she was done with Yagami. As I couldn't see a way to avoid the inevitable, it looked like I was living on borrowed time.

Just like someone else I knew.

I would have to go see Cal. It was selfish of me, reacting the way I did the last time I saw him. The man was dying. The least I could do was be there for him in his final weeks.

Assuming that I was still around myself for that long.

"How's your throat?" I asked Daisy as she came and sat down beside me on the couch with a glass of water in her hand.

"Well," she said, "considering I got choked out by a were-wolf, pretty good I'd say." She chuckled at this, and I smiled back at her.

"What's your mother going to say about all that bruising? She'll probably think it was me who did it."

"Why would you think that?"

"Because your mother hates me, that's why. I think she thinks I'm leading you astray or something."

"I don't care what she thinks. She's just a stupid drunk."

"Hey," I said. "She's still your mother."

Daisy sighed. "I know. I mean, I love her and all, but she just makes things so difficult, you know what I mean? She could be so much better if she didn't drink or do drugs."

"I know. People are who they are, though. You just have to deal with them, and that's it."

"The way you deal with me?"

I frowned. "I don't know what you mean."

"Come on," she said. "I'm sure you could do without some messed up teenager hanging around you."

"I don't think that at all. I like having you around."

"Because I remind you of your daughter?"

I shook my head, getting exasperated by her now. "No, I mean you sometimes do, I suppose, but that's not why I like you, Daisy. I like you for who you are. Don't be so damn down on yourself. You'll meet enough people who are down on you without you being like it as well. You're awesome. Start believing that you are."

Daisy smiled at me and then put her head against my shoulder. "Your daughter was lucky to have you as a dad."

I closed my eyes for a second when she said that, then took another slug from the whiskey bottle.

"Yeah," I said.

AFTER TAKING A SHOWER AND PICKING FRAGMENTS OF
werewolf bone out of my face and hands with tweezers, I
changed into some fresh clothes, binned yet another trench,
and then jumped in the Dodge and drove over to see Cal at
the scrap yard.

When I got there, I found him inside his trailer, throwing
up in the bathroom. I waited for him on the couch, and when
he finally emerged, he looked like hell, his face haggard, dark
circles under his eyes, looking ten years older than he was. It
broke my heart to even look at him.

When he saw me sitting there, he stopped to stare at me,
frowning as if he didn't know who I was. I half expected him
to ask me just that, but after a moment, a look of recognition
came into his eyes. "It's you," he said, heading into the kitchen
and returning with two beers, handing me one as he sat down
on the couch next to me.

"Should you be drinking?" I asked him.

Cal turned his head to give me a look. "Are you kidding?
Drink is the only thing keeping me going."

"I had no idea you were this bad."

"I hid it well."

"I guess so."

Cal glanced at the cuts on my face. "What happened to
you?"

"Had a run-in with a bunch of werewolves."

"Werewolves?" he said as if he didn't know what they
were. "Oh yeah, those things. Why?"

I shook my head. "It doesn't matter."

Cal sighed. "Yeah, I guess nothing much matters anymore,
does it?"

"I'm sorry for running away last time I was here."

"I guess I laid it all on you at once, didn't I?"

"Kind of, yeah. It was a shock."

"Imagine how *I* felt when I found out."

"You really only have weeks left?"

He nodded. "If I'm lucky. My brain feels like mush. I have a permanent migraine, and my memory has been obliterated. I had to think about who you were a minute ago. I didn't even recognize you."

Jesus.

Cal got up for a moment and then came back with a joint, which he lit, filling the trailer with pungent smoke. "This helps with the headaches."

I took a few drags of the joint myself when he passed it to me before passing it back to him. "What is this?"

"Northern Lights from my own grow."

"It's good shit."

"The grow is yours now, along with everything else here."

"What?"

"Don't look so surprised. Who else was I gonna leave all my shit to, the dogs?"

Hearing him say that, it made it all seem real, the fact that he would soon be dead. Before, when he told me, it was like a hallucinatory idea. Now it seemed set in stone.

He was gonna die.

"I don't care about your stuff."

"Well, you damn well better," he said. "This place is my legacy. Your name is on all the papers now. You don't have to worry about running the scrap business. Petey can run that for you. The only thing I'm not leaving you is my library. The girl can have all my books."

"Daisy?"

"Yep, she'll appreciate them more than you. I taught her a few things in the smithy as well. If she wants to work in that place, let her. She's a smart kid. She'll pick it up eventually."

"And the dogs?"

"They can look after themselves. Petey'll make sure they get fed every day."

"What about all your customers? The blade buyers?"

"Word'll spread I'm not around anymore. They'll stop coming, least until Daisy starts making her own blades. The girl has an interest in the craft."

"She never mentioned it."

"You're not her father. She doesn't have to tell you everything."

"I never said I was."

"You don't have to."

I took a swig of my beer as we sat in silence for a while, me hardly knowing what to say to him. In his mind, he was done. He'd washed his hands of this life and was now just waiting around to die. It pained me to think about where he might end up when he did die. Was he destined for the cold space of the Void? Or even Hell? Surely there had to be some other place to go? Surely Heaven's gates were still open somewhere? Or some place like Valhalla? A man like Cal didn't deserve to end up nowhere after he died. He deserved better than that, though he would probably disagree.

"Cal—" I began, but he stopped me.

"You don't have to say it," he said. "I already know."

I swallowed as I struggled to hold back tears. As he didn't want my words, I took his hand and held it instead, half-expecting him to pull away when I did.

But he gripped my hand tight.

"It's been a hell of a ride, kid," he said with a plaintive smile. "I'm glad you were on it with me."

I turned my head away, unable to hold back my tears any longer.

Me too, Cal. Me too.

To say I was out of sorts for the next couple days would be an understatement. After I left Cal, I became consumed with anger and depression, and I ended up locking myself away in The Brokedown Palace for a full day while I drank myself into oblivion and consumed enough Mud to have me trippin' balls the whole time I was there.

Being inside that place felt like being inside my own private Hell.

Thanks to the Mud and alcohol, I was tormented by many ghosts from my past, every insecurity I had made manifest in some way. If you'd walked in on me, you'd've seen me talking seemingly to myself, but I was actually drunkenly talking to the ghosts I just mentioned.

Not just talking, but crying, shouting, wailing, and bawling.

In short, I was a total fucking mess, until eventually I keeled over onto the floor and fell into oblivion for I don't know how many hours until I woke to the sound of my phone ringing.

When I was somehow able to answer it, a voice on the line started telling me that they'd come back, and I said who came back, and the voice said the sharks, and I was like, the fucking sharks? What are you talking about? And then the voice said their name and I heard the word Gemma and I realized who I was talking to finally, which seemed to sober me up a little, enough that I could listen and utter a few words.

As my mind began to kick into gear again, I realized Gemma was talking about Delphina and her crew, who had apparently shown up at the square and beat the living shit out of couple kids who had allegedly been accused of stealing from the convenience store, only they didn't take nothing according to Gemma, the crew just felt like beating on somebody. Something like that anyway. I just knew that Delphina had been causing trouble again, and that was enough for me.

In my fucked up state, I knew I had to do something about it this time.

Somehow, when I left The Brokedown Palace, I was able to drive home without crashing the Dodge. Once I was inside my apartment, I cleaned myself up and took a big line of Snake Bite, which was enough to sober me up and allow me to think clearly once again.

I SAT IN THE CAR, PARKED OUTSIDE THE OLD AQUARIUM NEAR the docks. It was sometime in the afternoon, and the rain was streaming down the windshield as I sat with a cigarette in one hand and my phone in the other.

Captain Edwards was on the line. He'd just called me a minute ago.

"You hear me, Drake?" he said.

"I heard you," I said in a distant voice.

"Your time is up. You're officially off the force. I expect you to turn your badge and gun in soon. Drake? Drake? Are you still there?"

I hung up the phone and dropped it onto the passenger

seat as I stared out the window at the rain streaming down the glass.

So it's finally happened. I'm not a cop anymore.

"Fuck," I breathed as I closed my eyes.

It felt like I was standing on the edge of a precipice as it slowly crumbled beneath my feet, about to be pitched into the abyss below, to be lost forever in the darkness...

"Come on, Ethan. Get a fucking grip..."

Fuck it. It was just a job. I'd find something else to do.

I had to.

Exiting the car, I stepped out into the rain as it pelted the leather coat I was wearing. Walking around the car, I faced the front of the old aquarium, which was formerly known as Shark Land. There used to be a whole water park built around the aquarium, but that had all been dismantled now, and only the aquarium remained. I remember taking Callie here when she was little, just before the place closed down. She always loved sharks and this place had more sharks than anywhere else, bar the nearby ocean. Even though she was only little, Callie had loved the place. She cried when I told her she couldn't go again because the place had closed down.

Exactly what Delphina was doing here, I didn't know. According to my tracking app, she had gone back and forth from here several times, which made me think she was hanging out here in between terrorizing people at the square.

Of course, there was also the fact that Delphina was a shark herself, so she may have been making use of the tanks inside. We'd see. The tracking app told me she'd got dropped off here a little while ago, so I was sure she was inside somewhere.

The front of the building was constructed from stone blocks, most of which had gone green with algae over the years. The lettering above the arched doorway had also faded, the various stuck-on fish shapes I remember being around the arch itself now gone, probably stripped by vandals.

The front entrance had been boarded up, but the boards had been pulled back just enough for someone to slip through.

Someone like Delphina.

Because of my size, I had to pull the boards further back so I could squeeze through the entrance, making a lot of noise in the process as the nails screeched in the wood. If Delphina didn't know I was here before, she sure as shit did now.

Not that I minded. I wasn't here to surprise her. I was here to talk some sense into her, to warn her off before there was no going back. I had taken on this case, and I wasn't about to walk away from it. Delphina had to understand that. I was here to give her a last chance before things got violent.

Or at least, more violent.

As I walked cautiously into the gloomy interior of the aquarium, I thought about the conversation I'd had with Routman a while ago, when I'd asked him if it was okay for cops to be judge, jury, and executioner. He'd told me to open my eyes, that we already were. And he was right, we were, and even though I wasn't a cop anymore, the same still applied.

I wanted Delphina to understand that before she inevitably told me to go fuck myself.

I crossed the entrance hallway into a short corridor that led into a large opening. Glass tanks covered in algae lined the walls on one side, most of which were still full of murky sea water. In the center of the floor was a vast tank set into the floor itself. At one time, the tank had glass over the top, so you could walk over it and look down at the fish inside. Now the glass had been removed or broken by vandals, leaving behind a very deep hole that was three-quarters filled with water.

There was a strange, dark feeling in the air, the sense of festering threat, though that could've been just the Mud…or my imagination.

"Delphina!" I called out as I paused by the tanks lining the graffiti-covered walls. "I know you're in here. It's Detective Drake. Why don't you come out so we can talk?"

If Delphina was here, she wasn't answering. I paused and listened for signs of her moving about, but in the empty silence of the place, all I heard was the steady drip of water somewhere, and the odd scratching sound, which was probably rats.

"Come on, Delphina," I said as I started walking toward the center of the room near the floor tank. "What's the point in hiding when I only wanna talk to you? I just wanna try to get this whole thing sorted out, so there's no more violence."

No more violence. Who was I kidding? If Delphina was listening, she was probably thinking the same thing.

As I neared the floor tank, I stopped suddenly out of some instinct. I frowned for a second and then turned my head to the left, looking down toward the blue-tiled floor.

And then I saw it.

A flashing red sensor light.

A motion sensor.

Too late, I realized what it was.

I'd just walked into a boobytrap.

"Son of a—"

There was a loud bang as a small explosion shattered the glass in the tanks along the wall. As the glass exploded outward, hundreds of gallons of water came gushing out at a rapid rate, taking me off my feet and washing me down into the tank on the floor.

The whole thing happened so fast.

One second I was standing on the floor. The next, I was submerged in a tank full of dark, briny water, which I wasn't happy about because I'm not the strongest of swimmers. When I was seven, a foster parent thought it a good idea to teach me to swim by tossing me in a lake. I almost drowned. Ever since I'd done my best to avoid going in the water.

As panic began to set in, I started to claw my way to the surface, but as I did, something big and hard bumped me on my side. When I looked down, my eyes widened in shock as I saw a massive shark swim underneath me.

What the fuck? How could there still be sharks here?

I didn't care how the shark got here. The only thing I cared about was getting to the surface and climbing out of this cursed shark tank.

But before I could reach the surface, something grabbed my ankle and started to pull me back down into the water. Despite kicking with my other leg and flailing my arms, whatever was pulling me down was too strong to fight against.

To my dismay, I was dragged deeper and deeper into the tank by god knows how many feet, the surface just a dark memory as I struggled to hold my breath.

As I was dragged down farther, I began to panic that I wouldn't be able to hold my breath for much longer and that soon, my lungs would fill with filthy salt water. Then I would drown, and my body would get eaten by the shark in here with me, and no one would ever know what happened.

At some point, I realized I wasn't being pulled anymore, and that I was sinking of my own accord. The shark that had nudged me a moment ago was still swimming in circles around me. The fucking thing was a monster with the coldest eyes I've ever seen, and a mouth big enough to swallow me whole if it wanted.

But that wasn't even the worst of it, because I soon discovered there were two of the bastards in here with me. Two massive sharks that were no doubt about to rip me asunder with those infinite rows of teeth that flashed white in the murky water.

Once again, I began to struggle toward the surface, even though at this point, I could no longer *see* the surface. There was only darkness above me.

And then a face appeared in front of me.

At first, I thought I was facing another shark, for I could see sharp teeth and thick gray skin and flapping gills.

But there was also dark hair and human eyes, and I soon realized I was looking at Delphina in her shark form.

The bitch was smiling at me with her wide mouth, and every time I went to move, she would pull me back down again, like a cat playing with a mouse, or a shark playing with a seal. It didn't matter that I was three times her size.

In here, in the water, Delphina was the predator, and I the prey.

My chest was getting tight and uncomfortable as I struggled to hold my breath. Soon, it was burning, and I didn't know how much longer I could keep my mouth closed. Every instinct I had told me to open my mouth and breath, and it was all I could do to stop myself.

All the while, Delphina continued to smile her shark smile, and the real sharks continued to swim in circles around me.

One last time, I made a bid for the surface, but once again, Delphina almost playfully pulled me back down, and when she did, I knew that was it. I could hold my breath no more.

All I could do was stare at her as I prepared to drown.

And then I closed my eyes and thought of Callie for a second just before my mouth flew open of its own accord.

But as I waited for the water to gush in and flood my lungs, nothing happened.

Somehow I was breathing air.

Or at least it seemed that way. I still had my eyes closed, and I was almost afraid to open them in case I was hallucinating as I drowned.

"You can breathe now," a voice said.

A familiar voice. Delphina's voice.

Opening my eyes, I saw that although my body was still surrounded by water, and I was standing on the floor of the tank, my head was inside a pocket of air, which is how I could breathe.

"What the fuck?" I gasped as I filled my lungs again.

Delphina, I saw, was naked as she stood before me, her head encased in the same pocket of air. Not only did she have gills, but she also had a dorsal fin and a shark's tail.

"Neat trick, huh?" she said. "I bet you thought you were gonna drown."

"This is…a bit much…Delphina," I said, still shook up from nearly drowning. "I only wanted…to talk to you."

"You set off my boobytrap. I didn't ask you to do that."

My body shivering in the freezing water, I asked: "Why would you even need a boobytrap?"

"In case nosey parkers like you come sniffing 'roun, that's why."

"These your pets?" I asked her, nodding toward the sharks circling us.

"Not my pets, my *friends*."

"Your friends?"

"Yeah, my friends, and they'll eat you alive if I tell 'em too, so you best not piss me off."

"I thought I'd already done that by coming here."

"Believe me, buster, you ain't never seen me pissed off. If you did, you'd run."

"Why d'you have to act so tough all the time?"

"Cus I am tough, that's why."

"Then why pick on people who aren't tough? Like Sam Sidwell?"

She sighed and looked away for a second. "That was an accident. He pushed me too far."

"By refusing to pay you?"

"By threatening to go to the cops and the newspapers so he could tell all about our little operation." She shook her head. "I dunno. I just snapped. You know how it is, I'm sure. You a tough guy as well, ain't you? Most people are afraid of me, but not you. Maybe I should *make* you afraid, huh…use these lovely big teeth o' mine to"— she thrust her head forward and snapped her jaw closed—"bite your head clean off."

"There's no need for that," I said as I warily eyed the sharks still swimming idly by.

"Well, there was no need for you to come sniffing around my hideout, now was there? But yet here you are, sniffin' aroun' like an ole bloodhound, albeit one who's out of his depth right now…literally and figuratively."

"How'd a girl like you end up running with the mob, anyway?" I asked her, hoping to steer the conversation in a different direction.

Well, actually, I wanted to ask her if we could continue our talk out of the water away from the damn patrolling sharks, but I knew she would never do so. She knew she was safe down here in the depths, and that she had the definite advantage.

"Oh, you know," she said, rolling her eyes slightly. "I was just an orphan girl that came here with her boyfriend with hopes and dreams until that boyfriend got killed one night by a bunch of street thugs. I gone killed two of 'em back, and the rest run off after they beat the shit outta me. Snake Tongue, he found me in the street after it happened, and he took me home and said he would look after me if I came to work for him. So I did. He could see I was tough, so he made me an enforcer just like my crew are now. But I soon realized I was more than just a mob bruiser."

"How so?"

"Well, I would often find myself heading down the docks and just sitting there, you know, staring at the great ocean. I felt a connection to the water that I couldn't explain, least not until I found this place here, and these two beautiful creatures in here with us. Once I found them, they opened my eyes to who I really was."

"A shark goddess?"

"That's right. A goddess."

"Does Snake Tongue know who you are?"

"Of course, and he loves me for it."

"I'm sure he does. He doesn't strike me as the type of person that would love anyone but himself."

"And how the hell would you know that? You never even met the man."

"I don't need to meet him to know that he uses people," I said. "Including you, Delphina."

"Watch it, mister," she said. "This little lifeline of yours right here, this pocket of air, I can fill it right back up with water in seconds, and then I'll have my friends here eat you for dinner."

"I'm just saying. You said it yourself, you're a goddess. I don't think a goddess is supposed to bully and extort people outta their money for the mob."

She stared at me a moment with her cold eyes. "What else I gonna do?"

"I'm sure there's plenty you could do, Delphina, that didn't involve working for the damn mob. Your friends here know what kind of person you are?"

Delphina turned her head to stare at the sharks. "They the only ones who know me."

"You say that Ka'ahu Pahau has been reborn in you somehow," I said.

"Yeah…"

"Then you know that Ka'ahu Pahau is actually a protector. She protected people from sharks and was said to guard the entrance to Pearl Harbor, sending menacing sharks on their way. Seems to me you're going about things the wrong way, Delphina. You should be protecting people *against* the mob, not working *for* the mob."

She went to say something and then stopped, turning her head away.

"I can see you're a decent person underneath all the bravado," I went on. "You probably just feel indebted to Francetti, and he plays on that, forcing you to be his attack dog."

"What the hell would you know about it? Ain't you just the same thing for the cops? An attack dog, as you put it?"

"Maybe I was, but I'm not anymore."

"What do you mean?"

"I mean, I'm no longer a cop."

She laughed and shook her head. "You mean you came here and you ain't even a cop anymore? Why?"

"Because I want to help the people of Nelson's Square, that's why," I said.

"You wanna help them, huh? Well, good luck with that, because once Snake Tongue has his hooks in a place, that's it. He'll always own it."

"Then help me stop him. I'm sure Nelson's Square isn't the only place he puts the squeeze on. Think of all the people you'd be helping. Think of all the people you'd be protecting. You say you're Ka'ahu Pahau, then act like it. You have a legacy to live up to, a duty to fulfill that doesn't include terrorizing innocent people. Help me, Delphina, keep the menacing sharks away."

"You're good," she said. "I'll give you that. Snake Tongue would kill me if I went up against him."

"How? With your powers, you could literally eat him alive."

"There's more to him than you know," she said. "There's more to all this than you know."

"Then let me out of this damn tank and explain it to me," I said. "This water is freezing."

Delphina floated for a long time as she seemed to debate things in her head. "It would be so much easier just to let you drown," she said.

"Maybe so, but goddesses don't take the easy way, do they?

They do the hard things on behalf of the people, so they can protect them. It's literally your job, Delphina, whether you like it or not."

"And what about Sam Sidwell, the guy I killed?" she asked, suddenly seeming remorseful for the first time.

"What's done is done," I said, knowing Gemma Sidwell would see things differently. She'd probably hate me if she knew I was having this conversation with Delphina right now. "You can't change things, but you can make up for it."

"Redemption, huh? You believe in that?"

"Not really, but it's not about that. It's about at least trying to do some good, that's all. Nobody's asking you to be a saint."

"Well, that's good, because that's the last thing I am is a damn saint."

I laughed a little, as did she. "Can we head up now? Your shark friends are making me nervous, and my balls are about to drop off."

I'D NEVER BEEN MORE GRATEFUL TO CLIMB OUT OF ANYWHERE in my life when I finally crawled out of that shark tank. If I never saw water again, it would be too soon. Delphina had transformed back into her human form, and I stood shivering as I waited on her saying goodbye to her two shark friends before climbing out of the tank herself, seeming oblivious to the fact that she was naked as she stood before me.

"Let me get my clothes," she said.

"I'll meet you…in the car," I told her, my teeth chattering so much I could hardly talk.

"I guess you need to warm up, huh?" she said, smiling like she found my discomfort amusing.

"Some of us are warm-blooded."

"Coulda fooled me."

Throwing her a look, I headed outside and took off my

coat, tossing it on the back seat, glad I'd left my phone in the car. Starting the engine, I turned the heat up full and reveled in its comforting warmth until Delphina showed up and got into the car with me, plonking herself down on the front passenger seat like she owned the place. She was dressed now in dark jeans and a leather jacket, smiling across at me, cocky as ever.

"You look like a drowned rat," she said.

"Gee, thanks. I feel like one as well."

I opened the glove compartment and rummaged until I found a small black hip flask and a half pack of cigarettes with a plastic lighter inside. I drank from the hip flask first, the whiskey helping to warm my insides. When I offered the flask to Delphina, she shook her head.

"I don't put poison in my body," she said.

"I guess you don't want a cigarette either then," I said as I popped one into my mouth and lit it, filling the car with acrid smoke, much to Delphina's annoyance.

"Jesus, if you're gonna kill yourself, at least open a damn window."

Smiling, I wound the window down halfway, recoiling at the cold air blowing over my sodden clothes and skin. "So, now that we're on the same page——"

Delphina raised her hand. "Wait a minute now, I didn't say anything about being on the same page, or about helping you. I'm still deciding on that."

"Okay." I turned my head slightly to blow smoke out the window. "Well, while you're deciding, perhaps you'd like to tell me about Snake Tongue and his operation."

"There's not much to tell," she said. "He runs things for Don Giordano, that's all. It's just business. You don't need the details, do you? He extorts money from people and gives it to the don. The mob business is just like any other business. We just do things differently, that's all."

"You mean, you hurt people."

"It's business. Someone always gets hurt."

"True, I guess."

"What you really wanna know about is Snake Tongue himself, am I right?"

"Tell me about him."

Delphina mashed her lips together as she stared out the window, seeming to debate whether to tell me anything. "He helped me——"

"He helped you to help him. There's a difference. His motives were selfish."

"Ain't everyone's motives selfish? I'm sure yours are. Why you really wanna take Snake Tongue down? And don't tell me it's to help people."

I stared at her a moment and then turned away as I continued smoking my cigarette. "You're overthinking this. I stop bad guys, and Snake Tongue is a bad guy. That's it."

"Bullshit."

"What?"

"I said, bullshit. You're doing this because you feel guilty over somethin'. It's written all over your sorry face. You trying to make up for something? I thought you didn't believe in redemption."

"I don't."

"Then why you doing this? Especially since you ain't even a cop anymore."

"Has anyone told you you'd make a good interrogator?"

A smile creased her lips. "I got some experience in that area, now that you mention it. Don't change the subject. How am I supposed to be honest with you if you won't be honest with me first?"

Sighing, I shook my head. "Maybe you're right, okay? I've got a lot to make up for."

"Does it help, doing what you do? Taking down bad guys, as you put it? Helping others?"

"Honestly? I don't know. Maybe. A little."

"Jeez," Delphina said, and then puffed her cheeks out a little. "And you expect me to change my tune after hearing that? What's the point if it doesn't change anything? I might as well carry on being the same self-serving SOB if that's the case."

"Because it's about at least trying," I said. "That's all that matters. That's all anyone can do."

"So you want me to *try* and be a good person, is that it?" she asked, looking at me with much skepticism.

"That's about it, yeah."

"Even if it brings me nothing but grief like it does you?"

"Your soul will thank you."

Delphina snorted. "Shit, even you don't believe that."

"You're not making this easy."

"Then don't say shit like your soul will thank you, especially when it's blatantly obvious that your soul thanks you for jack shit."

She was perceptive, I'd give her that. "Maybe you're right. I've done a lot of stuff over the years, stuff I can't come back from. It's not too late for you, though. You're still young. I'm just trying to save you from going down a dark path that you'll later regret."

"You do realize you're not my keeper, right?"

"No, I'm not your keeper," I said as I tossed my cigarette butt out and wound the window back up. "But neither is Snake Tongue or Giordano. Only you are, and only you can decide what's best. It's you that has to live with your decisions."

After sitting in silence for a moment, Delphina said, "Why the hell you ever have to cross paths with me? I was doing fine before you came along. Things were simple, and now you gone and complicated everything."

"Like it or not, Delphina, you have a gift, and with that gift comes—"

"Great responsibility? Yeah, I saw that movie too, you know."

"I was gonna say responsibilities, but same thing, I suppose. Either way, it's true." I paused to take another swig from the hip flask. "So, you wanna tell me what's going on with your bosses or what?"

"You mightn't believe me if I told you."

"You'd be surprised. Try me."

"Okay, I will, but only to get you off my damn back."

"Whatever you have to tell yourself."

She pursed her lips at me before continuing. "So ole Don Vito, he ain't what he seems. I mean, he's the don and all, but he's more than that. Even I'm not sure how much more."

"What do you mean? Is he like you? A Mytholite?"

"A what?"

"You aren't the only person in this city to develop powers, Delphina. There are many others, all different in their own way."

She nodded as if I'd confirmed something for her. "That explains a lot."

"So Giordano, what is he?"

"Well, according to Snake Tongue, the don is a god, just like me."

"Which one?"

"Osiris."

"Jesus. Don Giordano is the god of the underworld? That's fitting."

Delphina smiled. "Ain't it just? I mean, I don't know just how *much* of a god he is. The few times I met him, he seemed pretty normal to me."

"You seem normal as well. Doesn't mean you are."

"Yeah, I know. I mean, Snake Tongue makes him out to be Superman or something, like he can do all these things."

"What things?"

"Like he has superhuman strength, speed and agility," she said. "And he controls elements."

"Which ones?"

"All of them apparently—wind, fire, water, maybe even the earth itself."

"Is he the reason your crew members are so strong?"

Delphina nodded. "Once a year, the don has this big banquet at his house. Everyone who works for him is invited. The whole reason for it is so everyone can drink the Liquid Gold."

"Liquid Gold? What's that?"

"You ever heard of Ambrosia from Greek myth?"

"Yeah, it grants people abilities."

"Right. Liquid Gold is like that. When you drink it, you get yourself some superhuman strength, and depending on how much you drink, you get other abilities as well. The top dogs, they get more than the rest, so they end up with increased powers of persuasion and higher charisma, among other things."

"You've drunk this stuff?"

"Me? No, I don't need it, do I?"

"I guess not."

"Snake Tongue drinks it, though. It's what makes him such an effective businessman."

I nodded. "So that's how he was able to persuade everyone at the square to get into business with him. It's why Mrs. Honeysuckle, the florist, won't say a bad word against him."

"Precisely. Don Giordano got it all sewn up."

"We'll see about that."

Delphina turned her head and stared at me. "I hope you ain't dumb enough to think you can take the don on. Jesus Christ, you are, aren't you? Well, I ain't fucking helping you, that's for damn sure."

"Why not? This would be our chance to change things. Think of how many people you'd be helping."

"Man, you still don't get it, do you?" She turned slightly in her seat to face me. "Don Giordano is more of a god than I'll ever be. Me? I'm still me, despite all these powers. But the don, he's something else. He absolutely *believes* he's Osiris. Hell, he *is* Osiris. Snake Tongue refers to him as an Avatar. I don't think he can even be killed if that's what you're thinking about doing."

"One step at a time," I said. "I want Snake Tongue first."

"Even if you manage to kill Snake Tongue, whatta you think the don will do, huh? Sit back and do nothing? You dreamin' if you think you can take these guys on by yourself, or even with a damn army behind you. Gods can't be defeated. If I were you, I'd just let this go. Some things you just can't change. Some battles you just can't win."

I sat staring out the window for a few moments while I contemplated everything, annoyed by her insight and how right she was. Maybe Don Vito Giordano, a.k.a. Osiris *was* above my paygrade.

For now, anyway.

But Antonio Francetti wasn't.

I could take him out of the picture, and no one would have to know it was me. The people of Nelson's Square would be free from him then, as would Delphina. If she chose to stop working for the mob, at least she could be safe in the knowledge that Snake Tongue would never try to find her. She'd be free of him.

"So tell me now," I said to her. "Are you gonna walk away from the mob or not?"

She stared at me like I'd some nerve even asking, then shook her head as she looked out the window for a long time, her face serious now as she appeared to contemplate her future.

Eventually, she said, "I wish I'd never met you."

I smiled. "Listen, there's a girl I'd like you to meet. She has powers like you. Her name's Charlotte. I think you two would get along."

"I don't need no one else."

"We all need someone."

"Yeah? Who you got?"

Hannah's face flashed through my mind, her smile, her dark eyes, but the image was quickly replaced by Xaglath's sharp features and cobalt eyes. "I got someone. She's just... lost at the moment."

"Lost, huh? How do you just lose someone?"

"It's a long story," I said as I finally pulled away from the aquarium. "By the way, how do you feel about spiders?"

I thought I could kill two birds with one stone by introducing Delphina to Charlotte. Both girls were alone in the world with powers they weren't sure what to do with, so I figured they might work things out between them.

Delphina got a bit freaked out when I took her to the Great Woods, demanding that I drive her back to the city immediately, or she would bite my head off, even showing me her shark teeth when she said it. It took me a few minutes, but I managed to calm her down and explained to her that she didn't have to stay if she didn't want to, but first she had to meet Charlotte.

Reluctantly, she agreed, and off we went into the woods to Charlotte's cottage. I had to tell her not to freak out too much when we got to the cottage.

"Charlotte has a few issues at the moment," I said. "I'm hoping you can help her work through them."

"I ain't no damn social worker," Delphina said as she trudged through the forest alongside me. "And neither are you, come to think of it. Why the hell you doing this?"

"Think about it," I said. "What else are you going to do?

Drift around from place to place? You need time to figure out your next move, and a place to hide out until I sort Snake Tongue out."

"If you kill him, the mob will know I had something to do with it if I'm not around no more."

"They won't."

"You sound awfully confident for someone who isn't even a cop anymore."

"Just trust me."

"Yeah. You know how many times people have said that to me in my life? And every time they've been full of shit."

"I'm not one of those people."

"You better not be, for your sake."

Despite saying she wouldn't, Delphina freaked out when we came upon the cottage and saw all the spiderwebs everywhere. She even stopped and refused to go any further.

"What's wrong?" I asked her.

"I hate fucking spiders, that's what wrong," she said. "I mean, they scare the shit outta me."

"You're a damn shark. You shouldn't be afraid of spiders."

"Well, I am, so…"

"There are no spiders here."

"Then what's all this web, huh? Christmas decoration?"

It took a minute, but I persuaded her to follow me through the webs, and then she freaked out again when she saw the vampires cocooned within them.

"No spiders, huh?" she said, stopping again. "Then what the hell is this?"

"They're just vampires. Don't worry about them."

"Vampires? You're shitting me, right?"

"You don't believe in vampires?"

"You really should, my dear," a male voice piped up from within the web, and we turned to see a head poking out of a cocoon suspended between two trees. "We are everywhere."

Delphina just stared at the vamp. "Jesus. And I thought I was fucked up. Who the hell did all this?"

"I did," said another voice, and we turned again to see Charlotte standing outside of the webs.

"Charlotte," I said, ripping the webs so I could step through. "Hello again."

"I thought I told you not to come back," she said, standing naked, but thankfully not in her spider form. I think Delphina would've run for the hills if Charlotte had been full-on arachnid.

"I know you did," I said. "But I've brought someone I'd like you to meet. This is Delphina." I turned to Delphina, who stood warily behind me. "Delphina, meet Charlotte."

"Hey," Delphina said. "Nice place you got here."

"It's my grandmother's," Charlotte said, her face expressionless.

"Kinda reminds me of where I grew up," Delphina said. "Only without the creepy spiderwebs. You did all this?"

"Yes," Charlotte said, then frowned at Delphina. "You're different. What are you?"

Delphina smiled wide. "Top of the damn food chain, that's what I am."

A slight smile appeared on Charlotte's face, the first time I'd ever seen her show any real emotion. "You haven't seen what *I* can do."

"Oh," Delphina said. "I got a pretty good idea what you can do."

Charlotte smiled again, wider this time.

"And by the way," Delphina added. "Is there a reason you buck naked, girl?"

"I'm alone out here," Charlotte said. "Clothes also get in the way when I change."

Delphina nodded. "Yeah, I have that same problem."

The two of them locked eyes for a second and smiled at

each other until Charlotte dropped her gaze, still socially awkward despite her newfound powers.

"So," I said to Charlotte. "I thought you two could hang out for a little while, get to know each other, maybe help each other figure some stuff out."

"The big man thinks he's doing us both a favor here," Delphina said to Charlotte. "What do you think?"

Charlotte looked at me, and then at Delphina. "I think we'll see. Are you hungry? I have trout cooking."

"Well," said Delphina, stepping toward Charlotte. "I wasn't before, but I am now. Lead the way, girl."

Charlotte smiled, awkwardly this time, as if she wasn't used to such company, which I guess she wasn't.

"Alright," I said. "Since you two are good, I'm gonna go now, leave you to it."

"You let me know what happens," Delphina said as she stood next to Charlotte. "And hey, be careful. Don't underestimate Snake Tongue."

"Thanks. I won't."

As I went to walk away, Charlotte said, "Hey."

I turned. "Yeah?"

She stood staring at me a moment, her dark eyes still seeming lost, her face harrowed. "Anytime you want to visit my sister's grave, you can just, you know, drop by. If you want to, that is."

"Thanks," I said smiling. "I appreciate that."

I stood where I was for another moment as I watched the two of them walk inside the cottage together, two souls in need of nourishment that didn't involve violence.

I hope you're seeing this, Scarlet, I thought, before turning and walking back to the car.

～

ON THE DRIVE BACK TO THE CITY, I TURNED THE RADIO ON TO a local rock station as I drove along the highway in a Mud-induced daze, snapping of it when the news came on and started talking about The Ripper Tripper. Apparently, police had tracked the guy down and made an assault on his house, but when they did, the guy wasn't there. Surprise surprise.

"The murderer's name is Jensen Michaels," the newscaster said, before going on to give a description of him, finishing with the usual warning that no one should approach Michaels if they see him as he is "very dangerous".

No shit.

Turning down the radio, I picked up my phone from the front seat and called Jim Routman.

"Yeah?" he said after answering, sounding as tired and stressed as I'd ever heard him. This case would put years on him by the time it was all over. If it was ever over, given how adept this man Michaels was at staying hidden.

"Jim, it's Ethan," I said. "Just thought I'd see how the case was going."

"The case? Are you fucking kidding? This case has me ready for the goddamn rope."

"Yeah," I said, suppressing a chuckle. "I'm sure it has. What happened? Why didn't you get him?"

"I thought we had him," he said, pausing to suck on a cigarette. "We got to the house, broke the door down. His wife screams that her husband—Michaels—is upstairs. Only he wasn't, but the wife still swears he was there, and that he must've run. But the thing is, we had the whole house surrounded, so there was no way he could've gotten past us, not unless the guy is a fucking ghost, because that's the only way he could've got out of that house without us seeing him."

"You're sure he was there? Could the wife have been lying?"

"No. She had no clue what he was up to. As usual, right? She swears he was in the house when we arrived."

"Did you find much at the house?"

"We found a bunch of stuff in the guy's private office," he said. "Knives, syringes full of LSD, and get this, the guy had a safe. Guess what we found in it?"

"I dread to think."

"A fucking jar of pickled clitorises. Can you fucking believe that? That goes no further, by the way."

"Of course. So you have no idea where Mr. Michaels is now?"

"None," he said. "We're questioning the wife and son, but they're as in the dark as we are. I dunno, Ethan. I'm not sure we'll ever catch this guy. Or if we do, it'll be because he just walks into the station one day and gives himself up."

"You'll get him, Jim. You always do."

"Yeah, thanks for the vote of confidence," he said. "Listen, I heard you got kicked off the force. That true?"

I sighed as I stared straight ahead at the city looming in the distance. "Yeah, it's true, I'm afraid."

"I'm sorry, Ethan. I mean it. I know we had our differences, but you're the best cop I know. It should've been you running this task force."

"Nothing I can do about it now, Jim. I just gotta move on, I guess."

"Any idea what you're gonna do now?"

"I'm not sure yet."

"Well, don't be a stranger, Ethan. Good luck."

"You too, Jim."

Despondency set in when I hung up the phone, the sting of being kicked off the force once again raw in me. In one sense, I should've been relieved that I didn't have to deal with the bullshit that went along with the job, the politics especially. But when you don't have much else going on in your life, the job is all you have. It gets you out of bed in the morning. Now I'd have to find something else to pay the rent, especially since

I likely didn't have a pension to fall back on. No doubt Edwards had made sure of that.

Before hitting the city again, I stopped at a roadside diner and ordered some food from the waitress when she came to serve me. For the next hour or so, I sat staring out the window, watching the traffic go by as I slowly ate my burger and fries, hungry but not enjoying the meal. I had too much on my mind for that. Besides Francetti, I kept thinking about the person who had impersonated Hannah and set up the murders of my wife and daughter. Clearly, the person was some sort of Spell Freak, and a powerful one at that if they were able to shift their appearance at will the way I saw them do. It was tempting to drive to the address where this person lived and put a bullet in them, after I'd found out why they did what they did, of course.

But I knew it would never be that easy. To get this person, I had to reign in my emotions and take things slow, as torturous as that would be. Before I did anything, I had to find out exactly who I was dealing with. If this was revenge, I didn't know what for. I'd crossed paths with so many people over the years, I didn't even know where to begin. And that's if this was personal, and the Spreak hadn't just been hired by someone else.

Despite trying to put it out of my mind, I still found myself dwelling on the Spreak when I drove back into the city. So much so I headed into Bedford and parked across the road from the building I'd seen the Spreak go into on the video footage.

It was early evening when I cut the engine and settled back into my seat with a cigarette and started staring across at the brownstone building. The street itself appeared busy. A constant stream of pedestrians ebbed and flowed, most of them making their way to the nightclub down the street a ways, or to the movie theater up the other end.

I sat for over an hour, not really knowing what I was doing

there until eventually I angrily bashed the steering wheel and went to start the engine.

But as I did, I noticed the front door of the brownstone opening, and a moment later, a man stepped out. The same tall, blond-haired man I'd seen in the video.

My jaw set tight as I glared over at him and watched him walk down the steps to the street where he paused and looked around like some sort of arrogant king surveying his kingdom.

Then he turned his head, and his eyes settled on me, and for long seconds, we stared at each other until a smile spread across his face.

Unable to contain myself any longer, I opened the door of the Dodge and stepped outside just as the Spreak started walking down the street with his back to me, moving into the crowd.

Without even thinking, I took my gun out and ran across the street and into the crowd, some people gasping and moving aside when they saw I had a gun, but I didn't care.

My eyes were focused on the Spreak until I reached the steps of his brownstone. And then…he just seemed to disappear into the crowd.

I moved down the street as I searched the crowd for signs of him, but there were none. The bastard must've changed his appearance, just like he'd done in the video.

"Fuck!" I said as I stood helplessly in the middle of the sidewalk with people giving me a wide berth because of the gun in my hand, and my no doubt crazy appearance.

Holstering the gun, I ran across the street and got back into the car again, lighting a cigarette to calm myself.

The Spreak had seen me. He knew who I was. Of course he fucking did. He probably knew I was here long before he came outside.

He was toying with me, the bastard.

That's what this whole thing felt like, in fact, as if someone were pulling my strings for their own twisted amusement.

If not the Spreak, then someone else.

Well, no more. Sooner or later, I'd get the Spreak, and then I'd find out what's really going on, and I'd put an end to it once and for all. Even if it fucking killed me. I didn't care.

I just needed to know.

I needed it to end.

A fter my encounter with the Spreak, my blood still boiled with so much anger and frustration that I hardly knew what to do with it. Normally, I'd calm myself with a dose of Mud, but the bottle in my pocket was empty.

As I sped across the bridge to Old Town, I intended to go home and put myself right, maybe even get some much-needed sleep.

But as I came off the bridge, I started thinking about Antonio Francetti and the misery he'd caused for the people of Nelson's Square, not to mention the fact that he'd clearly taken advantage of Delphina, using her as his own personal attack dog, putting her in a position where she ended up killing Sam Sidwell.

Francetti was no better than the hellots, feeding off people's pain and misery for their own gain, blackening the soul of the city along the way.

I'd had enough of assholes like him taking advantage. I couldn't stop the Spreak—not yet—but I could sure as fuck stop Francetti.

Turning the steering wheel sharply to the left, I banked across the road and cut across town to the bar I'd seen him go into before. According to the tracking app, the SUV was parked there, which meant he was probably in there.

It was time I had a word with old Snake Tongue.

But not just yet.

I couldn't just storm into the bar in full view of everyone. The plan was to permanently take care of the problem and to do that, no one could know it was me.

As much as I wanted to, I couldn't just go in there and put a bullet in Francetti. If I did that, I'd have the full force of the mob down on me in no time. So instead, I parked down the street and waited on Francetti to come out.

After an hour, there was still no sign of him, and I was down to my last cigarette. There was a store on the corner of the street, so I got out of the car and jogged across the road to replenish my supply.

"Nice night," the store clerk, a young guy with longish hair and acne said. "At least it isn't raining, right?"

"Yeah," I said as I passed him the money for the cigarettes.

"I'm surprised you haven't switched to vaping yet."

"Excuse me?"

He held up a long contraption that looked like a big pen. "I switched months ago. Haven't looked back since. We sell them here if you're interested."

"I'll just take the cigarettes," I said with a tight smile. "I don't need a douche flute."

The clerk looked offended as he handed me my change. "Hope you don't die of lung cancer. Have a nice night."

I shook my head at him. "Yeah, you too."

Upon leaving the store, I saw that the black SUV was still outside the bar, and I wondered as I crossed the road how much longer Francetti would be.

Nothing worse than waiting around to kill somebody.

Back inside the car, I opened the new pack of cigarettes

and put one between my lips, but stopped suddenly as I went to light it.

A frown came over my face as I realized something wasn't right.

It was only when I looked in the rearview mirror did I see the face of the person who had suddenly appeared on the back seat, dressed in black, the eyes cold and murderous.

Eyes belonging to Officer Mike Williams.

"Snake Tongue sends his regards," Big Mike said, as he brought the wire over my head and jerked it back, pulling it across my throat and pinning my head to the seat, the cigarette falling out of my mouth as I started to gag, the sharp wire slicing into the soft flesh of my throat and neck. "You should've left well enough alone, Drake."

In response, the best I could do was grip each side of the garrote with my fingers, the wire immediately slicing into them as I did my best to take some of the pressure off.

But Williams was pulling so hard there was no way I'd be able to free myself.

With every passing second, I could feel the wire biting further into my throat.

I had about five seconds to do something before the wire sliced through my windpipe, and then I'd be done for.

So with what little breath I had left, I managed to utter the words to summon the Hellbastards.

But after saying the words of power, the demons never showed, and all the while, Williams kept pulling, and the wire kept biting deeper into my throat, slicing into my fingers like they were made of cheese.

Son of a bitch, I thought. *I can't believe I'm getting taken out by this fat fuck Williams.*

"Give my regards to your wife and kid, Drake," he said, and I caught his reflection in the mirror as he smiled at me.

I had no breath left at this point. The only thing keeping

me alive was the pressure I was holding off with my fingers, the wire now almost through to the bone.

But as my vision began to blur around the edges, I heard the back door open and the sound of Williams going, "What the fuck?" and then the sound of him screaming as the Hellbastards piled into the back of the car and dived on him.

Then finally, the pressure on the garrote was released, and I fell forward in my seat, the garrote falling into my lap as blood dripped from my neck and fingers at a rapid rate.

Gasping for air, I covered my throat with my bloody hands and felt to see how much damage had been done. Luckily the wire hadn't sliced into my throat too much, but it would leave a hell of a mark.

Meanwhile, in the back, the five Hellbastards were busy beating the shit out of Williams as he screamed and thrashed around, his blood all over my back seat, with Cracka screaming, "I sick of assholes trying to hurt the boss! We...will... make...you...SUFFEEEER!"

"Hold on, boys," I said as I started the car and made a U-turn, my bloody hands slipping on the steering wheel, driving erratically down the street a ways before pulling into an alley and screeching to a stop at the far end.

With blood spilling down my neck, soaking my shirt, I angrily exited the car and pulled open the back passenger door. When I did, Williams spilled out of it along with most of the Hellbastards.

Williams was only half conscious by this stage, his face a bloody mess as the Hellbastards kept battering him with their fists, and stabbing him all over with their sharp claws.

Cracka was busy punching Williams repeatedly in the balls with his tiny fist, shouting, "You gonna die, asshole! You gonna die hard!"

"Alright, boys," I said as I looked down the alley to make sure no one was around. "Leave him be, least for a minute."

"Ahhhh," Cracka moaned.

"We just getting started, boss," Scroteface said.

"I know you are, Scroteface," I said. "I just need a quick word with Officer Williams here, and then you can do whatever you want to the bastard."

"No, please—" William's moaned as he regained consciousness.

"Shut up!" Cracka said and punched William's in the balls again, who gave a high-pitched squeal in response.

I crouched down and grabbed William's by the scruff, pulling his head up close to mine as my blood dripped onto him.

"You fucking scumbag! You think you can kill me?" I punched him twice in the face, further ruining his good looks.

"Drake…" he croaked, barely able to speak properly, the state he was in. "Don't…kill me…please…"

After laughing bitterly at his audacity, I spat blood on his chest. "You were gonna take my fucking head off, you fat fuck! For Francetti!"

"He—he made me…he made do it…" Williams said through bloody teeth, just as I got a whiff of something god awful and realized the cunt had shat himself.

"You disgust me, William's, you know that?" I said. "As a cop and as a human being, you fucking turn my stomach."

"He shit himself," Cracka laughed.

"Shitty pants," Toast joked to a chorus of laughter.

Despite the pain he was in, William's still had it in him to be terrified of the Hellbastards as they stood around him, itching to get going on him again, and he knew it. He *should* be fucking terrified. "Take me in, Drake," he pleaded. "My wife, my kids—"

I stood up and looked down at him, unable to bear the smell anymore. "You shoulda thought of that before you tried to kill me. And you forget one thing, Williams."

"What?" he mumbled.

"I'm not a cop anymore."

I turned to the Hellbastards, who were waiting like anxious gundogs to retrieve a kill. "Do your worst, boys."

The Hellbastards dived on Williams en masse like a pack of hungry zombies on a corpse.

"NO!" Williams screamed. "NO…AHHHHH-HHHHHHH…"

WHEN I DROVE OUT OF THE ALLEY AGAIN—AFTER TELLING THE Hellbastards to clean up after them—I saw that the black SUV was gone. It didn't matter. I'd track its movements later.

In the meantime, I had to get cleaned up. Initially, I called at The Tattoomb to see if Larry was there, but the parlor was locked up, and despite me banging on the door, Larry didn't appear.

Looks like I'm sorting myself out then.

It wouldn't be the first time.

With the car stinking of blood, I drove home to my apartment, only to find Daisy sitting in there when I opened the door. Her eyes widened when she saw me. "Oh my god, Ethan," she cried. "What happened to you?"

"No need to worry," I said. "I'm fine. Mostly. How come you're in here?"

Daisy was already over examining my cut fingers and peering up at the garrote wound in my neck. "I just needed somewhere quiet to sit, that's all," she said like it hardly mattered. "Who did this to you?"

"A cop."

"A cop? Why?"

"Because he's a scumbag, that's why."

"Where is he now?"

"With the Hellbastards."

"Oh." She knew what that meant. "Well, good riddance."

"My thoughts exactly."

"Sit on the couch," she said. "I'll get the medi kit from the bedroom."

"You'll need the key."

"Actually, I won't," she said, almost apologetically. "It's already open. Did I mention I've been practicing lock picking?"

"Nope, you didn't."

She gave a nervous laugh. "Well, I have. I'll just be a minute."

"Yeah, okay."

Shaking my head—though not exactly annoyed—that she'd clearly been snooping in my storeroom, I sat down on the couch after I'd grabbed a bottle of whiskey from the kitchen.

Jesus, what a day.

First, I almost get drowned by a shark goddess, and then a cop tries to kill me. Sometimes I wonder how I'm still alive at all.

Daisy came back into the living room a few moments later as I sat drinking whiskey from the bottle, smearing bloody prints all over it.

"Take your coat and shirt off," she said, sounding like she'd done this same routine countless times before. It scared me at times how confident she was getting, and how unafraid she was of the world I existed in, the world she was being drawn inexorably into herself.

"What's the damage, doc?" I asked her as she cleaned the wound on my neck with gauze soaked in a saline solution.

"It's not as deep as I thought," she said. "It's still pretty bad, though. What did this?"

"Wire."

"Nasty."

"Yes, it is." I glanced down at the jars of ointment she had brought in. "How'd you know which ones to get?"

"Lucky guess?"

"Hardly."

"I've been reading your books."

"When?"

"When I'm supposed to be in school."

"Daisy," I scolded. "You can't be skipping school like that. You'll have the authorities calling at your door."

"I hate school. It's stupid and full of stupid people."

"It doesn't matter, you still have to go."

"It's Fall break soon, anyway."

"Still. Don't make a habit of it."

"I bet you didn't go to school."

"That was different."

"How?"

"It just was."

"I'm sure."

I sighed, too tired to argue with her as she applied ointment from one of the jars, dabbing it around the wound on my neck, which would prevent any heavy scarring and speed up the healing process. When she was done, she wrapped a bandage around my entire neck.

"You're good at this," I said. "Maybe you should become a doctor."

"You trying to get me to stay in school?" she asked, throwing me a look as she began to inspect my fingers.

"Yeah, unless you wanna end up like me, sitting covered in blood as a thirteen-year-old tends to your wounds."

She smiled and shook her head. "These cuts on your fingers are deep. I can see the bones."

"Those bones stopped me from losing my head," I said. "Apply the red ointment. It'll heal them pretty quick."

"You really need stitches."

"Trust me, the ointment is as good as stitches."

"You know best." She cleaned the cuts on all of my fingers and applied the ointment. When she went to bandage my digits together, I told her not to. "I still need my fingers. Do them individually."

As she applied the bandages, she asked, "So why did another cop try to kill you?"

"Well, first of all, it's *a* cop. As of today, I'm not a cop anymore myself."

She stopped wrapping the bandages to look up at me. "I'm sorry."

I shook my head. "Don't be. Maybe it's for the best."

"Really? I thought you liked being a cop."

"There are other ways to do what I do. I'll sort something out."

"So why did this cop try to kill you then?" she asked again.

"He was acting on the orders of someone else," I said. "A mobster named Antonio Francetti. I'm investigating his operation, and he obviously wanted me taken care of."

"Won't he come after you again?"

"I don't intend to give him that chance."

"You're going to kill him?"

"Let's not talk about that."

"Why not? It's not like I haven't killed anybody, is it?"

Kids. Always thinking they know best.

"You had any more dreams lately?" I asked, changing the subject.

"I had one last night. It was pretty nasty."

"Why? What happened in it?"

"I just remember pieces," she said. "There was a battle and monsters...and lots of blood."

"And you were fighting in this battle?"

"Yes. So were you."

"And was this a...vision of the future, do you think?"

She shrugged. "Maybe. Or it could've just been a dream. I guess time will tell."

Let's bloody hope not.

"Listen," I said when she was done. "You should go see Cal."

She frowned at me as she gathered everything up. "Why?"

"He's—" I stopped, unsure of what to tell her. On the one hand, I didn't want to burden her with the knowledge that Cal was about to die, but on the other hand, I knew she had a soft spot for him, and that she would want to be there for him if she could. "He's pretty sick."

Daisy stopped and stared at me for a long moment, no doubt able to tell from my face what I meant by that. "How sick?" she asked. "Is he—"

I sighed and looked away. "I'm sorry, Daisy."

Seeming in shock, Daisy dropped everything she was holding and sat down on the floor, a range of emotions reflected in her eyes before she nodded to herself. "Okay," she said. "What's wrong with him?"

"He has a brain tumor. He doesn't have long."

She nodded as she stared hard at the floor. "Okay, well, then he's going to need somebody there with him."

"I don't think—"

"I'll go tomorrow. He shouldn't be alone." She wiped tears from her eyes and stood up to carry the ointments and medi kit back into the storeroom. "I'll just put these away."

"Are you okay?" I called after her.

But she didn't answer.

19

The next morning, I awoke refreshed after getting some sleep. In the bathroom, I peeled the bandage off my neck to check the wound underneath, and was glad to see that it was healing nicely, the ointment Daisy had applied doing its job well. With any luck, there would only be a slight scar left behind, and my dashing good looks wouldn't be impacted too much.

To cover the damage and to avoid any awkward questions from people, I dug out a black turtleneck and put it on, wearing a scuffed black leather jacket over the top.

According to the tracking app, the SUV had made a stop in Hill Valley last night in north Bedford. Going over the history, I saw the vehicle had made several visits to the same address, so it was a safe bet that Francetti lived there.

This didn't surprise me, because the place was a haven for movie stars and celebrities, and Francetti struck me as the type to enjoy fraternizing with the vapid brigade, probably pulling them unwittingly into his illegal business schemes and supplying them with drugs and fuck knows what else.

The Hellbastards hadn't returned home yet. I guessed they were still enjoying themselves with Big Mike, though I doubted he was enjoying himself as much. I almost felt sorry for him as I thought about what the Hellbastards were doing to him.

Almost.

Before leaving the apartment, I pocketed a suppressor for the Sig Sauer. The plan was to let myself into Francetti's house and quickly take him out, assuming he was home. If he wasn't, I would wait on him.

Then I would kill him quick.

No talking. No messing about.

What was there to say, anyway?

Sure, I could probably question him about his boss—Osiris as it turned out—but he wasn't likely to tell me anything, and would probably try to use his powers of persuasion to talk me out of killing him.

I only wanted Francetti anyway. Vito Giordano wasn't on my hit list. He was too big a fish, and if I wanted to take him down, it would take a ton of research and planning.

I wasn't here to take down every bad guy in the city anyhow. Just the ones that crossed me, and Giordano hadn't crossed me.

Yet.

Out of habit, I clipped my badge onto my belt. I felt slightly foolish doing so, but a part of me wasn't ready to give it up just yet. When I went to see Captain Edwards for the final time, that's when I would give up my badge.

Until then, in my mind, I was still a cop.

Even though I was about to go kill somebody.

BUT AS IT TURNED OUT, I DIDN'T HAVE TO KILL FRANCETTI. Somebody else beat me to it.

When I rolled up to the house in Hill Valley, the place was swarming with cops.

"What the fuck is this?" I said, spotting Routman's car up ahead.

I sat for a few moments, watching the forensic techs come and go, before deciding to check things out for myself. The road was cordoned off, but I flashed my badge to the uniform standing there, and he let me through.

But as I walked up the path to the front door, Routman came out, doing a double-take as he spotted me coming.

"Ethan," he said, frowning at me. "What the hell are you doing here? You can't be here."

"I was just passing," I said casually. "Thought I would see what was going on. Whose house is this?"

Routman mashed his lips together and started shaking his head. "Ethan, you're not a cop anymore. This has nothing to do with you."

"Come on, Jim," I said, pretending to be the sad sack ex-cop who couldn't let go. "Humor me. Just this once, for old time's sake."

Routman sighed. "Just this once. If the captain knew I was doing this, he'd send me down the road along with you."

Smiling, I followed Routman into the post-modern night-mare of a house, and into the spacious living room to find it full of forensic techs, including Gordon Mackey, who looked surprised to see me.

"Ethan," he said. "What are you going here? I thought—"

"I am. I'm just taking a look."

"Well, since you're here," Mackey said, turning to look at the back wall as if he was presenting a great work of art. "Feast your eyes on this bloody masterpiece."

My jaw went slack as soon as I saw what he was talking about. On the pristine white wall was Antonio Francetti, naked and spreadeagled, stuck to the wall in a giant spider-web. His head hung slack against his chest, and there was a huge chunk taken out of his side, almost like something had bitten him.

"The guy's a mobster named Antonio Francetti," Routman said. "You know him?"

"I've heard of him," I said. "He ran the extortion racket I was investigating in Nelson's Square. Never met the guy, though."

Routman looked at me like this was news to him. "That why you're here?"

"No," I said. "I told you, I was just passing."

"Just passing, huh? If you know anything about this, you need to tell me."

"What would I know?" I said as I gazed at Francetti's body, who had obviously died from extreme blood loss. Every drop he had seemed to be pooled underneath him on the floor and splashed around the white walls. "I'm not even a cop anymore."

"What I want to know," Mackey said, "is why the vic is stuck on what appears to be a giant spiderweb, and more importantly, why he seems to have what looks like a shark bite in his side."

"Yeah," I said as I turned to leave. "Good luck figuring that one out."

NEEDLESS TO SAY, MY NEXT PORT OF CALL WAS THE GREAT Woods. When I clawed my way through the mass of spiderwebs, ignoring the pleas of the stuck vampires, I stopped outside the little cottage and called the girls' names out. A moment later, Delphina came walking out of the cottage with a smile on her face.

"Detective," she said. "What brings you here this fine day?"

Giving her a look, I stood shaking my head at her. "I think you know why I'm here, Delphina."

Delphina kept on smiling innocently as Charlotte emerged

from the cottage, clothed this time in a black, lace dress. She sorta dropped her gaze when she saw me, not quite adept at pulling off the innocent act as Delphina. "Hi," she said.

"Hi," I said. "So, you'll never guess where I've just come from."

With her hands on her hips, Delphina said, "The city?"

"Yeah," I said. "From Antonio Francetti's house in Hill Valley. Guess what I found there?"

Both girls looked at each other and shook their heads. "We don't know," Delphina said. "What did you find?"

I sighed in annoyance at their feigned ignorance. "Snake Tongue dead on the wall, held there in a giant spiderweb, with a massive chunk bitten out of his side, almost like, you know, a shark bit him."

"A shark?" Delphina laughed. "Man, you must be trippin' or something. There ain't no sharks in Hill Valley. Sharks only live in the ocean. Didn't you learn anything in school?"

Charlotte dropped her head slightly as she tried not to smile, and I stood there staring at the two of them, knowing I would not get a straight answer out of either of them. "I'm so gonna regret bringing you two together, aren't I?"

Delphina and Charlotte glanced at each other and smiled before looking at me. "Yep," they both said in unison, and then started laughing their asses off.

Give me strength.

WITH NOT MUCH LEFT TO DO, I STOPPED OFF AT NELSON'S Square to let Gemma know the news. Later, I planned on going down to the precinct for the last time so I could—reluctantly I have to say—hand in my badge and gun.

Just the thought left a bitter taste in my mouth.

Gemma was working in the shop when I walked in, stacking shelves. Her expression as she turned to see who had come in was almost fearful as if she was continually dreading that Delphina would come barging in along with her gang.

When she saw it was me, she smiled. "Hey there," she said, moving a lock of red hair behind one ear.

"Hey there yourself," I said, smiling back. "I come bearing good news."

"You arrested my uncle's killers?" She seemed hopeful as she walked up the aisle toward me.

"Not exactly."

"Oh, I thought…"

"Turns out, there'll be no need to arrest Francetti."

"Why not?"

"Because he's dead."

"Dead?"

"Yep."

"How?"

"Does it matter? You won't be seeing him in here again."

"Well, I hate to gloat over anyone's death, but…"

"It's fine. The guy was an asshole. He deserved what he got."

"And Delphina? What about her, and the rest of her gang?"

"Well, I can't speak for her gang, but Delphina won't be bothering you again."

Gemma shook her head like she didn't understand. "How do you know?"

I paused, about to lie to her, but when I looked in her eyes, I thought she deserved the truth. "Look, Delphina is just a mixed-up kid who was under Francetti's thumb." Despite the deep frown of concern on Gemma's face, I carried on. "I spoke with her and persuaded her to leave him. I helped her get away from the mob, in fact."

Gemma's jaw dropped as she looked at me with disbelief. "Wait a minute," she said. "You helped her? You helped the psychopath who killed my uncle?" Tears came to her eyes. "Are you serious right now?"

"Gemma, there's more to it than that. I—"

"I think you should go," she said, walking past me to stand behind the counter, hardly able to look at me now.

I wanted to explain everything to her, but I knew she wouldn't listen, so I just said, "I doubt anyone from the mob will come back here, but if they do, you have my number."

"Yeah," she said with some bitterness. "Maybe you could help them as well. I mean, they're all just under their bosses' thumb, right?"

"Look," I said with a sigh. "I know you wanted justice for your uncle, but this is the best you're going to get. This is how things get done here, Gemma. Black and white, good guys and bad guys, those concepts only exist in movies. In real life, everything is a shade of gray. You'll come to realize that someday."

She stared at me with bitter tears in her eyes. "I'm realizing it now. Goodbye, Detective."

There was nothing more I could say, so I turned and left the shop.

Feeling like shit over how I left things with Gemma, I stopped off on the way home to grab some groceries for the apartment since my fridge and cupboards were all empty, especially since Daisy was spending so much time at my place. That girl could eat, I tell you. Her favorite food seemed to be pizza, as she'd cleared out of every one I had in the freezer, so I bought a load more, along with a couple bottles of whiskey for myself and a juicy T-bone steak that I intended to fry as soon as I got home.

When I pulled up in my street, however, I spotted a familiar dark shape standing in the mouth of the alley.

Haedemus.

My heart sank, for I knew trouble had found me again.

Leaving the groceries in the car, I got out to talk to him. He appeared to be alone.

"Finally," he said. "You know, Ethan, in all the time I've been here in this world, I'd say I've spent at least half of it waiting around on you."

"Well, sorry to keep you," I said. "I didn't know we had an appointment. What's going on? Where's your mistress?"

"Probably out killing people for that little gangster man."

"Yagami?"

"Yes, that's the one."

"I'm not sure I follow."

"Well, Ethan, there's been a turn of events, hasn't there? You see, when Xaglath went to finish off this Yagami man—because she was so eager to get to you next—she inadvertently walked into a trap."

I nodded, remembering that Yagami had said he was going to find a way to control Xaglath. "He used a spell on her."

"Yes," Haedemus said. "Obviously I wasn't in the building when it happened, but I saw her when she came out some hours later, and she explained to me what happened. She has no choice now but to do what Yagami tells her to do."

"Which is what exactly?"

"Well, at present, she's busy taking out a number of rival gangs and business competitors. She's creating quite the mess."

"I'm sure she is. Why aren't you with her?"

"I left her when she entered some casino to destroy the place," he said. "I thought to myself if anyone could help it would be Ethan, and here I am."

"So what the hell am I supposed to do?"

"What?"

"You heard me. If Yagami has used magic—clearly

powerful magic—to bring Xaglath under his control, how am I supposed to break it? Magic isn't my thing, Haedemus."

"I can't believe I'm hearing this," he said as he towered over me. "You're the reason she's in this mess in the first place, and now you're telling me you won't do anything to help her out of it? I must say, Ethan, I'm extremely disappointed. I thought you were better than this. I thought you had morals, a sense of justice, a sense of—"

"Alright, alright," I said, sighing as I took out my cigarettes. "I'll try to help her."

"Good man yourself, Ethan," Haedemus said. "I knew I could guilt trip you into it."

"Screw you." I stabbed a cigarette into my mouth and lit it. "There's something we need to consider here before we go gallivanting off, or at least something *I* need to consider."

"And what's that?"

"Say I manage to get Xaglath out from under Yagami's control. What then? I'd just be freeing her so she could turn around and set her sights on me. She wants to punish me, remember?"

"Yes, and?"

"What do you mean, and? She'll torture and kill me!"

Haedemus shook his big head dismissively. "Don't be a ninny, Ethan. Once you save her, she'll have no choice but to let you go."

"Fuck off, Haedemus. Who do you think you're talking to, some desperate damned soul down in Hell?" I pointed my finger at him. "You know she's an evil bitch. She'd never let me go no matter what I did."

"Fine," he said. "Then do it for Hannah, if not for Xaglath. You know she's still in there somewhere."

"I don't, actually. Do you?"

He paused before answering. "Truth? I'm not sure."

Sighing, I shook my head. "So I'm supposed to go on faith, am I?"

"I guess so," he said. "I have faith in you, Ethan."

"Stop trying to butter me up. You're just afraid Yagami will make Xaglath banish you back to Hell."

"Well—I—yes, actually. I am. I'm afraid, Ethan, alright? There, I said it. But I'm not afraid for the reason you said."

I frowned. "Why then?"

"Because, my dear Ethan, I may just be an ugly Hellicorn who most people can't even see, and I may live in a world where I don't really belong, but it's more than I had before in Hell. I never felt fear until I came here, least not in Hell." He walked past me a little and peered up and down the street before turning back to face me. "Now, I fear losing what little I have here. I fear losing you as well, Ethan, but I think saving Xaglath from a life of servitude is the best chance you have of surviving her. If you don't, Yagami will send her after you anyway. And from what I can gather about the man, he doesn't like loose ends. You pissed him off, so your days are numbered, anyway. So you see, Ethan, you may think you have a choice here, but you really don't."

"Well," I said, "you're right about one thing."

"And what's that?"

"You *are* ugly."

We stared at each other a second, and then we both laughed at the same time. "Oh, Ethan," he said. "How I've missed your sarcasm."

I came forward and patted him on the head, my fingers avoiding the gaping hole under his serrated horn. "You know what, buddy? As much as you can be a pain in the ass, I've actually missed you too."

"Oh…" he said, melodramatically. "I think I'm going to cry."

"Like you did after fucking that near-dead guy on the battlefield that time?"

Haedemus' eyes narrowed, his voice going deadpan. "You just had to bring that up, didn't you?"

20

With my groceries abandoned in the back of the Dodge —including my juicy T-bone sadly—I rode Haedemus through the city to Little Tokyo, unseen by anyone thanks to his invisibility, unless you happened to be an Aware, in which case you would've seen us galloping hard down the congested streets, Haedemus expertly avoiding cars and pedestrians, sometimes even leaping over the top of them if the need arose.

I had to admit, I'd missed riding the Hellicorn and the sense of freedom that came along with it, not to mention the rush of galloping at great speed toward a destination.

Only I wasn't looking forward to reaching this particular destination very much.

Yakuza headquarters.

And the formidable Xaglath.

Before I'd hit the road with Haedemus, I made a call to Richard Solomon. I figured if anyone knew how to break the spell Yagami had Xaglath under, it would be him. But when I asked him about it, he merely laughed darkly down the phone and said there was only one way to break such a spell, and proceeded to tell me what it was, but only after he made me tell him a secret first.

"A secret you have never told anyone," he'd said. "And be careful, for I will know if you have or not."

"Really, Solomon?" I'd said. "You can't just do this one thing without asking for something in return?"

"There is always a price to pay, Ethan," he'd said. "Surely you've figured that out by now."

Unfortunately, I had, so I thought for a minute or two as I dredged up whatever dirty little secrets I had locked up inside me—and believe me, there are quite a few—some minor, some as big as houses. I figured he wasn't interested in the minor secrets, like the string of affairs I had when I was married, or the corners I cut as a cop. No, Solomon always wanted me to go deeper, so I found the one secret I hardly even knew I had myself it was buried so deep, and I told it to him. And if you think I'm going to say what it is, you can think again. It's a secret, after all.

"You continue to surprise me, Ethan," he'd said. "The darkness would welcome you with open arms if you would only give yourself over to it."

"Just tell me what I want to know, Solomon."

He told me what I wanted to know, and it wasn't what I was expecting. Far from it.

Now, as I rode toward Little Tokyo, I felt like a kid riding into battle with a plastic sword.

"I hope this plan of yours works, Ethan," Haedemus said as he galloped down a side street. "If it doesn't, we're both fucked."

"Yes, you've already made that abundantly clear, Haedemus."

"I was thinking, though, that if it doesn't work, at least we'll have each other in Hell. I could show you the sights."

Spending an eternity in Hell with Haedemus as he rode

me around pointing out all manner of horrors wasn't exactly a prospect I relished.

You better be right about this, Solomon, I thought.

~

I DISMOUNTED HAEDEMUS AROUND THE BACK OF THE YAKUZA corporate building since I didn't think it was a good idea to just walk in the front door. "Is she in there now?" I asked Haedemus.

"She is," he said. "I can feel her presence near."

I swallowed, not exactly thrilled about what I was walking into. "Oh, goody."

"If anyone can do this, it's you, Ethan," Haedemus said as he looked down on me with his red eyes. "In fact, you're the only one who can do this."

"I hope you're right, Haedemus." I took out my gun as I walked toward the back exit door, trying the handle and finding it locked.

"Allow me." Haedemus strode toward the door before turning around and kicking it with his two back legs, sending the door flying inward on its hinges. "If I could, I'd go in with you, but you know, stairs..."

"Yeah, I know."

With my gun held close to my chest, I stepped through the doorway and started making my way up the stairs, keeping an eye up ahead in case any of Yagami's men were waiting somewhere.

But after four flights of stairs, it soon became apparent that no one was waiting anywhere, and I made it to the top floor without incident. Even when I stepped out into the hall-way, everything was quiet.

Too quiet.

There should've been guards posted outside Yagami's office doors, but there were none.

Nonetheless, I stayed cautious as I made way down the long hallway toward the heavy double doors at the far end. When I reached the ornately carved wooden doors, I stopped to listen but heard no noise from inside.

Fuck this.

I was uneasy and would've preferred if I'd been met by a bunch of angry Yakuza. At least then, I would've known what I was walking into.

But this? This sinister silence and lack of opposition just put me further on edge.

Taking a deep breath with my hand on the door handle, I readied myself for a second and then opened the door, pushing it open wide before stepping inside with my gun pointing out in front of me as I quickly did a sweep of the massive room, checking either side of me and seeing no one.

No one but Yagami, who was seated behind his desk with his fingers steepled in front of him as if he'd been expecting me all this time.

"Mr. Drake," he said with his usual thin smile, completely composed despite the fact that I was pointing my gun at him. "It's nice to see you again."

"I wish I could say the same," I said. "Where is she?"

Yagami smiled as another voice said from behind me, "I'm right here, Ethan."

Spinning around, I instinctively pointed my gun at Xaglath, who seemed to have materialized from nowhere because she wasn't there a second ago.

She looked as demonic as she did the last time we'd met, still wearing her black leather outfit, the long back trailing behind her as she took a few steps nearer to me, her cobalt eyes as icy as it was possible to get.

Despite how fearsome she looked, however, there was something different about her. She wasn't as forthcoming as she normally was, and I realized it was because she had been rendered impotent by Yagami's spell. She had no choice but hang back and await whatever order her new master gave her.

Though she did use her power to take my gun from me, telekinetically ripping it from my hands so it went flying across the room away from me.

Yagami wasn't stupid. He knew if I killed him, his spell over Xaglath would be broken. Besides, he didn't go to all this trouble just to get shot.

"Didn't I tell you, Mr. Drake," Yagami said, "that I would find a way to bring the beast under my control?"

"Congratulations," I said after reluctantly turning my back on Xaglath to face him. "You have your own weapon of mass destruction now. Bully for you."

"I have more than that, Mr. Drake." Yagami got out of his seat to look out the massive window which gave him a decent view of the sprawling city below. "I have the means to do whatever I want, and what I want is to take over this entire city."

I shook my head in disdain. "You're nothing if not predictable, Yagami."

"As are you, Mr. Drake," he said, turning to face me. "My daughter and I—"

"Stop. That right there"—I turned slightly to point at Xaglath—"is not your daughter."

Yagami smiled. "You are right, she is more than that. She is, in fact, the daughter I always wanted."

"You're a sick fuck, Yagami."

The aging gangster stared hard at me. "As I was saying, Xaglath and I counted on her Hell Beast to go running to you. She said you would come here, though, to be honest, I really didn't think you'd be that stupid. I mean, what are you planning on doing, Mr. Drake? You know you can't stop us. Though clearly, Xaglath knows you better than I do, for here you are, a willing participant in your own death."

Standing there with Xaglath behind me, it was hard to

disagree with him. This absolutely felt like I'd just sentenced myself to death—and to Hell—just by coming here.

Turning to look at Xaglath, seeing no trace of Hannah in her inhuman face at all, it was becoming ever more difficult to believe that my plan was going to work. Staring into those eyes, I didn't think there was a chance in hell I'd be able to get through to her, which is what my plan required.

If Hannah didn't exist anymore, nor any trace of her former celestial self, I was done for.

Suddenly, I had visions of roaming Hell with Haedemus, but only after an eon of horrendous torture at the hands of Xaglath.

"So what's the plan, Yagami, huh?" I asked as I started walking toward him, thinking if I could close the gap quick enough, I could break the bastard's neck before Xaglath got a chance to do anything. "You gonna have your new pet kill me, is that it? Is that why you lured me here, so you could watch me die? So you could—"

I started running toward him, my hands already out so I could grab his neck and—

Something hit me on the back, and I went flying forward, crashing onto the floor, my face smashing against the carpet tiles, my nose bursting open as my vision went black for a second.

Before I could even recover, the same force that had flung me forward lifted me up and pulled me back through the air until I once again crash-landed on the floor just past Xaglath, who was the cause of all this ragdoll physics.

As I lay in a daze, groaning at the pain in the back of my head, I saw Xaglath thrust a hand out in front of her. Next thing I knew, I was telekinetically hoisted off the floor and then thrust through the air until I hit the wall, where I remained, pinned like a dead butterfly next to the tank of piranhas.

Xaglath held me against the wall while Yagami walked

into the center of the room to stare at me, his expression one of mild disdain, like I was just a nuisance he couldn't wait to get rid of.

"It's fitting that you aren't a cop anymore, Mr. Drake," he said. "Yes, I did hear you were dismissed from the police force. It's fitting because you are going to die anyway. I'm sure no one will miss you, given your family is already dead."

"You fuck!" I raged as I tried to free myself from the wall, but it felt like I was trapped in one of Charlotte's webs, unable to move my head or limbs a single inch.

Yagami, ignoring my angry retort, turned to Xaglath. "Kill him, my daughter."

Xaglath didn't look too happy about being ordered to do anything, nor at Yagami referring to her as his daughter, but she nodded once and then started walking toward me with her hand still out, seeming to increase the pressure on my chest the closer she got.

"Wait!" I said to her while I still had the breath to do it.

"Alas, Ethan, it is too late for you," she said. "I would've liked to have had my way with you, but fate has conspired against me."

"No!" I said as I stared into her eyes. "Hannah! I know you're in there. Please! Fight this!"

"Hannah's dead," Xaglath said almost matter-of-factly. "How many times do I have to repeat it?"

"Hannah!" I said again, ignoring Xaglath. "Hannah, you have to listen to me! You have to—"

"Kill him!" Yagami barked at Xaglath.

The pressure increased in my chest, and this time I felt another pressure around my heart. Xaglath was crushing it, but I resisted with everything I had.

"Hannah!" I shouted again, my voice so strained now it was becoming too difficult to even form the words. "Remember...your...True Name!"

Xaglath visibly froze when I said it, and for a moment, the pressure around my heart and chest eased up.

"What?" she said.

"Ignore him!" Yagami ordered her. "Finish him!"

"Hannah, I know you're in there somewhere," I said. "I can still feel you. I've always felt you. You can break free, Hannah! All you have to do is—"

"Silence!" Xaglath roared.

Blood exploded from my mouth like crimson vomit, as if she had crushed something inside me, but I kept on at her. "You're stronger than she is, Hannah! You can defeat her! You can—"

I screamed as something cracked in my chest. Then more blood followed, exploding from my ears, my nose, my mouth. The pressure was crushing, like being caught between two freight trains.

But I didn't stop.

"*Hannah…*"

"I SAID FINISH HIM!"

"*Please, Hannah…*"

Xaglath looked confused now as she stared at me. The cobalt glare of her eyes seemed to have faded, and her features appeared to be changing, the sharpness becoming rounded out, the bluish-white skin changing color.

"*No…*" she whispered.

As blood continued to pour from my every orifice, I gave one last push.

"*Come back to me, Hannah!*" I all but wailed. "*I need you…to remember your… True Name, Hannah…remember…me…*"

Unable to speak any further, my head fell forward, and as it did, my body followed, and I pitched onto the floor. The crushing pressure on my body had gone now, but I was still weak as hell.

The only thing I could do was look up at Xaglath…no,

not Xaglath. She was changing, but into who or what, I had no idea. I hoped it was Hannah, but I just couldn't be sure.

In any case, I smiled at her and said, "Just remember... your True Name. That's...all you have to do."

"Enough of this!" Yagami roared, and I saw him cross the room and pick up my gun from the floor. "I'll finish you myself, Mr. Drake!"

As Yagami pointed the gun while he stomped toward me, I closed my eyes as I awaited the inevitable.

But the inevitable didn't come.

Almost fearfully, I opened my eyes to see that Yagami had been flung across the room, the gun now lying on the floor far away from him. With blood running down his face, he cowered in the corner, seeming frightened now, and as I looked up at Xaglath, I could see why.

For she was changing.

Against her will, Xaglath floated up into the air until she was halfway between the floor and ceiling. In amazement, I watched as her clothes just seemed to fall from her, revealing her naked form underneath.

And then the light shone through.

The most beautiful light I had ever seen, so bright it should've blinded me instantly, and yet it didn't.

And as I watched, the demon that was Xaglath became transformed, as another being entirely subsumed her—a being of pure light that brought with it a heavenly sound of a thousand angels singing at once, a sound that rightly should not have been fit for my human ears, and yet I heard every note and vibration as every fiber of my being sang along to its celestial chorus.

Tears of sheer joy flooded from my eyes as I looked upon this glorious sight, this perfect-in-every-way heavenly being, and right then, I took back every bad thing I'd ever said about God, because any god who could birth something as utterly perfect as this being of pure love and of pure creation deserved to be revered.

This celestial perfection floated down to me and stretched out a hand for me to take, and even though it was pure light, I could still feel it. I could feel the warmth and love coming from it, and within seconds, every bit of damage that Xaglath had done to me was healed as that glorious light raced about my body.

And if that wasn't enough, the being before me then took a step back and, unbelievably, started shifting into a solid form that was just as beautiful to my eyes as the being of light it was before.

For that form was Hannah, and she was standing there, naked and beautiful and smiling, and all I could do was cry tears of joy and gratitude as I looked upon her finally.

"It's really you," I whispered.

Hannah smiled beautifully. "Hello, Ethan."

"Hannah…"

I could still hardly believe she was standing in front of me after all this time. After I'd thought I'd lost her forever.

"Are you okay?" she asked as she held her hand out, and when I took it, she helped me get to my feet so I was finally standing in front of her.

"I—I'm fine," I said as I stared into her eyes, glad when I could see no trace of Xaglath in them. "I'm sorry, Hannah. I'm sorry for what I did to you. This is all my fault."

Hannah merely smiled as she placed her warm hand on my cheek. "I know why you did it. I understand."

"Hannah, no, I—"

She placed one finger against my lips to shush me. "I'm here now. That's all that matters."

Slowly, I pulled her hand away from me so I could lean in and put my arms around her, pulling her soft, warm body into me. "I didn't think I'd ever see you again," I whispered.

"Your faith in me is the reason I'm standing here," she said. "If it weren't for you, I'd be lost to the darkness forever."

"If it weren't for me—"

"Don't. What's done is done. It's time to move forward now."

"No, it isn't!" Yagami screamed.

Without us noticing, he had moved behind his desk, and he was now leaning over it with a gun in his hand. From his wild eyes, I could see what he was going to do. Before I could even shout for Hannah to move or pull her out of the way, Yagami fired twice, both bullets hitting Hannah in the back.

"NO!" I screamed.

Hannah's eyes went wide with the shock of getting shot, but she didn't fall. She didn't register any pain in her face, either.

Instead, she turned to face Yagami, who was on his feet now as he aimed the gun at her once more and fired another three shots, every one of which Hannah took in the chest.

But as she calmly walked toward Yagami—who looked more shocked than Hannah did at this point—I looked at her back and saw the bullets that entered her push their way out of her body again, the holes they'd created in her flesh closing up, leaving hardly a blemish on her skin.

As she carried on walking toward Yagami, the other three bullets fell to the floor.

I could only stand and shake my head in amazement, grateful that Hannah was unharmed.

"Why won't you die, you bitch?" Yagami screamed out in frustration, raising the gun again so he could shoot her once more, but as he started firing—the noise deafening as it echoed through the room, the air filling with gunpowder smoke—Hannah raised her hand and held it so her palm faced outward. This time, the bullets Yagami fired didn't get a chance to enter her body, for they were stopped in mid-air, where they then fell harmlessly to the ground. It was the same trick that Xaglath had employed against Yagami's men in the street that night.

In frustration, Yagami threw the gun at Hannah, who avoided it by moving swiftly to the side.

"I'll get you now!" he raged and grabbed a katana from the display rack on the window ledge, sliding the long blade out of it's *saya*, letting the *saya* fall before jumping up onto his desk and then leaping off of it, the sword held high as he brought it down toward Hannah's head with a scream of effort.

Hannah, as calmly as I've seen anyone do anything, caught the blade between her palms before it could touch her skull. She then held the sword there for a second as Yagami struggled to bring it down onto her, failing miserably.

Then he just seemed to give up, the fight finally gone out of him as he let go of the sword and sank to his knees. Hannah lowered the katana and held it in one hand by her side, saying nothing as she stared down at Yagami.

"Just do it," he said in defeat. "Kill me."

Hannah took a few steps forward until she was standing right over him. For a second, I thought she was going to do as he asked as she held up the katana, but instead, she tossed the sword away.

Yagami had his head bowed almost in shame now, and Hannah stretched out her hand and gently lifted his chin to raise his head, showing the tears in his eyes, and the disgrace on his face. "Hannah..." he began.

"Shh," Hannah said quietly. "I forgive you."

Yagami stared at her for a long moment, and then burst into tears, sobbing as he seemed to sink down into himself.

I watched all this happen with mixed feelings, to say the least. I didn't share Hannah's sense of forgiveness, and nor did I feel any sympathy for Yagami. He had tried to kill Hannah after all, his supposed daughter, and before that, he had been happy to keep her as a demon, using her for his own ends. He didn't deserve forgiveness. As far as I was concerned, Yagami only deserved one thing.

So as Hannah turned away from him and started walking toward the door, I spotted my gun lying on the floor, not three feet away from me. Without giving it a second thought, I went and picked up the gun before walking straight to Yagami with it.

"Ethan—" Hannah started to say.

"She may forgive you," I said to Yagami as he looked up at me, and I pointed the gun at his head, "but I don't."

Without hesitation, I squeezed the trigger and shot Yagami point-blank, his blood and brains spraying all over his desk as he fell back dead onto the floor. I stood for a second, staring down at him, before turning to look at Hannah.

"I forgave him," she said.

"He didn't deserve your forgiveness after everything he did to you."

"Everyone deserves forgiveness," she said, giving me a pointed a look.

I stared back at her. "Not everyone."

"ETHAN, YOU BEAUTIFUL BASTARD, YOU DID IT!"

Haedemus was practically jumping up and down as Hannah and I walked out of the Yakuza building, Hannah now wearing my coat.

"Just about," I said to him as I looked at Hannah. "It was a close call."

"Hello, Haedemus," Hannah said as she stroked his head, though Haedemus still seemed a little wary.

"It's great to see you, Hannah," he said. "Though I have to ask, where is Xaglath? Is she still...*in you?*"

"Xaglath will always be a part of me," Hannah said.

"So she could still take over?" Haedemus asked, sounding worried now.

Hannah shook her head. "No, my powers lie with me now that I've been reminded of my True Name."

"So balance has been restored?" I asked her.

"I think so," she said, smiling.

"Well, let's bloody hope so," Haedemus said. "For I never want to see that bitch Xaglath ever again. My, the things she did. How much do you remember, Hannah?"

"Not much," she said.

"Oh, well, that's probably for the best."

"We should get out of here," I said, "before Yagami's men turn up. God knows what they'll do when they find their boss dead." I looked at Hannah. "I seem to remember you mentioning he had a son. Where is he?"

Hannah shook her head like she didn't know. "Japan, maybe? Yagami never really spoke of him. I think they may have had a falling out."

"Well, you can rest assured he'll be back here when he finds out his father is dead," I said.

"Oh great," Haedemus said. "So there's another war in the pipeline then?"

I shrugged. "If there is, we'll deal with it. Right now, I just want a drink. Let's go back to my place."

"I've been thinking," Haedemus said as he started transporting Hannah and me back to my apartment.

"Always a bad sign," I said.

"Shut up, Ethan," he said. "I've been thinking you should find somewhere else to live, somewhere I can interact freely with you all. I'm sick of waiting in alleyways while people languish in their cozy homes."

"So, what do you suggest?" I asked as Hannah hugged my back, her warmth and touch feeling so good right now.

"I don't know," he said. "Maybe a house in the country-side, with a stable...and a few lovely mares. That sounds nice."

"Hmm, lovely."

"Don't be flippant, Ethan. We're a family now. You need to upgrade your living arrangements."

"A family?" I said, not wholly opposed to the idea.

"Yes," he said. "Like it or not, Ethan, that's what we are now. A family."

"I agree," Hannah said as she hugged me tightly.

I couldn't help but smile. "A family it is then."

WHEN WE GOT BACK, HANNAH AND I WENT INSIDE THE apartment while Haedemus reluctantly stayed outside, and for once, I actually felt bad about leaving him there. Before we went inside, he made me promise to consider finding somewhere to live that was more amenable to his needs. To appease him, I said I would.

The Hellbastards went pretty wild when they saw Hannah walk in, immediately surrounding her and hugging her legs like kids who hadn't seen their mother in weeks. I indulged them for a bit while I got myself and Hannah a drink, before banishing them back to the couch where they previously where watching cartoons. Reluctantly, they did as they were told while Hannah and I went into the kitchen for a little privacy, both of us taking a seat at the small table in there.

Now that Hannah was back and things had begun to settle, I couldn't help feeling a little awkward as we both sat in silence for a while. All I could think about was the fact that I'd shot her and had caused all this mess in the first place.

Hannah, no doubt sensing my guilt, broke the silence by saying, "I meant what I said earlier. What happened before, it's over with now. You don't have to feel bad about it."

"But I do," I said. "I mean, I shot you, for Christ's sake."

She shrugged slightly. "You thought I arranged to have your wife and daughter killed. You were angry. You weren't thinking straight."

"Maybe not. It still doesn't excuse what I did. I jumped to conclusions when I shouldn't have."

"So who was in the video pretending to be me?"

"Some Spreak as far as I know."

"Spreak?"

"A Spell Freak. A warlock."

"Do you know why he did it?"

I shook my head. "Not yet, but I'll find out."

"I'm surprised you haven't confronted him yet."

"It's not that easy," I said. "This guy is powerful. I went rushing in last time and look what happened."

"Fair point."

"Anyway, I'll get the bastard, once I figure out a plan."

"If you need my help…"

I nodded. "Of course, but I think you should take some time. You've been through a lot."

"So have you," she said. "I can see it in your face."

"Things have happened. I've been kicked off the force for a start."

She raised her eyebrows in surprise. "Really? I didn't think they'd do it."

"Well, they did."

"I guess I'm not a cop anymore either then."

"That's probably a safe bet."

"Even if I could go back, I wouldn't. What would be the point without you there? We were partners."

"We still are…I hope."

Hannah put her hand on mine and smiled. "Of course we are."

I remained silent for a moment, enjoying the feeling of her hand on mine, before asking, "So what do you remember about the last while?"

"Not much. Bits and pieces. From the moment you shot me that night, it's all seems like some crazy dream."

"You remember killing those Yakuza, and blowing up their cars? And saving me from the werewolves?"

She frowned as if trying to remember. "I don't. Did I... hurt you?"

"Not really," I said. "It wasn't you anyway, was it?"

"It was a side of me, I guess, that took over completely, facilitated by my hurt and anger."

"So who or what are you now?" I asked her as I refilled our glasses.

"I'm...Hannah," she said, as if it was that simple, also looking a little offended that I would even ask. "I mean, we are who we chose to be, right?"

I lifted my glass and held it out toward her. "That sounds good enough to me."

She smiled as she chinked my glass with her own. "And me."

"So listen," I said. "The way you healed me earlier. Could you do that again?"

"I'm...not sure," she said. "I was my original celestial self when I did that. Why do you ask?"

"It's Cal. He's sick. He's dying."

Hannah stared at me in shock. "Oh. I'm sorry, Ethan."

"Do you think maybe you could try to heal him as you did me?"

"I could try, but—"

"You can't promise anything. Of course."

"I'm sorry, Ethan. You must be devastated."

"It hasn't been easy."

"I wish I could've been there for you."

"You're here now," I said, just as my phone rang inside my coat pocket, which Hannah was still wearing. She fished the phone out and handed it to me. "Speak of the devil. It's Cal. Cal, hey—"

"Not Cal, asshole," said a gruff voice.

I jumped to my feet immediately. "Who the fuck is this? Where's Cal?"

"You know who this is," the male voice said. "We met the other night when your demon bitch killed our leader."

"What the fuck do you want?" I asked him as I glanced at Hannah, who was looking at me in confusion now. "What have you done with Cal? If you've hurt him, I swear to—"

"The old guy is right here. Say hello, old man."

Cal's voice came over the phone, strained, sounding like he was in pain. "Don't come here, Ethan!" he shouted. "They'll kill—" There was a grunt of pain as if someone had hit him.

"Cal!" I shouted.

The other guy came back on the phone. "You better get over here now," he said, "or we kill the old man. Come alone. If we see any sign of that demon bitch, or anyone else for that matter, the old man is dead. We'll be waiting."

The line went dead, and I stared at Hannah for a moment. "They have Cal."

"Who?" she asked.

"The werewolves."

"What werewolves?"

"The ones from the other night. I don't have time to explain. I have to go."

"Wait, Ethan," Hannah said. "You're going alone?"

"I have to. They'll kill him if I don't."

"But.. they'll kill you as well. You know that."

I stared at her, knowing she might be right. "It's a chance I'll have to take."

Before she could say anything else, I rushed out of the apartment and went to save my friend.

22

Despite Haedemus insisting that he take me to the scrap yard, I took the Dodge there instead. The guy on the phone had said to come alone, so that's what I was going to do. I didn't want the mutts freaking out when I rode in on a Hell Beast, least they think the demon they're so afraid of wasn't far behind. I already knew the werewolves wouldn't need much of an excuse to kill Cal, so I wasn't about to give them one.

Darkness had fallen when I reached the scrap yard. Outside, the sky was clear, and the air cold, with hardly a breeze as the full moon shone its silvery light over everything. The werewolves had picked a good time to do this. They could transform themselves anytime, but they were particularly powerful during a full moon, not to mention notoriously more bloodthirsty.

I didn't know how many of the werewolves there were waiting on me as I navigated the Dodge along the dirt tracks that wound through the mountains of scrap metal. Nor did I know what was going to happen. My only concern was saving Cal.

Beyond that, I didn't know.

The werewolves were waiting for me outside Cal's trailer.

As I pulled up, I counted at least ten of the bastards standing around, all men except for the woman who had made first contact with me a few nights ago. My eyes settled on her face first as I slowly got out of the car. She stared at me for a second and then looked away, uncomfortable with what was happening, but having no choice but to go along with the rest of the pack.

And what was happening was, Cal was on his knees in the dirt as the werewolves formed a semi-circle around him. Anger rose in me as I saw the blood on his face and naked torso, the claw marks across his chest and shoulders.

Motherfuckers.

As I stood by the car, I made a point of not making eye contact with any of them, except for Cal. "You alright, Cal?" I asked him, trying to seem calm, though inside I was seething.

Cal raised his weary head, seeming not to recognize me for a moment, before saying, "You dumb bastard. You shouldn't have come here. They're gonna fucking kill ya."

One of the werewolves stepped forward and stood behind Cal. He was a massive man in his early thirties with dark hair and a beard, wearing a leather jacket, his barrel chest bursting out of it. He was clearly the new pack leader. His dark, wolfish eyes fell on me as I remained by the car.

"Glad you could join us, asshole," he said in a gruff voice, a voice I recognized from the phone. "You better be alone this time, or…" He grabbed Cal by the hair and pulled his head back, gripping Cal's neck in a clawed hand as if he was going to rip the older man's throat out.

"Let him go," I said as I started to walk toward them. "You don't need him. You have me now."

"No," the pack leader said. "You're wrong. We have both of you."

Before I knew what was happening, two pack members grabbed Cal and started dragging him across the ground toward one of the huge mounds of scrap metal nearby. "Wait!" I shouted. "What the hell are you—"

Something hit from me from behind, knocking me to the ground, though I broke my fall with my forearms and rolled over onto my back.

Standing over me were two more pack members, their faces half-transformed, their eyes blazing yellow as they growled down at me, showing me their pointed teeth.

Before I knew it, both of them dived on me and started raining down blows like they were working out in the gym, their huge fists powered by powerful arms as they battered me relentlessly. All I could do was try to cover my face with my arms as the punches kept coming.

It was inevitable that more than one would connect with my head, and soon, I was lying in a daze, half-unconscious, and unable to defend myself properly.

"Enough!" I heard the pack leader shout. "Get him up!"

"Ah, come on, Linc," one of my assailants said. "We just getting started here."

"Don't worry," Linc said. "You'll get another chance soon enough. For now, I want him to watch the old man die. Get him up."

"No…" I mumbled as blood spilled from my mouth.

"Shut up!"

A heavy boot came down on my gut, forcing the air from my lungs, and I started coughing and wheezing as each of my arms was grabbed, and I was dragged across the dirt just like Cal was.

A moment later, I was brought to a halt, and someone behind me grabbed me by the hair and yanked my head up so I could see what was ahead of me.

And what was ahead of me was Cal.

The werewolves had constructed a makeshift cross out of scrap metal, which they'd stuck into the ground. Cal was tied to it with thin wire wrapped around his wrists and ankles, his arms spread out like Jesus himself. His head hung down to one side as if he didn't have the energy to hold it up any longer.

As if he'd given up.

He was done, and he knew it.

And so did I.

I struggled against the three guys holding me, but between them, they were far too strong, ensuring I didn't stand a chance of escaping their clutches.

I had no choice but to stay on my knees and watch what happened next.

And what happened next was the worst thing I've ever had to witness.

One by one, each of the pack members took turns in going up to Cal as he hung on that makeshift crucifix, and one by one, they swiped at him, raking their claws across his flesh, slicing him open as surely as any razor.

"Stop this!" I roared.

"Keep watching, asshole," Linc said, standing next to me now, sounding like he was enjoying my anguish. They all were. "This is half the price you pay for fucking with us. The other half you'll pay with your life."

Another pack member approached Cal and raked his claws slowly down Cal's face, causing Cal to scream as I've never heard him scream before.

In a rage, and with tears streaming down my face, I struggled to break free from my captors, but the harder I struggled, the harder they held me, until Linc punched me in the side of the head, causing me to go limp for a moment, though the person behind me didn't allow my head to drop forward. He continued to hold me up so I could look upon Cal, who by this stage was covered in so much blood, his whole body sliced up so much, I was almost certain he was dead until I heard a moan escape from his mouth.

"Shit," someone said. "The old guy sure can take some punishment."

"Keep watching," Linc said quietly into my ear. "Because you're next, asshole."

Shifting my eyes away from Cal, I caught the eye of the woman, who looked even more disturbed by this whole thing than she did earlier. With my eyes, I pleaded with her to make all this stop, but once again, she dropped her gaze and moved away to where I couldn't see her.

"Is he dead yet?" one of the guys holding me said. "I wanna see how much this asshole right here can take before he starts crying like a fucking bitch."

"Fuckin-A!"

"Yeah!"

"Check the old guy," Linc said, and I watched with dread as one of the pack members felt Cal for a pulse.

"Jesus," the guy said. "He's still fuckin' hanging in there. You fuckin' believe that? I mean, he looks like shredded fuckin' beef!"

"Leave him there," Linc said. "He'll soon die on his own, anyway." He stepped around in front of me and smiled. "You ready to get what's comin', asshole?"

I spat blood at him. "Fuck you!"

Linc continued to smile. "Yeah, we'll see how much of that attitude you keep in a minute." He crouched down, so his head was level with mine. "We're gonna do something a little different with you." His eyes moved up to the men holding me. "Let him go."

A second later, I was dumped forward onto the ground, and when I got up, I saw that I was encircled by the whole pack, including the woman. Every one of them then stripped off their clothes, laying them in piles behind them.

Then as I watched in horror, they all began to transform themselves, their bodies shifting and changing shockingly fast, until I was no longer encircled by men, but by monsters, each of them growling and roaring at me, some of them throwing their heads back so they could howl at the full moon hanging massive above us.

Then, one at a time, they started coming at me.

The first werewolf broke from the circle and ran at me with shocking speed as if he was going to railroad me into next week. I did my best to dodge him by jumping to one side, but his claws caught me across the abdomen as he ran past, slicing through my clothes and into my flesh, causing me to yell in pain.

Barely a second later, another of the pack charged me from the side, barreling into me so fast I somersaulted in the air before crash-landing on my back.

Despite the pain and shock, I jumped immediately to my feet again, knowing if I stayed down, I was done for.

The next one who came at me grabbed me by the shoulders as if he was about to lift me and toss me, but before he could, I jammed my thumbs into both of his large eyes and pressed as hard as I could as a satisfying howl of pain came from the werewolf's mouth. With my thumbs buried to the hilt in his eye sockets, I drove the werewolf back away from me, and then kicked him in the chest, sending him careening back into the circle again.

After that, they came at me faster, leaving less time between each attack. Sometimes I would get the better of one of them, but mostly, they were too fast and too strong for me to handle, especially with there being so many.

Before long, it was like being caught inside a meat grinder, with claws slicing me in all directions, and massive bodies slamming into me, ensuring I remained disoriented the whole time.

Breathing hard and bleeding all over, it felt like I'd been inside the circle for hours, even though I knew that only minutes had probably passed.

As the werewolves kept coming, sometimes in twos or threes, I soon had to admit that I couldn't keep defending myself against them for much longer. It was like a clowder of cats playing with a single mouse, and I didn't stand a chance.

Sooner or later, one of the werewolves would deliver a blow that I couldn't come back from, or I'd end up bleeding to death from the multitude of wounds on my body.

As I desperately moved around trying to avoid the onslaught of attacks, I would occasionally catch a glimpse of Cal, who was still tied to the makeshift cross, his ravaged body unmoving, leaving me doubting he was even still alive.

The attacks continued unabated, blow after bloody blow until I could take no more. After a particularly devastating swipe to my head, I fell to the ground for the final time, unable to get up again.

Until Linc, the pack leader—bigger than all the rest— emerged from the circle and pulled me up off the ground with his massive hands, holding me up because I didn't have the strength left to hold myself up anymore.

His face was in front of me, his eyes boring into me, and I realized he had shifted out of his full wolf form so he could talk.

But even as he spoke, I didn't listen. I couldn't tell you a single word he said to me, for my thoughts were elsewhere. I was thinking about Callie, picturing her smiling face and bright eyes.

If I was going to go out, I was going to go out thinking of her, not some stinking werewolf.

But then something pulled me out of my thoughts.

My eyes came into focus for a brief moment, and I was able to see past the werewolf holding me, to the dirt track running between the piles of scrap.

Something was coming, and at first, I thought I must've been hallucinating. I even blinked a few times to see if the moving shape would go away, but it didn't. It just kept getting closer, and the closer it got, the more into focus it became until I could finally tell what it was.

A galloping black shape in the night.

Haedemus.

And there was someone on his back.

Someone small and holding a blade out to the side that glinted like silver under the bright moonlight.

But even as Haedemus drew near, I still couldn't be sure if I was hallucinating or not. Nor could I be sure who was riding him.

At first, I thought it was Hannah, but as Haedemus drew ever closer, I saw it wasn't Hannah. This person was smaller and had short, dark hair.

It looked like a boy riding Haedemus.

And as Haedemus burst through the circle of shocked werewolves, I smiled to myself as if to say, "Huh."

Because it was Daisy on top of Haedemus, and out of her mouth came a bloodcurdling scream, a battle cry like none I've ever heard as she raised her shining blade high above her.

Linc let me go then, as he spun around to see what was happening.

But by the time he turned around, it was too late.

As I fell to the side, Daisy charged toward Linc and swung her blade, lopping Linc's head clean off.

I watched as if in slow motion, as Linc's head spun around in the air before thumping down into the dirt. Then his massive body toppled over like a felled oak, thudding down beside me.

WHAT CAME NEXT CAN ONLY BE DESCRIBED AS BLOODY CHAOS.

While the werewolves recovered from the shock of seeing their leader beheaded, Daisy started attacking them, expertly steering Haedemus as she used her other hand to swing her sword—one of Cal's swords—at the werewolves who had begun attacking back.

Haedemus himself was spearing everything in sight with his horn, and stamping downed werewolves with his enormous hooves.

And then, as I sat in the middle of all this as if in a dream, the Hellbastards came charging out of nowhere and started attacking the werewolves as well, Toast sending fireballs flying everywhere as the rest of them fearlessly jumped on whatever werewolf was closest, biting and battering, clawing and tearing, and in Snot Skull's case, vomiting.

And to make matters even more surreal, the Hellbastards were all wearing their superhero costumes. Batman, Spiderman, Superman, Robin, and Wonder Woman had all arrived to save the day and fuck shit up.

As this dream-like scenario continued to play out, in my concussed state I watched as two werewolves got lifted into the air as if by some invisible hand, and I knew then that Hannah had entered the fray.

And indeed, she appeared a moment later, just before she used her powers to rip apart the two werewolves she had control of.

Throughout all of this, I continued to sit on the ground, looking around in a near daze as blood and fur and limbs and everything else flew past me as if in a blender.

Then at some point, it all stopped.

The chaos subsided.

Silence descended.

Beautiful silence.

Which was broken by Cracka standing next to me.

"Your friendly neighborhood Spiderman has come to save you, boss!" he said, his tiny costume covered in werewolf blood and god knows what else.

Smiling, I patted the little demon on the head. "Thanks, Cracka."

"You don't look too good there, Ethan," Haedemus said as he stood over me. "Are you—"

A scream from behind us cut him off before he could finish.

It was Daisy.

And suddenly I realized why she was screaming.

"Cal—" I said as I struggled to get up.

"Let me help you." Hannah came over and helped me get painfully to my feet, every inch of my body feeling like it was on fire.

But I didn't care about the pain. I just needed to get to Cal.

As I hobbled across the dirt with Hannah's help, I saw Daisy standing before the metal crucifix, just staring at Cal, and I thought, *He's dead...*

But incredibly, he wasn't.

When I approached with Hannah, Cal somehow managed to lift his head up as he tried to say something.

"We have to get him down," I said.

The Hellbastards were on it, climbing up the cross and undoing the wire that bound Cal's wrists. Then Hannah held Cal up as the Hellbastards undid the wire tying his ankles to the steel post until finally, Cal was free, and Hannah laid him down.

Hardly able to stand myself, I all but crawled across the dirt and sat beside Cal, lifting his head as gently as I could and placing it in my lap. I'd never seen someone in such a bloody mess.

"Cal..." I whispered. "I'm so sorry."

"I can try to heal him," Hannah said quietly.

"Yes," Daisy said as tears rolled down her cheeks. "Save him."

It was then that Cal somehow found the strength to reach up and grip my wrist, opening his swollen eyes to look at me, and I realized he wanted to say something. Leaning down, I put my ear near his mouth.

"*Let...me...go,*" he whispered.

I lifted my head to look into his eyes. "Cal, no," I whispered back. "Hannah can——"

I felt his grip tighten on my wrist. "*No…*" he insisted in a hoarse whisper.

I could only stare down at him as his eyes closed again, and tears started streaming out of my own.

Up until then, I'd felt his body rising and falling as he struggled to keep breathing. But as his eyes closed, that almost imperceptible movement slowed.

And then stopped altogether.

When I realized he had gone, I broke down as tears flooded my eyes, and I sat gently rocking his head back and forth in my lap, as though doing so would somehow bring him back.

At that point, everyone else walked away, leaving me alone with Cal, unable to believe that my one true friend in all the world was now gone forever.

A WHILE LATER, AFTER I COULD FINALLY BRING MYSELF TO LET Cal go, I staggered across the yard, picking my way through bodies, to find that Daisy and the Hellbastards were crowded around somebody——a surviving werewolf.

The woman.

Daisy had her sword to the woman's throat as she threatened to kill her.

"Wait," I croaked as I approached them.

Daisy stared at me. "She's the last one. We finished all the rest. Toast is going to burn their bodies."

"Not her," I said.

The woman, a naked, bloody mess herself, looked at me gratefully.

"What?" Daisy said. "But she's one of them. Cal is dead

because of her and her pack." She pressed the sword harder against the woman's throat.

Painfully, I crouched down to look into the woman's eyes. "I trust I won't ever see you again if I let you go?"

The woman nodded. "I never wanted this."

"I know." I looked up at Daisy. "Let her go, Daisy."

Daisy stared at me before finally removing her sword from the woman's throat and stepping back, as did the Hellbastards. Cautiously, she got to her feet and backed away a little. She stopped for a second to stare at me and then nodded once before turning around and scurrying off into the night.

"Why did you let her go?" Daisy asked.

"Because not everyone deserves to die," I said, and then collapsed onto the ground as blackness swallowed me up.

23

I came to several hours later in Cal's trailer to find myself naked in bed, my body covered in claw marks, bruises, and several deeper wounds that appeared to have been partially healed.

"I did my best," Hannah said, who I noticed was sitting in a chair next to me. "You were in bad shape. You still are."

"I'll live," I croaked, my throat parched. "I always do."

Hannah smiled. "I know you do, though Lord knows how."

After she gave me some water, I sat up in the bed, groaning in pain as I did so. "Where's Daisy?" I asked.

"With Cal," she said. "We moved his body into your trailer."

"Is she okay?"

Hannah shrugged. "She's distraught. I had no idea she and Cal were so close."

My heart ached just thinking about him, and about Daisy. "I guess they got close in the short time he knew her."

"Something is going on with her. She seems very different."

"I know. She's…changing. More so every day, it seems."

"She's like a different person."

"That's 'cause she is in a way. Have I told you about Mytholites yet?"

"I'm not sure. If you did, I can't remember. I remember being aware of them when I was Xaglath. They have powers, right?"

"Yeah. I'll explain it to you later."

Hannah stopped me as I went to get out of bed. "What are you doing? You need to rest."

Ignoring her, I gritted my teeth against the pain and swung my legs onto the floor. "I have to bury my friend."

Hannah nodded. "Okay. At least let me help you."

"I'll have to wear some of Cal's clothes," I said as I stood up. "No doubt mine are in tatters."

"They are," Hannah said as she looked around for clothes for me to wear, finding a pair of jeans and an old Zeppelin T-shirt, handing them to me.

"Why did you all come here?" I asked her after I was dressed, the smell of Cal's clothes almost bringing tears to my eyes again. "I told you I had to come alone."

"Yeah," she said. "And look where that got you. Almost killed."

"I thought they'd at least have let Cal go."

Hannah gave me a look. "Really, Ethan? For such a smart man, you can be incredibly stupid sometimes."

I nodded as if I knew full well what she was talking about. "How did Daisy end up here? And what's with her new haircut, not to mention the leather body armor she's wearing? I have no idea where she would even get that."

"Well, she got it from somewhere, and as for the haircut, I don't know about that either."

"You told her where I'd gone?"

"I told her you'd gone to save Cal. Once she heard that, she was gone, even taking Haedemus with her. I didn't know she could ride so well."

"She couldn't. Another skill she just acquired from nowhere."

"Anyway, I took the Hellbastards and went after her."

"What in?"

"I stole a car."

I nodded. "Nice."

"I'll return it, don't worry."

I smiled and shook my head at her as we went outside, the bright morning sunlight hurting my eyes as I squinted against it. I stood for a few moments, basking in the comforting rays, suddenly realizing that everything I could see around me was now mine.

"Where do you intend to bury Cal?" Hannah asked as she stood beside me.

"His favorite place," I said. "The Secret Garden."

THE SECRET GARDEN WAS LOCATED AT THE VERY BACK OF THE scrap yard. It was about half an acre of cleared land that had all manner of plants and herbs growing in it, including several of Cal's beloved marijuana plants, all of which looked ready for harvesting at this point.

In the center of the garden was an oak tree that Cal had planted years ago. He always maintained that when he died, this was where he wanted to be buried, right next to the oak tree. He'd even left a patch of ground free for the grave.

As I wasn't fit to do so, it fell on Hannah and the Hellbastards to dig the grave. While they went about that, I sat with Daisy in a different part of the garden, on a bench that was nestled inside a little grove surrounded by fruit trees.

"Are you okay?" I asked Daisy as she stared around the garden.

"It's beautiful in here, isn't it?" she said as if she hadn't heard me.

"Yeah, it is."

"It's like all that hard iron out front was Cal on the outside, and all of this beauty was Cal on the inside, don't you think?"

I smiled. "That's a nice way of putting it, and true, I guess."

"I'm really going to miss him." She looked at me for the first time since we had sat down. "Does that sound weird? We didn't even know each other that long, but he taught me so much in that short time."

Putting my arm around her, I pulled her gently into me. "Not at all. Cal had a soft spot for you. So do I."

She pulled away from me then. "You have to promise me you'll never do anything like that again. I don't want to lose you as well, Ethan. I—I can't."

There were tears in her eyes now.

"I promise," I said. "And don't worry. If a pack of were-wolves can't kill me, what can?"

She smiled but said, "You know what I mean."

"I know what you mean."

"Good."

"So, what's with the new haircut? It's very…"

"Boyish?"

"I was gonna say short, but now that you mention it, it is boyish. I'm still getting used to it, I guess."

"So am I," she said. "My mom hates it. She thinks I'm gay or something."

"Okay," I said.

"I mean, she hardly notices much else. She's doing some heavy drugs at the moment."

"Any reason for that? I thought she'd dialed everything back."

"She did, for a short while. Now she's not. She barely even notices if I'm there or not these days."

"That must be hard for you."

Daisy shrugged her shoulders slightly as if she didn't know how else to react. "It's the way it's always been, I guess. Things will never change. One day I'll wake up and I'll find her dead on the couch."

"Jesus, Daisy, don't say shit like that."

"You don't live with her. You don't know what it's like. The constant criticism, the put-downs, the—"

"What?"

"Nothing. I don't want to talk about it anymore."

I nodded as we both fell into silence for a few moments, the serenity of the garden seeming to wash over us, creating a stillness that made it okay to be quiet.

"I think I know who I am now," Daisy said eventually, breaking the silence. "Or at least, who I'm supposed to be. I had a dream about it last night."

"Okay. Who?"

"I can't believe I'm even saying this, but Joan of Arc."

Daisy stared at me like she expected me to laugh. But how could I when a version of Jack the Ripper was running about out there? Not to mention a shark goddess, the living embodiment of Osiris, and god knows who else. "That...makes a lot of sense, actually. The visions, the fighting abilities."

"The haircut."

I laughed. "Yeah, the haircut."

"I'm scared, Ethan," she said, staring up at me.

"That's okay," I said as I put my arm around her. "What you're going through, I'm sure it isn't easy. But hey, you've got me, and you've got Hannah. We're here for you."

"You forgot Haedemus and the Hellbastards."

"Yeah, how could I forget them? We're just one big happy F-ed up family."

Daisy laughed, then said, "I wouldn't have it any other way."

"Neither would I kiddo," I said. "Neither would I."

It didn't take Hannah and the Hellbastards long to dig the grave. When they were done, Daisy helped me carry Cal's body—which was wrapped in a sheet—to the Secret Garden, before we all helped lower him down into the grave.

We stood for a few moments, me with tears running down my cheeks as Daisy and Hannah stood next to me, with Haedemus and the Hellbastards (sans superhero costumes thankfully) standing on the other side.

We all stood in silence for a while as we stared down into the open grave before I said something.

"Before I met Cal, I was lost," I said. "I was an angry, scared kid, terrified of where I would end up. Then I met Cal, and he terrified me as well."

Everyone chuckled at that before I carried on.

"But anyway, despite me being a colossal pain in the ass, he took me in, and he showed me how to control all that anger I had, how to channel it into something worthwhile. And while we had our disagreements over the years, he taught me many things. He taught me how to be a man when no one else would, and for that, I'll be forever grateful."

I had a bottle of Cal's favorite beer with me, which I poured into the grave. "I hope you're at peace, my friend, wherever you are."

After a moment, Daisy stepped forward and said, "I'd like to sing something if that's okay."

"Of course," I said, slightly surprised, having no idea she even could sing.

Daisy smiled at me and then took a second to compose herself before beginning to sing in the most beautifully haunting voice I've ever heard, surprising me further by singing "Seasons" by Chris Cornell.

When she was done, she bowed her head and then bent

down to pick up a handful of dirt, which she threw into the grave.

"Goodbye, Cal," she said, before turning and walking away.

Soon, everyone else followed her, leaving me alone by the gravesite. "Goodbye, old friend," I said. "It was helluva ride indeed."

24

For the rest of the day, I mostly pottered around Cal's trailer, drinking beer and looking through the papers he'd left behind for me. There were the deeds to the land and scrap business, and the details of his various bank accounts, which combined, amounted to a hefty seven-figure sum. I had no idea Cal had accrued so much over the years, though I wasn't surprised by it either. He was the tightest son of a bitch I ever came across, spending nothing unless he had to.

It was a Sunday, so thankfully, none of the men had turned up for work. I called Petey, the guy that ran the scrap business for Cal, and told him the news, telling him that Cal had died in the night from his illness, which Cal had already informed Petey about anyway. Petey was obviously devastated by the news, but I assured him nothing would change, and that he would still run the business. I also told him to tell the rest of the scrap workers to take the coming week off, and that we would talk again once he came back. It was a difficult conversation for me, for it felt like losing Cal all over again.

Daisy was still distraught as well. She had gone home to see to her mother, who apparently had taken a fall last night and had hurt herself in the process.

Hannah had also gone off to sort some things out, firstly at the precinct. If she wasn't already let go, she said she would hand in her badge. After that, she wanted to sort things out at her apartment. She was planning on telling her landlord she would be moving out, assuming the landlord hadn't evicted her already given what happened the night I shot her.

Hannah would take my old trailer to live in from now on, while I would take Cal's. At least that way, we would still have our own space when we inevitably pissed each other off. Neither of us was under any illusions about the relationship we had. We were partners first, at least in my mind.

After that, we'd have to see what happened.

As for Haedemus, he took himself off somewhere because he said he "needed to think about his future" as if he had options. I was happy enough for him to go so he wasn't hanging around annoying me, given my fragile mental state at the moment.

And the Hellbastards, they were running around the yard somewhere, exploring their new home and probably terrorizing Cal's dogs, Ace and Apollo, both of whom I'd seen moping around the Secret Garden earlier, knowing full well that their beloved master was no longer around. I felt sorry for the two dogs, and I vowed to look after them from now on as they both whined and licked my face by Cal's grave.

When evening rolled around, and the sun set behind the mountains of scrap in the yard, I reluctantly made the decision to head down the precinct to do what I'd been putting off for days, which was to hand my badge in.

"Fuck it," I said as I sat outside with a beer in my hand, cigarette in the other. "It's time to move on. Maybe you were right, Cal. Maybe it's for the best I'm not a cop anymore. You always were right about everything."

Smiling at the nonetheless painful memory of him, I wearily stood up and groaned at the pain that still wracked my body. The werewolves had done a number on me good and proper. I was still amazed I'd taken so much punishment without dying. Hell, I probably would be dead if Hannah hadn't healed me, or partly healed me. She wasn't Jesus, after all. She was just a person like the rest of us, struggling to find where she fit into the world. She'd been through the mill so much, I doubted even *she* knew who she really was or what she was capable of.

But that's why we're all here, right? To find all that out, for good or bad.

As I headed toward the trailer to grab my coat and car keys, I heard my phone ringing inside. Thinking it might be Hannah, I quickened my step and went inside to answer it.

"Hello?" I said without looking at the caller ID.

"Ethan," said a breathy voice. "It's Vic."

"Vic?" I said, surprised to hear from her, but also knowing that something was wrong. "Are you okay? You sound—"

"Hurt? That's because I am."

"Tell me where you are. I'll come right now." I was already grabbing my coat and car keys and heading out the door.

"The slaughterhouse," she said, her voice weak.

"Which one?" I asked as I got into the car and put the phone on the dash, putting it on speaker so I could drive.

"Cas—"

"Castle Street, near the Red Light District?" I put the car in gear and sped off.

"Yes…and Ethan…"

"Yeah? Hold on, Vic. I'm coming."

"He's here."

I frowned at the phone, having a good idea of who she was talking about. "Who Vic?"

"The…Ripper."

Jesus.

"Alright, Vic. Can you stay safe till I get there?"

"He's …here…"

The line went dead.

"Fuck!"

I slammed the steering wheel and then called Hannah, who thankfully answered straight away as I drove the car through the open gates and out onto the road.

"Ethan," Hannah said. "I was just about to——"

"I need you to meet me at the slaughterhouse on Castle Street near the Red Light District right away," I told her.

"Why? What's——"

"Just get there. Now!"

Before she could say anything else, I quit the call and hit Vic's number, but all I got was her voicemail. "Fuck!"

Putting my foot down, I drove like a maniac toward the Red Light District and prayed Vic wasn't dead yet.

WHEN I REACHED THE SLAUGHTERHOUSE TWENTY MINUTES later, I drove through the already opened front gates and brought the Dodge to a screeching halt by the loading bay, noticing that the side entrance door was lying open.

Before exiting the car, I opened the glove compartment and took out the Glock 19 that was in there, ejecting the magazine to check if it was full before slamming it back in again.

I was about to close the glove compartment when I noticed the Karambit knife. The same one Daisy had got me for my birthday. I'd forgot I'd put the knife in there after I took it from Daisy the night she used it to kill Dormer. Taking it now, I put into my coat pocket before shutting the glove compartment.

Once I was outside, I hurried toward the open side entrance door with my gun held close to my chest, pausing in the doorway to look inside first.

The place was in darkness, so I blinked rapidly three times

to activate my infrared vision until I picked up a heat signature off to the left in the large packing room.

"Vic?" I called out in a hushed voice as I moved toward the heat signature, which seemed to be moving.

"Ethan…" a weak voice said.

"Vic." I hurried over to her as she lay on the floor, deactivating my infrared vision as I did. Although it was dark, I could still make out it was her lying on the cold floor, a pool of her blood around her. "Jesus, you're hurt bad."

Vic was dressed in her vigilante outfit, green and black, crafted from leather, and lined with kevlar. Unfortunately, her neck wasn't protected, and there was a slash wound across her throat, which would explain the huge amount of blood around her.

Placing my gun on the floor next to me, I put my hand over her wound and applied pressure on it, praying that Hannah would get here soon.

"He's …*here*," Vic whispered.

I couldn't help but look around when she said it. Was he really in here somewhere, or was Vic just babbling?

"Help is coming," I said. "Don't talk."

She grabbed my wrist. "*I…shot…him.*"

I was surprised to hear that. I didn't think Vic used guns. She always carried two batons with her when she went out as The Rook. Clearly, when it came to the Ripper, she didn't want to take any chances. "Okay," I said. "Stop talking now. You're gonna be okay, Vic."

A noise made me turn my head toward the side entrance door. With my other hand, I picked up the Glock and pointed it at the approaching figure, sighing when I realized it was Hannah.

"What's going on?" she asked as she crouched down beside me. "Who is this?"

"Her name's Vic," I said. "Her throat has been slashed.

She's lost a lot of blood. Can you help her, at least until she can get to a hospital?"

"*No...hospital*," Vic whispered.

"Just do what you can here," I said to Hannah. "Then take her to Wilshire. They'll just think she's another victim."

"A victim?"

"Of the Ripper. He's here. I'm going after him." I took my hand away from Vic's neck just as Hannah placed her own hand there.

"Be careful, Ethan," Hannah said.

"Save her. Please."

Hannah nodded. "I'll try."

25

After leaving Hannah with Vic, I made my way from the loading area into the cold storage room where dozens of animal carcasses hung on steel hooks from railings.

With the Glock held close to my chest, I paused in the doorway and looked around using my infrared vision. When nothing showed up in the darkness, I switched spectrums by blinking rapidly four times. If the Ripper was here, he wouldn't be able to hide from me.

Not for long anyway.

Slowly, cautiously, I made my way into the massive room, scanning for anything that contrasted against the darkness. The room was deathly silent, and every footstep sounded too loud to my ears. The smell of dead meat and disinfectant mingled in the freezing air that prickled the skin on my hands and face.

Then a noise above me and to the left made me look up at the walkway that ran along the side of the room.

I froze when I saw a white figure standing up there, perfectly still, like a ghost in my thermal imaging. A tall figure dressed in a cloak and top hat, with something long and metallic held by their side.

It was the Ripper.

Without hesitation, I pointed the Glock at him and fired twice in quick succession.

But before I'd even finished firing, the Ripper had vanished.

Just like that, he was gone.

What the fuck?

"You think you can catch me?" a voice said from somewhere, and I looked around until I spotted the white figure again, this time on the opposite walkway across the room.

Once again, I fired.

And again, the Ripper vanished.

"No one can catch me," the voice came again, sounding like it was behind me this time, and I spun and saw him standing by the doorway.

But even as I squeezed the trigger on the Glock, he had vanished once more.

Fuck! How is he doing that?

"No one could catch me back in London," the voice came again, seeming to echo around the whole room now, making it impossible to pinpoint where it was coming from. "And no one will catch me now."

I cried out as I felt something slash across my forearm—a blade—causing me to yelp in pain and drop my gun. But when I looked for the cause, no one was there.

Laughter echoed throughout the room.

Despite the blood pouring from my arm, I quickly picked up my gun and hurried over to hide among the hanging carcasses, thinking it would make things harder for the Ripper to ambush me if there was a bunch of dead cows in the way.

The bastard was enjoying this; otherwise, he'd be long gone by now. Maybe just evading capture wasn't enough for him anymore. Maybe he wanted to prove himself face to face, to show that he was the superior predator.

Whatever his motivations for hanging around here and

engaging in this game of cat and mouse with me, only one of us would leave this place alive.

And I would make sure it was me.

"Enough with the games, asshole," I said as I moved slowly among the carcasses. "Stop hiding and come out and face me. You think you're so superior? That you're the apex predator? Come and prove it!"

No sooner had I called him out than a carcass came flying toward me, sliding at speed along the railing until it hit me full on, sending me flying back into another carcass until I lost my balance and fell, the Glock releasing from my hand and skidding across the floor into the darkness.

"Shit!" I said.

But before I could even begin to search for the gun, the Ripper appeared above me, his ghostly white figure showing up in my thermal imaging like a malevolent ghost, his top hat making him seem supernaturally tall.

I could make out his features just enough to see that he was smiling.

I could also see the massive butcher knife he was holding out in front of him, pointing down at me.

"You think you can goad me into making a mistake?" he said as he suddenly lunged at me with the knife, driving it down toward my stomach before I could scramble back away from him.

Instinctively, I grabbed his wrist and forearm with both of my hands, but I wasn't quick enough to stop at least two inches of the blade penetrating my belly just below the solar plexus.

A scream left me as the point of the knife went in, but I held his arm tight to prevent it from going any further.

"Nothing can stop me," he said as he leaned his weight onto the knife, pushing it into me another fraction of an inch, causing me to scream in pain again. "Not even a bullet from that bitch's gun. The Rook." He laughed as he pushed harder on the knife. "I soon clipped her wings."

Realizing I had to do something before I ended up gutted like a fish, I suddenly remembered the Karambit knife in my coat pocket.

But to get it, I would have to release one hand from his arm, which would make it easier for him to push the knife further into my belly.

But I had no choice. It was that or die anyway.

So I released my grip from his arm and continued to hold on with my left hand while I used my right hand to get the knife out of my pocket, feeling for the release button, pressing it so the blade sprung out in my pocket. The Ripper was so intent on what he was doing he didn't hear the mechanism click.

But even though I now had the knife in my grip, he still seemed too far away for me to slash him with it.

I needed him closer.

Which meant allowing him to press down further on his own knife until he got to within striking distance.

Gritting my teeth, I released some of the pressure on his arm, and as I did, he pushed down as the knife went deeper into me.

I screamed with the pain, but my ploy had worked.

He was close enough now.

Within striking distance.

When the Karambit blade was turned to the right position, I pulled it out of my pocket as quickly as I could and then slashed his neck with it, the curved blade digging deep into his flesh and slicing through his carotid artery and most of his larynx, blood erupting immediately from the wound.

Letting go of the butcher knife, the Ripper slapped one hand onto his neck to try to stem the flow of blood from his carotid artery, staggering back away from me as he did so.

Bracing myself, I dropped the Karambit knife and then

pulled the butcher knife from my belly, crying out with the pain.

Still holding onto the knife, my hand slick with blood, I scrambled to my feet to see the Ripper leaning back against one of the hanging carcasses as blood continued to jet from his slashed neck.

Knowing this would be my only chance before he did his disappearing act, I charged at him with the butcher knife, screaming as I did so until the knife plunged into his belly.

Even in the thermal imaging, I could see the shock on his face as his top hat fell from his head and landed on the blood-soaked floor between us.

"Who's the apex predator now, motherfucker?" I said through clenched teeth as I forced the butcher knife further into him, using the last of my strength to jerk it upward, slicing through his insides until the blade reached his sternum, and then I pulled it out, and half his innards came spilling out along with it.

Breathing hard, I took a step back, still holding onto the knife just in case.

But I didn't need it.

The Ripper fell backward between two carcasses and landed on the floor.

With his final breath, he uttered, *"Death…is not…the end."*

"It is for you, motherfucker," I said.

A few seconds later, the Ripper was dead.

His reign of terror having finally ended.

26

Dripping blood from my stab and slash wounds, I left the body of the Ripper on the slaughterhouse floor while I went outside and popped the trunk on the Dodge, rummaging for a moment until I found a first aid kit. Then I wrapped a bandage around the slash wound on my forearm and stuck a gauze and some tape over the stab wound in my stomach. Both injuries needed proper medical attention, but they could wait.

I had other things to take care of first.

Grabbing my phone from the front seat, I called Hannah. "Are you at the hospital?" I asked her when she answered. "Is Vic okay?"

"She'll be fine," Hannah said. "I healed her wound a little before taking her here. The doctors are seeing to her now. They said she's stable, though she might have trouble speaking for a while. What about you? Did you find the Ripper?"

"I found him."

"Well, are you okay? You sound like you're in pain."

"I'm okay. Nothing a few stitches won't sort out."

"Do you want me to come to you? I'm just hanging around here…"

"No," I said. "Stay with Vic. Make sure she's okay. I'll come to you soon. There's just something I gotta do first."

~

A SHORT TIME LATER, I PULLED UP OUTSIDE THE POLICE precinct, got out of the car, and went around to the trunk. I was just about to pop the lid when a man approached from behind, a look of mild horror on his face as he took in all the blood on me.

"Are you alright?" the man asked, who was maybe in his fifties, dressed in a dark suit. I didn't pay him much attention.

"What's it to you?" I asked him, giving him a hard stare, in no mood for nosey strangers.

"Actually, I was just hoping to talk to you for a minute."

"I don't got time," I said and popped the trunk, revealing the Ripper's body inside, half his guts hanging out of his belly, a gaping wound in his neck.

"Dear God," the man behind me said. "Is that…"

"It's none of your fucking business," I snapped, turning to stare him down. "Now fuck off before you end up just like him."

Without waiting on a response, I turned around and lifted the dead body out of the trunk, struggling for a moment as I turned the corpse around and then hoisted it up onto my shoulder, before heading inside the precinct with it.

Needless to say, I turned heads as soon as I entered the building, every cop in the place staring at me with a mixture of horror and fascination as I made my way up the west stairs, passing the main conference room and then the bullpen, where every detective in the place, including Jim Routman, froze and stopped what they were doing to gawp at me as I carried on walking past them, paying them no attention as I went down the corridor until I reached the captain's office.

When I got there, I kicked the door open, to the shock of Captain Edwards, who was seated behind his desk.

"What the fuck?" he all but shouted. "Drake? What the fuck are you—"

I dumped the Ripper's body down on Edwards' desk so hard that the desk broke in half and blood from the body's open wounds splattered everywhere, including over the captain, who could only stand there as he stared down at the dead body, first in sheer horror, and then in recognition as he realized who it was that I had brought in, though that didn't make him any less angry.

Not that I cared as I stared hard at him.

"There's your fucking Ripper Tripper," I said to him, and then reached into my pocket and took out my badge, tossing it onto the body of the serial killer. "And there's my fucking badge. Have a nice life, Edwards."

Turning, I started to walk out of the office, with Edwards behind me screaming my name, demanding that I stop immediately. But I carried on walking past the crowd of cops that had gathered in the hallway, most of whom were staring at me with a mixture of shock and admiration.

"Stop right there, Drake!" Edwards screamed behind me, and I stopped and turned around slowly to see that the bastard was pointing his gun at me.

"Put that away, Edwards," I said. "We both know you've never even fired it."

"Somebody arrest him!" Edwards shouted. "Now!"

I stared at all the faces surrounding me. "Which one of you is gonna do it?" I asked as each of them dropped their gazes, reluctant to even make eye contact with me, never mind arrest me. "That's what I thought."

As I moved out of the hallway and walked past the bullpen, Edwards started roaring again behind me. "You think you'll get away with this, Drake?" he screamed. "You'll go to prison for this! I guarantee it!"

"Yeah, yeah," I said without turning to look at him. "Fuck you too, Edwards."

When I reached the stairs, somebody called my name, and I turned to see Routman behind me. "Ethan," he said, walking up to me with a smile on his face. "I don't know what you're on, but that was fucking awesome. The look on Edwards' face is one I'll never forget."

"Yeah, glad you enjoyed it, Jim," I said as I went to head down the stairs.

"Ethan, hold up." Routman came around and stood in front of me, blocking my way. "How'd you do it? How'd you catch the fucker?"

"I didn't," I said. "I just killed him when he tried to kill me."

"Don't worry. No one's gonna hold this against you. I mean, it's the fucking Ripper Tripper, right?"

"Yeah. I gotta get going, Jim."

I went to move past him again, but he stopped me once more, this time thrusting his hand out. "You might be a pain in the ass, Ethan, but this place is gonna miss you. Hell, I'll miss you."

Taking his hand, I shook it, even though mine was covered in blood, which Routman didn't seem to mind. "Thanks, Jim."

"Take care of yourself, Ethan."

"Yeah, you too, Jim."

Walking out of the precinct, I reflected this would be for the last time, but it didn't bother me anymore. I'd devoted ten years to being a cop.

It was time to move on.

When I reached the car, the man from earlier was still standing there waiting for me.

"It must've been a big surprise for everyone when you brought that body in," he said smiling.

"Yeah, like fucking Christmas," I said, stopping to stare at him. "Who the fuck are you again? And what do you want?"

The man reached inside his jacket and produced an ID wallet, flipping it open for me to see. "Raymond Bradley," he said. "FBI."

I stared at his ID and then at him. "Yeah? Whatta you want?"

"Well," he said, still smiling. "I'd like to offer you a job, Ethan."

I couldn't help but laugh. "Jesus Christ, are you serious right now? A job? You have to be kidding me."

"Why is that funny?"

I shook my head. "It just is. I mean, look at me. Do I look like an FBI guy to you?"

"No, not at all, but that's sorta the point," he said. "I've been following you closely for a while now, and you're exactly the kind of person I need."

"For what?"

"Well, we both know that not everything this city is as it seems," he said. "There are some powerful forces at play, supernatural forces you might say, with new ones emerging all the time. I've been tasked by the director to start looking into these forces, to investigate them, and if necessary, do something about them. We're the Federal government, after all, and it's our job to protect national security. If these forces aren't a threat to that national security, then I don't know what is. So I'm putting together a team, off the books, starting with you and your partner, Hannah Walker."

Puffing my cheeks out slightly, I could only nod at him. This was the last thing I expected to happen, to get recruited by the FBI of all people.

"Listen," I said. "It's not that I'm not interested—I am— but you caught me at a rough time. I just lost my best friend, and I'm also gonna need some time to consider things before I jump into anything, so—"

I stopped talking when I noticed a familiar face standing across the road. "Motherfucker…"

"Excuse me?" Bradley said.

"Not you," I said, my eyes on the person standing across the street.

The goddamn Spreak of all people. Was he following me? Trying to intimidate me or something?

Without saying anything else to Bradley, I started across the street in the direction of the dark-suited Spreak. "Hey!" I shouted.

"I'll be in touch," Bradley called, but I paid him no attention as I quickened my pace toward the asshole across the street who had now turned and walked up an alley.

When he disappeared into the alley, I ran after him, only to find that he had gone.

Vanished.

As I stood looking around in frustration, laughter suddenly began to echo around me, ceaseless and mocking, intended to make me feel small and helpless no doubt.

To make me feel like a fool for thinking I stood a chance against this person.

"Fuck you and your scare tactics!" I shouted, still looking around for the bastard, even though I knew I wouldn't find him. "You think you can get away with what you did? I'm coming for you, asshole! You hear me? I'm coming for you!"

As I walked away, the laughter continued.

Unabated.

And in my head, all I could think was…

The nightmare is just beginning…

~

DON'T FORGET! VIP'S get advance notice of all future releases and projects. AND A FREE NOVELLA! Click the image or join here: www.npmartin.com

ETHAN DRAKE WILL RETURN IN BOOK FOUR! COMING SOON! SIGN UP TO THE NEWSLETTER TO BE AMONG THE FIRST TO BE NOTIFIED!

MAKE A DIFFERENCE

For an indie author like myself, reviews are the most powerful tool I have to bring attention to my books. I don't have the financial muscle of the big traditional publishers, but I can build a group of committed and loyal readers...readers just like you!

Honest reviews of my books help bring them to the attention of other readers.

If you've enjoyed this book, I would be very grateful if you could spend just five minutes leaving a review (which can be as short as you like) on my book's Amazon page by clicking below.

And if you're still not motivated to leave a review, please also bear in mind that this is how I feed my family. Without reviews—*without sales*—I don't get to support my wife and darling daughters.

So now that I've shamelessly tugged on your heart strings, here's the link to leave the review:

Review Death Dealers

Thank you in advance.

TEASER: BLOOD MAGIC (WIZARD'S CREED # 1)

When the magic hit, I was knocked to the floor like I'd taken a hard-right hook to the jaw. The spell was so powerful, it blew through my every defense. For all my wards and the good they did me, I might as well have been a Sleepwalker with no protection at all.

The faint smell of decayed flesh mixed with sulfur hung thick in the air, a sure sign that dark magic had just been used, which in my experience, was never good. Coming across dark magic is a bit like turning up at a children's party to find Beelzebub in attendance, a shit-eating grin on his face as he tied balloon animals for the terrified kids. It's highly disturbing.

I sat dazed on the floor, blinking around me for a moment. My mind was fuzzy and partially frozen, as though I'd awakened from a nightmare. I was inside an abandoned office space, the expansive rectangular room lined with grimy, broken windows that let cold air in to draw me out of my daze. Darkness coated the room, the only real light coming from the moon outside as it beamed its pale, silvery light through the smashed skylights.

I struggled back to my feet and blindly reached for the

pistol inside my dark green trench coat, frowning when I realized the gun wasn't there. Then I remembered it had gone flying out of my hand when the spell had hit. Looking around, I soon located the pistol lying on the floor several feet away, and I lurched over and grabbed it, slightly more secure now that the gun's reassuring weight was back in my hand.

There were disturbing holes in my memory. I recalled confronting someone after tracking them here. But who? I couldn't get a clear image. The person was no more than a shadow figure in my mind. I had no clue as to why I was following this person unknown in the first place. Obviously, they had done something to get on my radar. The question was what, though?

The answer came a few seconds later when my eyes fell upon the dark shape in the middle of the room, and a deep sense of dread filled me; a dread that was both familiar and sickening at the same time, for I knew what I was about to find. Swallowing, I stared hard through the gloom at the human shape lying lifelessly on the debris-covered floor. Over the sharp scent of rats piss and pigeon shit, the heavy, festering stench of blood hit my nostrils without mercy.

When I crossed to the center of the room, my initial fears were confirmed when I saw that it was a dead body lying on the floor. A young woman with her throat slit. Glyphs were carved into the naked flesh of her spread-eagled body, with ropes leading from her wrists and ankles to rusty metal spikes hammered into the floor. I marveled at the force required to drive the nails into the concrete, knowing full well that a hammer had nothing to do with it.

Along the circumference of a magic circle painted around the victim was what looked like blood-drawn glyphs. The sheer detail of them unnerved me as I observed in them a certain quality that could only have come from a well-practiced hand.

I breathed out as I reluctantly took in the callous butchery on display. The dead woman looked to be in her early thirties, though it was difficult to tell because both her eyes were missing; cut out with the knife used to slice her throat, no doubt. I shook my head as I looked around in a vain effort to locate the dead woman's eyeballs.

The woman looked underweight for her size. She was around the same height as me at six feet, but there was very little meat on her bones, as if she was a stranger to regular meals. I also noted the needle marks on her feet, and the bruises around her thighs. This, coupled with how she had been dressed—in a leather mini skirt and short top, both items discarded on the floor nearby—made me almost certain the woman had been a prostitute. A convenient, easy victim for whoever had killed her.

If the symbols carved into her pale flesh were anything to go by, it would seem the woman had been ritually sacrificed. At a guess, I would have said she was an offering to one of the Dimension Lords, which the glyphs seemed to point to. The glyphs themselves weren't only complex, but also carved with surgical precision. The clarity of the symbols against the woman's pale flesh made it possible for me to make out certain ones that I recognized as being signifiers to alternate dimensions, though which dimension exactly, I couldn't be sure, at least not until I had studied the glyphs further. Glyphs such as the ones I was looking at were always uniquely different in some way. No two people drew glyphs the same, with each person etching their own personality into every one, which can often make it hard to work out their precise meanings. One thing I could be certain of was that the glyphs carved into the woman's body resonated only evil intent; an intent so strong, I felt it in my gut, gnawing at me like a parasite seeking access to my insides, as if drawn to my magic power. Not a pleasant feeling, but I was used to it, having been exposed to enough dark magic in my time.

After taking in the scene, I soon came to the conclusion

that the woman wasn't the killer's first victim; not by a long stretch, given the precision and clear competency of the work on display.

"Son of a bitch," I said, annoyed. I couldn't recall any details about the case I had so obviously been working on. It was no coincidence that I had ended up where I was, a place that happened to reek of dark magic, and which housed a murder that had occult written all over it. I'd been on the hunt, and I had gotten close to the killer, which was the likeliest reason for the dark magic booby trap I happened to carelessly spring like some bloody rookie.

Whoever the killer was, they wielded powerful magic. A spell that managed to wipe all my memories of the person in question wouldn't have been an easy one to create. And given the depth of power to their magic, it also felt to me like they had channeled it from some other source, most likely from whatever Dimension Lord they were sacrificing people to.

Whatever the case, the killer's spell had worked. Getting back the memories they had stolen from me wouldn't be easy, and that's if I could get them back at all, which I feared might just be the case.

After shaking my head at how messed up the situation was, I froze upon hearing a commanding voice booming in the room like thunder.

"Don't move, motherfucker!"

~

Get your copy of BLOOD MAGIC online today!

~

TEASER: SERPENT SON (GODS AND MONSTERS TRILOGY BOOK 1)

They knew I was back, for someone had been tailing me for the last half hour. As I walked along Lower Ormond Quay with the River Liffey flowing to the right of me, I pretended not to notice my stalker. I'd only just arrived back in Dublin after a stay in London, and I was in no mood for confrontation.

I was picking up on goblin vibes, but I couldn't be sure until I laid eyes on the cretin. The wiry little bastards were sneaky and good at blending in unseen.

As I moved down a deserted side street, hoping my pursuer would follow me, I weighed my options. There were several spells I could use: I could create a doorway in one of the walls next to me and disappear into the building; or I could turn myself into vapor and disappear; or I could even levitate up to the roof of one of the nearby buildings and escape.

Truthfully though, I didn't like using magic in broad daylight, even if there was no one around. Hell, I hardly used magic at all, despite being gifted with a connection to the Void —the source of all magic—just like every other Touched being in the world.

Despite my abilities, though, I was no wizard. I was just a musician who preferred to make magic through playing the guitar; real magic that touched the soul of the listener. Not the often destructive magic generated by the Void.

Still, Void magic could come in handy sometimes, like now as I spun around suddenly and said the word, *"Impedio!"* I felt the power of the Void flow through me as I spoke. But looking down the street, there appeared to be no one there.

Only I knew there was.

I hurried back down the street and then stopped by a dumpster on the side of the road. Crouching behind the dumpster was a small, wiry individual with dark hair and pinched features. He appeared frozen as he glared up at me, thanks to the spell I had used to stop him in his tracks, preventing him from even moving a muscle until I released him.

"Let me guess," I said. "Iolas got wind I was coming back, so he sent you to what...follow me? Maybe kill me, like he had my mother killed?"

Anger threatened to rise in me as blue magic sparked across my hand. Eight words, that's all it would take to kill the frozen goblin in front of me, to shut down his life support system and render him dead in an instant. It would've been so easy to do, but I wasn't a killer...at least not yet.

The goblin strained against the spell I still held him in, hardly able to move a muscle. To an ordinary eye, the goblin appeared mundane, just a small, rakish man in his thirties with thinning hair and dark eyes that appeared to be too big for his face. To my Touched eye, however, I could see the goblin creature for what he was underneath the glamor he used to conceal his true form, which to be honest, wasn't that far away from the mundane form he presented to the world. His eyes were bigger and darker, his mouth wider and full of thin pointed teeth that jutted out at all angles, barely concealed by lips like two strips of thick rubber. His skin was also paler, and his ears large and pointed.

"I don't know what you're talking about," the goblin said when I released him from the spell. He stood up straight, his head barely level with my chest. "I'm just out for a stroll on this fine summer evening, or at least I was before you accosted me like you did…"

I shook my head in disgust. What did I expect anyway, a full rundown of his orders from Iolas? Of course he was going to play dumb because he *was* dumb. He knew nothing, except that he had to follow me and report on my whereabouts. Iolas being the paranoid wanker that he was, would want eyes on me the whole time now that I was back in town. Or at least until he could decide what to do with me.

"All right, asshole," I said as magic crackled in my hand, making the cocky goblin rather nervous, his huge eyes constantly flitting from my face to the magic in my hand. "Before you fuck off out of it, make sure Iolas gets this message, will you? Tell that stuck up elf…tell him…"

The goblin frowned, his dark eyes staring into me. "Go on, tell Iolas what?" He was goading me, the sneaky little shit. "That you're coming for him? That you will kill him for supposedly snuffing out your witch-bitch mother—"

Rage erupted in me, and before the goblin could say another filthy word, I conjured my magic, thrusting my light-filled hand toward him while shouting the words, "*Ignem exquiris!*"

In an instant, a fireball about the size of a baseball exploded from my hand and hit the goblin square in the chest, the force of it slamming him back against the wall, the flames setting his clothes alight.

"*Dholec maach!*" the goblin screamed as he frantically slapped at his clothes to put the flames out.

"What were you saying again?" I cocked my head mockingly at him as if waiting for an answer.

"*Dhon ogaach!*" The goblin tore off his burning jacket and tossed it to the ground, then put out the remaining flames still licking at his linen shirt. The smell of burned fabric and roasted goblin skin now permeated the balmy air surrounding us.

"Yeah? You go fuck yourself as well after you've apologized for insulting my mother."

The goblin snarled at me as he stood quivering with rage and shock. "You won't last a day here, wizard! Iolas will have you fed to the vamps!"

I shot forward and grabbed the goblin by the throat, thrusting him against the wall. "First, I'm a musician, not a wizard, and secondly——" I had to turn my head away for a second, my nostrils assaulted by the atrocious stench of burnt goblin flesh. "Second, I'm not afraid of your elfin boss, or his vamp mates."

Struggling to speak with my hand still around his throat, the goblin said in a strangled voice, "Is that why...you ran away...like a...little bitch?"

I glared at the goblin for another second and then let him go, taking a step back as he slid down the wall. His black eyes were still full of defiance, and I almost admired his tenacity.

"I've listened to enough of your shit, goblin," I said, forcing my anger down. "Turn on your heels and get the hell out of here, before I incinerate you altogether." I held my hand up to show him the flames that danced in my palm, eliciting a fearful look from him. "Go!"

The goblin didn't need to be told twice. He pushed off the wall and scurried down the street, stopping after ten yards to turn around.

"You've signed your own death warrant coming back here, Chance," he shouted. "Iolas will have your head mounted above his fireplace!" His lips peeled back as he formed a rictus grin, then he turned around and ran, disappearing around the corner a moment later.

"Son of a bitch," I muttered as I stood shaking my head.

Maybe it was a mistake coming back here, I thought.

I should've stayed in London, played gigs every night, maybe headed to Europe or the States, Japan even. Instead, I came back to Ireland to tear open old wounds...and unavoidably, to make new ones.

Shaking my head once more at the way things were going already, I grabbed my guitar and luggage bag and headed toward where I used to live before my life was turned upside down two months ago.

As I walked up the Quay alongside the turgid river, I took a moment to take in my surroundings. It was a balmy summer evening, and the city appeared to be in a laid-back mood as people walked around in their flimsy summer clothes, enjoying the weather, knowing it could revert to dull and overcast at any time, as the Irish weather is apt to do. Despite my earlier reservations, it felt good to be back. While I enjoyed London (as much as I could while mourning the death of my mother), Dublin was my home and always had been. I felt a connection to the land here that I felt nowhere else, and I'd been to plenty of other places around the world.

Still, I hadn't expected Iolas to be on me so soon. He had all but banished me from the city when I accused him of orchestrating my mother's murder. He was no doubt pissed when he heard I was coming back.

Fuck him, I thought as I neared my destination. *If he thinks I will allow him to get away with murder, he's mistaken.*

Just ahead of me was *Chance's Bookstore*—the shop my mother opened over three decades ago, and which now belonged to me, along with the apartment above it. It was a medium-sized store with dark green wood paneling and a quaint feel to it. It was also one of the oldest remaining independent bookstores in the city, and the only one that dealt with rare occult books. Because of this, the store attracted a lot of Untouched with an interest in all things occult and magical. It also attracted its fair share of Touched, who knew the store as a place to go acquire hard to find books on magic or some aspect of the occult. My mother, before she was killed, had formed contacts all over the world, and there was hardly a book she wasn't able to get her hands on if someone requested it, for a price, of course.

As I stood a moment in front of the shop, my mind awash with painful memories, I glanced at my reflection in the window, seeing a disheveled imposter standing there in need of a shave and a haircut, and probably also a change of clothes, my favorite dark jeans and waistcoat having hardly been off me in two months.

Looking away from my reflection, I opened the door to the shop and stepped inside, locking it behind me again. The smell of old paper and leather surrounded me immediately, soliciting more painful memories as images of my mother flashed through my mind. After closing my eyes for a second, I moved into the shop, every square inch of the place deeply familiar to me, connected to memories that threatened to come at me all at once.

Until they were interrupted that is, by a mass of swirling darkness near the back of the shop, out of which an equally dark figure emerged, two slightly glowing eyes glaring at me.

Then, before I could muster any magic or even say a word of surprise, the darkness surrounding the figure lashed out, hitting me so hard across the face I thought my jaw had broken, and I went reeling back, cursing the gods for having it in for me today.

Welcome home, Corvin, I thought as I stood seeing stars. *Welcome bloody home...*

Get your copy of SERPENT SON online today!

BOOKS BY N. P. MARTIN

Ethan Drake Series

INFERNAL JUSTICE
BLOOD SUMMONED
DEATH DEALERS

Gods And Monsters Trilogy

SERPENT SON
DARK SON
RISING SON

Wizard's Creed Series

CRIMSON CROW
BLOOD MAGIC
BLOOD DEBT
BLOOD CULT
BLOOD DEMON

Nephilim Rising Series

BOOKS BY N. P. MARTIN

HUNTER'S LEGACY
DEMON'S LEGACY
HELL'S LEGACY
DEVIL'S LEGACY

ABOUT THE AUTHOR

I'm Neal Martin and I'm a lover of dark fantasy and horror. Writing stories about magic, the occult, monsters and kickass characters has always been my idea of a dream job, and these days, I get to live that dream. I have tried many things in my life (professional martial arts instructor, bouncer, plasterer, salesman…to name a few), but only the writing hat seems to fit. When I'm not writing, I'm spending time with my wife and daughters at our home in Northern Ireland.

Be sure to sign up to my mailing list:
readerlinks.com/l/663790/nl
And say hi on social media…

Printed in Great Britain
by Amazon